MICHAEL JOHANSEN

CONFESSION IN
MOSCOW

MICHAEL JOHANSEN

CONFESSION IN MOSCOW

BREAKWATER BOOKS

BREAKWATER
100 Water Street
P.O. Box 2188
St. John's, NL
A1C 6E6

National Library of Canada Cataloguing in Publication

Johansen, Michael, 1962-
        Confession in Moscow / Michael Johansen.

ISBN 1-55081-197-5   I. Title.

PS8569.O26763C66 2003   C813'.6   C2003-902846-1
PR9199.4.J64C66 2003

© 2003 Michael Johansen

Design & Layout: Carola Kern, Rhonda Molloy
Cover Design: Rhonda Molloy

The Canada Council | Le Conseil des Arts
for the Arts | du Canada

We acknowledge the financial support of The Canada Council for the Arts for our publishing activities.

 We acknowledge the financial support of the Government of Canada through the Book Publishing Industry Development Program (BPIDP) for our publishing activities.

Printed in Canada.

FOR LISE, who was there at the beginning,
AND FOR VALERIE, who was there to the end.

ONE

I WAS WAITING for Lise when the planes came. She was late. Her father had just returned home to a hero's welcome, so maybe she wouldn't come.

I was sitting by our pond in the woods, staring at the water, listening to the wind blow gently through the high branches of the surrounding trees. I had little on my mind—just the sun, the water, the wind.

A new sound came from behind me, a low buzzing so distant I listened for several seconds before I realized I didn't know what was making it. By the time I turned to peer through the new leaves the buzz had grown to a roar that filled the sky. Suddenly, one plane after another flashed overhead. They were coming from the south, heading for Rønne. I could hardly see them, but I knew who they must be.

The British had finally come! We'd waited days for their arrival and now they were here! They would free us from the Nazis at last!

I jumped to my feet, wishing I was in town. The event I had waited years for was about to happen and I was going to miss it. I pictured noisy, celebrating crowds and I laughed with the joy of it.

Suddenly I stopped, fear washing over me like a blush. I heard something I could not understand. I stood still and silent, and it came again: thunder from a clear, blue sky. Thunder was rolling from the town and lightning was striking again and again. Sirens began to wail their cries of warning. The planes were dropping bombs. They couldn't be British after all. But then who?

I ran away from the pond, through thick willows. Branches whipped me, grabbing at me, until I reached the railway tracks. I followed the tracks as fast as I could run, my feet slipping on the oily wooden ties. I had to get back to the town...I had to get back....

The old man sat trembling with the memory, his hands brushing the branches out of his way, his eyes focussed on the past. He looked up at me, his interrogator. His eyes searched my face. What was he looking for? Understanding? An answer to his childhood betrayal? Until then he had kept his eyes on his hands, which were resting with fingers intertwined on the table before him.

"I thought the war was over, you see. We all thought the war was over."

His gaze dropped back to his hands and his mind returned to the present.

"But why should you care what happened back then? It was long before you were born…"

This seemed an odd question to me. He had come to us; we didn't seek him out. I said nothing. I just stared at him. He seemed to take that for an answer. He nodded.

"Yes, of course…I remember now. Of course you have to know this. I have to tell you everything."

He continued his confession.

I have no idea how many bombs fell, or how long they rained down onto the lanes and houses of Rønne. The bombardment ended while I was running and the planes were gone by the time I entered the streets. This was my home, where I'd lived the last five years of my thirteen-year-long life. Now it was a strange place, a town I'd never seen before. The air was filled with smoke from the hungry fires. I tried to get to Lise's house, but found my way blocked again and again. In one street a wooden cart lay upturned and broken, filling the narrow space between the buildings. Two Danes, with rifles slung over their shoulders and the partisan colours wrapped around their right arms, struggled to free a panicky horse from its traces. I turned and searched for another route. I passed a woman plaintively calling out a name while she hugged a crying child. Her hand darted out and grabbed my sleeve. She begged me to tell her where her husband was. I broke free and kept running, dodging panicky crowds and horn-blaring cars. I was overtaken and almost knocked down by a troop of German soldiers hurrying down to the docks.

I was not going that far. I rounded a corner out of the little square and came to Lise's street, expecting to see her house a little way down. I stopped dead, wondering how I managed to go the wrong way. This wasn't Lise's street. Her house wasn't there.

But the judge's house was there on one side and the teacher's on the other.

They looked wrong. I realized their windows were all open to the smoke, the glass smashed from the frames. In between, where Lise's house always had been, always should have been, there was something else. There was smoke and fire and noise and nothing that looked like my friend's warm and comfortable home. I stood on the cobbles, my thoughts whirling in confusion, watching men in helmets—some wearing the red and blue resistance armbands, some in German uniforms—picking their way through a pile of bricks and wood and shattered furniture.

More men came carrying tools and boxes emblazoned with red crosses. They shouted to each other and they yelled at me to get out of the way. Two soldiers passed me, carrying a man on a stretcher. I could not recognize him. Dirt and blood obscured his face and clothing. He lay limp and motionless. I did not know whether he was dead or alive. Everything seemed to go quiet around me. The sunlight grew brighter and my head began to pound with a dull thumping. I felt hands on my arms pulling me backwards. Slowly I realized I was looking at Lise's father, or maybe at one of her bothers. In an instant, all the noise—the crack of falling bricks, the voices of the rescuers, and even sounds I hadn't noticed before, like a bell that was ringing somewhere far away—came rushing back to my ears. I suddenly understood what had happened with perfect clarity. I understood where Lise's house was. I understood everything.

Lise had not come to meet me. Lise had stayed home with her family. If she was here, she was beneath the rubble. If my friend—my best and only friend—was still alive, she needed help.

My thoughts exploded and I began screaming. I scrambled onto the shattered house, tearing boards away, desperately trying to dig down and find Lise. More hands grabbed me and lifted me away. I fought them, yelling her name over and over: "Lise! Lise! Lise!"

She didn't answer me. She couldn't answer me....

I looked at the man sitting across from me. He had gone silent. He was again staring down at his hands on the bare wooden table.

I tried to picture him as a thirteen-year-old boy digging for a body through a heap of smashed bricks. All I could see was a man who looked much older than his sixty-three years sitting here in the Moscow police station at Petrovka 38.

He said nothing for a long while, silently letting his tears fall. I was amazed these old memories of his could still make him feel so deeply. I sat and scribbled in my notebook, pretending not to notice. It embarrassed me. This kind of thing always embarrassed me. I wished he could control himself. Finally, he did. He pulled a wrinkled handkerchief out of his pocket, wiped his eyes and blew his nose.

I looked up and saw his eyes were now dry. I motioned for him to go on with his story. With a sigh, he continued.

My first memory of the war comes from the day the Germans invaded Denmark. I was eight years old. It was the middle of an April morning. I had woken up hours earlier to a low rumbling that went on and on and on. The noise seemed to be coming from overhead. When I peered out my window to try to see up into the sky, past the high roofs of the surrounding apartment buildings, I caught a glimpse of airplanes endlessly circling the city. I did not know what they were doing there and neither did my mother, or so she said.

My father had left our apartment while I was still asleep. It was a school day, but my mother kept me home, telling me only that there would not be many children going to classes that morning. That, more than anything, told me something very important was happening. My mother never kept me home from school for trivial reasons.

Although she excused me from classes, she did not excuse me from my school work. She sat me at the kitchen table where she could keep an eye on me, gave me a pencil and some paper, and told me to write a story.

"About what?" I asked.

My mother paused in her washing-up and thought for a moment.

"About summer," she finally said. "About what you want to do in the summer holidays."

Summer seemed so far away, but I quickly decided I wanted to do the same thing we'd done the summer before: visit my cousins in northern Sjealand and pass the sunny days playing with them on the beach. With this pleasant image in my mind I wrote rapidly and the morning passed quickly. While I was busy my mother finished washing the breakfast dishes, took a break with a cup of tea, spent some time in the living room with a dust rag, and eventually returned to the kitchen to begin preparing lunch.

She was cutting slices from a loaf of dark rye bread when the front door opened and closed. I heard the empty hangers chiming together as my father hung up his coat in the hall closet.

He was early and I saw my mother had a worried look on her face as she watched him come into the kitchen. He rarely missed a lunch although he was often late for supper, since evenings were always busier than mornings at his work, but it was unusual for my father to come home before noon. It was still only a quarter to. He kissed my mother absent-mindedly and came over to stand beside me. He put his hand lightly on the top of my head and looked at what I was writing. He picked up the pages and began to read out loud.

"'What I Want to Do at the Beach: by Mathias Finne.'" He continued reading silently. I watched his eyes moving rapidly over my written lines. He finished after a minute or so and handed the papers back to me.

He said, "That's fine, Mathias. Very nice. Maybe we can get you to the beach this summer."

My father knew about words. He was a writer. He wrote for a newspaper in Copenhagen. He brought it home every day and he tossed the copy he had with him onto the table. It flopped open. I saw large bold words over dense grey type and the photograph of a man with his arm stretched out in front of himself. I did not really know who it was, but it was someone who appeared often in my father's newspaper.

"They've come," my father said.

My mother ignored him.

"Things will change for us now," my father said, trying to overcome her silence.

I looked up. He was facing my mother. She had her arms crossed in front of her, over the top of her apron. She did not answer right away, but I could see she was about to say something.

"You've said that before, Carl," she finally answered, "but we still live in this little flat. We need more room. That's how things should change, if you want to know what I think."

I looked around our home. The idea that out flat was little came as a surprise to me. I had a room and my parents had a room and there was a kitchen and a living room. Why did she say it was little?

"We will get a bigger flat, Magda. There is a newspaper that needs someone to be an editor and manager. I have been offered the job. I would like to take it."

"Where is this newspaper?" my mother asked.

That's when I first heard the name of Bornholm, the island that was to be my home for the next five years of my life. I did not yet know how far away it was from Copenhagen, how beautiful were its beaches and hills and streams, nor how much it would mean to my future. I only knew that my mother did not want to go there.

"Bornholm!" she exclaimed. "But that would mean we must leave Copenhagen."

"But of course…there are not spare newspapers in this city. Not yet, anyway. I have a chance to prove myself. Later perhaps I will get an even better job and we will be able to come back. Bornholm won't be bad. You'll see."

This conversation—this argument—was going on over my head. I tried to follow what they were saying, twisting my neck back and forth as my mother and father threw words and gestures at each other. They spoke like this so often that I thought this kind of restrained fighting was a normal part of family life. Only later, when I came to know Lise's family, in fact, did I learn that smiles and gentle words should pass between parents, not hard looks and bitter thoughts.

I understood some of what they were saying to each other. I understood what it meant to move, but I did not fully grasp why it should be a topic of such emotion. We had only been in this flat in Copenhagen for about a year. Before that we lived in Berlin, where my father attended university and my mother attended to me.

I was born in Copenhagen, but we'd moved south when I was still too young to remember. I became aware of myself and the world around me while living in Germany. I started school in a Berlin kindergarten and most of my friends, except for a couple of expatriate Danish children like me, were all German. Being so young I learned German easily and spoke it fluently, so I didn't look or sound at all out of place in a gang of German school children.

I had not found the move north to Copenhagen traumatic in any way. I was excited about living in Copenhagen. My experiences with that city had been confined to short visits during vacations. My memories almost exclusively centered on friendly relatives who were determined to spoil me as much as possible in the short time they had.

I could not imagine anything bad in moving to Bornholm, either. Sure, I'd quickly made friends in Copenhagen and I'd miss them and my cousins, but I knew I'd make new friends. I saw the prospect of another move as exciting, not something to be dreaded.

My mother saw it differently.

"I don't care if Bornholm will be good or bad," she said to my father. "I want to stay here. You promised me we could stay here."

"Yes, I did," my father said, "but we've been here a year and now things have changed."

"Things have changed! Things have changed!" my mother parroted in a mocking tone. "In Berlin you said things would change, but they're not really any different. You're still doing what they tell you to do. You're still putting them ahead of Mathias and me."

I wondered who "they" were, but I didn't get the chance to ask.

"You don't understand!" my father shot back. "You've never understood. Why can't you see that what we do for the Party we do for ourselves?"

"For ourselves? How can this be for ourselves? In Berlin you promised me that when you were finished your studies we could come home. I want Mathias to grow up here where I grew up. I do not want him to become a model German child—a puppet like all those others! I want him to be a Danish boy in Copenhagen!"

"A puppet?" my father exclaimed, ignoring what my mother had said afterwards. "What do you mean—puppet? Why can't you understand what the Party is doing for us? What it will do for us?"

"Explain it to me," my mother said. "What is the Party doing for us? It gave you a small job on a small paper. Now it wants to send you away from Copenhagen. How is that doing anything for us?"

"If I'm not getting the best jobs, whose fault do you think that is? Do you think they don't know how you feel about them? God! You should see your face when they say something you don't like. Do you think they don't notice how you despise them? Maybe I could get a better job if you would only stop acting like you know better than they do. Sometimes I wonder if they pity me, or if they blame me, too."

"Pity you? Pity you?"

By now my mother and father were both red in the face, glaring at each other with fire in their eyes. I sat crouched between them, my homework forgotten in front of me. I wanted to escape, but didn't know how to slip away.

My mother, however, suddenly seemed to notice my discomfort. Or maybe she knew the argument was breaking out into open and bitter conflict.

"Mathias," she said, speaking gently. "Take your papers and pencils and go to your room, please. I'll call you when it's time to eat."

I left willingly, without saying anything or looking directly at either of my parents. I went down the short hall to my room and closed the door. But that didn't block out the sound of their fight. I couldn't make out the words any more, but I could hear their voices rising and clashing. I lay on my bed and tried unsuccessfully to pretend it wasn't happening. I must have finally fallen asleep, but not before my pillow was wet from my tears.

Finne paused, so I held up my hand and smiled briefly to prevent him from continuing. The air in the room was stuffy and hot; I needed something to drink. I walked a few steps to the door, opened it and spoke with the guard outside in the hall. It occurred to me the prisoner might also be thirsty, so I asked for a second glass of tea to be brought along.

I used the break to collect my thoughts. I crossed the room to open the window and stood for a moment inhaling the cool air as I gazed across the street at a small, old church, idly wondering if it would be torn down or repaired. I saw out of the corner of my eye that Finne sat without moving. It was as if he now lived his whole life solely through the story he told; when he was silent his only purpose was to wait until he could go on. I believe he didn't even realize he was hot and thirsty until the guard came back with two glasses of tea. The old man drank slowly but steadily, gradually draining his glass between his words.

My father won that argument. We were going to move to Bornholm and he was going to take that important position at the newspaper.

We began preparations almost immediately. All our things were packed into bags and boxes, some of which we were to take with us, others we'd leave behind in storage. I was given one suitcase to fill and my mother told me that I had to choose what I really wanted to bring along. Everything that couldn't fit into my case would have to stay in Copenhagen. However, my mother assured me it wouldn't be gone forever. We'd be back one day to get it.

We remained in Copenhagen for a week or two—long enough for me to see how the city had changed. I was used to seeing German soldiers, of course. Berlin was full of them. The sight of goose-stepping troops and grey staff cars was not a novelty for me. But that was in Germany. Here in Denmark they looked very out of place.

The war was still young and the German army stood undefeated. It certainly had had no trouble overcoming the Danish army. There had been some fighting down at the border, but the Germans quickly suppressed that resistance. The rest of the Danish army was ordered to surrender, so the conquest of Denmark took less than a day.

That probably accounted for the high spirits the German soldiers displayed and the low morale of the Danish citizenry. In those first weeks of the war we had little to celebrate and a whole country to mourn.

But I learned in the days before our departure that although we had been defeated, we weren't yet truly conquered. My mother taught me that lesson, with a little help from King Christian. I don't know if that had been her intention the morning she bundled me into my raincoat and boots and took me for a walk through the drizzly streets, but that's what she succeeded in doing. I suspect she was seizing her last chance to show me something that in all of the new Nazi empire we could only see in our own home city: open, untouchable rebellion against German rule.

We left our flat in Fredricksberg and caught a trolley car that headed towards the Copenhagen city centre. The ride was uneventful, but as it was still fairly early in the morning the car was full of men and women on their way to work. I sat by the window looking out and my mother protectively took the aisle seat. Because of the crowd conditions a drowsy-looking man was forced to lean over us and my mother pressed tight against me to avoid his touch. I looked out the rain-streaked window at the many pedestrians hurrying about their business. It grew hot in the car and I sat uncomfortably in my heavy slicker.

Finally we got off the car at the city hall plaza and caught another that took us to a large circular street known as *Kongens Nytorv*. We stepped off the second car there and set off on foot across the wide park in the middle of the circle, heading towards the new harbour with its colourful little fishing boats. We passed that and headed down several streets until I felt thoroughly lost and confused. My mother shushed me every time I asked her where we were going or what we were doing. Having already spent some years in Nazi Germany she knew well the value of silence.

Just when I was becoming tired of our mysterious trek and longing for a rest we came to a wide, quiet tree-lined street and we stopped. My mother led me to a bench. She wiped a spot dry with her handkerchief and we sat down together to wait—for what I did not know.

Fortunately we didn't have to sit there for too long. I welcomed the rest, but the damp weather soon started to chill me. I whined about this a little bit, but my mother only answered with a sharp rebuke. I kept quiet from then on.

There were few people in the street and I could see no reason for our presence. Some men in civilian clothes passed by without looking at us and entered a nearby building. Once, a woman, umbrella unfurled, hurried towards us, her eyes pinned to the sidewalk in front of her. She did not notice us until she was actually within reach. At that point she saw us on the bench and gave a startled gasp. She kept walking, but looked back at my mother and me with suspicion in her eyes. I greeted her look with a shy smile, but she did not return it.

Next came a couple of German officers, caps on their heads and pistols holstered to their sides. They also looked at us with some suspicion, but my mother ignored them, digging into her purse as if we had just sat down and would leave as soon as she found what she was missing. I gave them the same smile I'd given the woman and they passed on without a word.

Within a minute—the officers had barely gone twenty metres down the street—I heard the sound of a horse walking towards us. Horses were still quite common in Copenhagen in those days, so I did not consider the sound anything special, but it seemed to be what my mother was waiting for. She perked right up and peered down the street, trying to see the approaching horse.

"Pay attention, Mathias," she said. "Watch what he does."

"Watch who, mother?" I asked, but she just shushed me again.

I expected to see some tired old workhorse pulling a milk wagon, but I could not have been more wrong. What I saw was a magnificent beast, its head erect and proud. That pride was mirrored in the bearing of the old man who sat on his back. The rider was dressed in an old-fashioned military uniform. A sword, not a gun, hung from his side and his helmet was festooned with colourful feathers. Full, grey whiskers framed his stern face. He looked familiar, but I couldn't think of where I'd seen him before. I surely would have remembered this sight.

"Watch what the Germans do too, Mathias."

I took my eyes off the splendid old man and saw that the two German officers were standing at attention, saluting the old soldier. I looked back at him, but he was not returning their salute. He blatantly ignored them.

The horse and rider passed the Germans and they approached us. "Stand up, Mathias," my mother said, "and take off your cap."

I did as I was told and stood there gazing up at the rider as he drew abreast. For a second I saw his face in silhouette and suddenly I realized where I had seen him before: his head was on the front of just about every coin I'd ever seen in Denmark.

I gasped and blurted out with out thinking: "It's the King!"

He must have heard me. He didn't check his horse's stride, but he glanced down at me and smiled for a brief moment before passing us by and continuing up the street. We remained standing until he had turned the nearest corner and then we followed him a little while before turning a different corner to head back towards *Kongens Nytorv*.

Neither of us said anything until we were seated on a homeward-bound trolley car. My mind was full of wonder at what I'd seen and I was struggling to understand what it meant. My mother was also silent, but for a different reason.

"Mathias," she finally said to me, "you know I've always taught you not to lie to me and not to keep secrets from your father and me."

I nodded my head.

"Well, now…" Her voice trailed off and her eyes left mine. "Now I have to ask you to forget what I used to tell you. Now you have to keep what you've seen a secret. You must never tell your father where we were this morning."

She looked at me again.

"Do you understand?"

I didn't, but I nodded anyway.

"Your father…he would not approve. He would say I was wrong to show you this today."

"But that was the King," I said and added in my thoughts, how could it be wrong to see the King?

"I can't really explain that to you now," she said. "You must trust me and not say a word. But you must also promise me you'll never forget what the King did."

I thought back to what I had seen, but I could not think of what she was referring to. My mother must have seen the confusion in my face.

"He defied them, Mathias," she whispered. "He defied them!"

I interrupted Finne. This talk of a king puzzled me. He didn't sound like a serious monarch at all. I tried to imagine the old czars cantering about in the streets like that, smiling at little boys. It didn't seem credible. I wondered if I should disbelieve it.

"What did your mother mean?" I asked Finne. "How did your King defy the Nazis?"

Finne thought for a moment before answering me.

"Well, like I already said: he ignored them. The Germans were trying to placate us. They knew we loved our King, so the German soldiers were ordered to show proper respect towards him. Maybe Hitler thought we would accept the occupation more if he left our King alone. But Christian wouldn't play his game. He refused to acknowledge their respect. He ignored them and that way you could say he ignored the whole German Empire.

"But there was something else. He wore the red and blue armband."

"What red and blue armband?" I asked. "You've mentioned this before. Explain it."

"The resistance armband," Finne said. "When our army disbanded, our soldiers tore strips from their uniforms and wore them tied around their arms in secret. That was the start of the resistance. The King knew what they had done and what they wanted to do. He knew and he wanted to help, to lend those men and women his strength. So he wore the armband, too. But he wore his openly, in full view of any German who cared to see it."

This, I knew, must have taken courage, even for a king. The Nazis must have given him some sort of immunity, but what they give can also be taken away. Who knew the treachery of Adolf Hitler better than Mother Russia?

"What was your King doing riding around in the streets? Shouldn't he have been in his palace, safe? All alone in the streets with German soldiers all around him—what kind of king does that?"

Finne raised his head and scowled at me. He was obviously offended.

"A good king!" he answered. "A real king! Why should he stay locked up like a prisoner in his palace? Denmark was his country. There was nowhere he could not go."

Finne's expression hardened and I could sense a strong pride behind his words.

"We were a free people," he said. "And our King was a free man. He reminded us we were free and showed us that one day we would be able to exercise our freedom again."

"What, he did all that by riding around on his little horse?" I mocked.

"Yes," Finne shot back, "by riding around on his horse. It's something he did every morning for exercise and fresh air. He did it before the war started, so why should he stop just because the Germans had invaded? Don't you understand? He was showing us—and he was showing the Germans—that the occupation would end one day and things would go back to the way they'd been before. He ignored the German soldiers because they weren't really important. Their time would pass and Denmark would again be free!"

"He did all that?"

"Yes, he did all that."

"All right, then. Go on with your story."

Our boat left at dusk. We took a taxi from the flat down to the docks. The driver helped carry our bags down the three flights of stairs and loaded them into the trunk of his car. All three of us, my mother, my father and I, sat together in the back seat. I wanted to sit by a window to look out at the city, but my parents put me between them.

They didn't say on word to each other as we drove through Copenhagen. They each of them gazed out their own windows, leaving me to trade silent glances with the driver in his rear-view mirror. He seemed sympathetic, but he didn't say anything either.

The boat was larger than I had expected. Its tall sides towered over me as I stood on the dock and craned my neck to look up. We must have arrived quite close to departure time and we had to wait our turn to embark. A mob of paper-waving passengers crowded at the bottom of the gangplank. Some carried luggage and others had theirs carried for them, but all had to pass inspection by a couple of black-uniformed German soldiers.

In those days it wasn't enough to just have tickets if you wanted to travel, especially if you wanted to make a long trip like the one we were about to take. You had to have an official reason. You needed papers.

Not everyone who wanted to get on the Bornholm ferry that evening had the right papers. I saw one couple refused boarding. They were turned away, ordered into a nearby office and escorted there by armed guard. I wondered what would happen to them and I wondered if my parents and I would have the same trouble getting permission to climb aboard.

We did not have any trouble at all. In fact, my father's papers seemed to carry more weight than all the others did. The German officer who inspected them not only saluted my father, but he also instructed one of his soldiers to help carry out luggage up onto the boat. That must have been my father's first taste of his new importance. He was obviously enjoying the privilege and basked in the deference the Germans were showing him. He thanked the officer in German and nodded to the soldier who picked up his suitcase.

As we walked up the gangplank the eyes of many of our fellow passengers were upon us. We all noticed them, but it seems each of us saw them differently. I think they pleased my father. He reacted to them as if they were friendly looks. He smiled at these people and his expression combined his old shyness with a newfound smugness. The looks from these Danes puzzled me. I saw no friendliness. Instead I detected resentment and scorn, although I did not fully comprehend why they should feel these things about us. By the way my mother set her mouth firmly and held my hand tightly, pulling me close to her—even to the point of hindering me and I climbed the plank—I could tell she was afraid. She saw these looks from her fellow citizens as a threat. She feared them.

Our cabin on board the ferry—we were to spend one night en route—was made for four people, so we had an extra bed we used to hold our luggage. My parents each took one of the lower bunks while I was given an upper berth. I was happy with it. I liked heights; I liked being able to look down at things— to look down at my parents. I also liked the privacy the upper bunk gave me. Down below I would have been open to inspection by my mother or father. Up above I could lie against the wall and feel hidden away.

I also like the top bunk because my head was beside the small round porthole. A whitish grime somewhat obscured the outside of the thick glass, but I could still peer through it. We were on the starboard side of the boat and, as we were still tied up at the dock, my porthole looked out over the city. Unfortunately I couldn't see much. Night was falling, and since Copenhagen was under blackout orders, gloom prevailed. Nevertheless, as my parents unpacked the few things we would need for the trip I stared though the glass absorbing what little I could see: cars and trucks pulling up to the boat; more passengers climbing aboard; and finally the dimming outlines of nearby buildings. I knew I would not see Copenhagen again for a long, long time.

We were still in the cabin when the boat pulled away from the dock and out of the harbour. I wonder about that now. My parents had no desire to stand with all the other passengers up on the deck. Perhaps it was because no one had come to see us off. My mother's sister and her family were too far away in the north of Sjealand to make the trip and my father's family didn"t speak with him anymore. At the time I did not understand why that was so, but I have since learned that politics kept the family apart. My uncles did not approve of my father's membership in the Danish Nazi Party.

The trip was uneventful. It was not my first time on a ferry, so the experience was not completely novel for me. Today they are busy building bridges and tunnels all over Denmark, but in those days you could not travel anywhere without spending time on a boat. The train journey we took from Berlin to Copenhagen a year before was broken by an overnight sailing.

There's a saying in English about the calm before a storm. That's what that trip was like for me. The seas were flat and dull. The passengers were subdued. My parents were in foul moods, barely speaking to each other.

I moped around the boat, avoiding their company when I could. I watched the other passengers and gazed out to sea, longing for our arrival at Bornholm. I was anxious for this new life of ours to begin.

Two

MY FIRST SIGHT of Bornholm came with the sun setting behind me. Rønne, the island's main town, glowed orange in the thick light. I stood shadowed at the bow, looking out over the calm waters towards my new home. I liked what I saw, so different as it was from both Copenhagen and Berlin.

I was used to large cities and this was a small town. I could see almost all of it from my vantage point on the boat. Directly in front of me were the docks, dominated by a massive warehouse built on a wharf right in the harbour. The land rose quickly away from the shore, creating a steep escarpment to my right, but climbing gently enough to my left to allow streets and houses to have been built on the slope. A white church stood on top of the steepest part, somewhat behind the warehouse. Further to the south, further to my right, that is, I could see a massive round stone tower. Trees surrounded this imposing structure and the woods continued beyond it. To the north I could see homes strung along a sandy shoreline, but I lost all sight of them as the ferry passed the breakwater and entered the harbour. Now we were surrounded by seagulls in the air above us and on the water by boats of all kinds: large freighters, small fishing vessels, and fast German patrol boats. We were soon docked and I returned to our cabin to find my parents.

We were met on the dock by a soldier who saluted my father and led us to a large black car. He opened the rear door for us and went off again in search of our luggage. We left after the driver assured my father, in German, that our bags would be brought to our hotel. The driver told us the commander of the German naval forces on Bornholm, Captain Werner Reinhardt, requested our presence for dinner.

On this ride I was again stuck in the middle of the back seat, so I couldn't see much of this new town. I craned my neck to peer out of the windshield, but I only managed to get a vague impression of low, steep-roofed houses lining narrow winding streets. The sun had already set, the sky was darkening, and the streetlights were not being lit; blackout rules were being applied in Rønne as they were everywhere else in Denmark.

We arrived at our destination and were quickly ushered out of the automobile and into a large old house by yet another German officer. He took us down a long hallway and showed us into a plush sitting room. Speaking in German, he told us to make ourselves comfortable and asked us if we desired anything to drink.

"Ale? Spirits? Something for the boy?"

My father asked for a beer. My mother requested a cup of tea for herself and a soda pop for me. The officer said he would have them sent in and that Herr Commandant would join us presently.

We received our drinks as quickly as promised and sat in silence, enjoying them. My father leaned back comfortably in a soft armchair, one hand holding his beer, the other stroking the knot of his tie as if he longed to loosen it. My mother sat perched on the edge of a couch, taking quick sips of her tea, as if fully absorbed in the simple pleasure of the taste. I sat beside her and drank my pop as fast as I could—not because I was particularly thirsty, but because it seemed the most delicious drink I'd ever had. When the bottle was empty I looked at it mournfully and wished the servant would reappear with another one. He didn't.

Captain Reinhardt came instead and his sudden, noiseless appearance startled all of us. One minute the door was closed and we were alone. Then without seeing or hearing the door open we saw the captain had entered the room and was smiling at the three of us. My parents sprung out of their seats in surprise.

"Good evening Mr. and Mrs. Finne and you, too, young man," Reinhardt said in Danish. "Welcome to Bornholm. I trust your journey was a pleasant one?"

He didn't wait for an answer

"Sit down. Sit down," he said as he crossed the floor and opened a large wooden cabinet.

"I see you already have something to drink. I hope you won't mind if I join you."

The cabinet contained various kinds of bottles. He chose one and poured a dark liquid into a glass. He took a large sip, gave a satisfied sigh, and turned back towards us. I kept wishing this man would offer me another soda pop, but he did not seem to notice I needed one.

"You must forgive me for bringing you here before you have had a chance to settle in to your hotel," Reinhardt said. "I have a busy schedule tonight and I cannot spare you much time. I decided we should eat together and get to know each other over a good meal. Are you hungry? I cannot imagine the food was very good on the boat. My chef is quite skilled. I know you will enjoy what he is preparing for us."

The German commander went on describing exactly what he had ordered his chef to cook. The captain barely allowed my mother or father to respond to anything he said. I noticed he asked many questions, but rarely listened for an answer. I quickly got the impression that his good humour and his good manners—his friendly attitude towards us—were false and insincere. I found myself disliking him quite strongly.

Werner Reinhardt was a tall, slim man. His face, animated by conversation, appeared pleasant, but he had sharp features that I imagined could instantly turn cold and fearsome. Steely grey eyes looked out over a hooked nose and thin lips. All his movements were tightly controlled. I ceased wishing he would offer me more to drink and instead I hoped he wouldn't notice me at all.

My father, on the other hand, drank in the German officer's presence as avidly as I had consumed my pop. He made a couple of attempts to speak, to answer the commander's questions, but he took no offence when the German's banter steamrolled right over him.

My mother remained quiet. She cradled her near-empty teacup in both hands and her eyes flitted back and forth from Reinhardt to my father. By her stillness I sensed she did take some offense from the German's manner and she liked him no better than I did.

Eventually a servant knocked on the door to announce that the meal was ready. Reinhardt offered his arm to my mother and we made our way down the hall and through a set of double doors. A large table, covered with a white lace cloth, was set for the four of us with silver cutlery, crystal glasses, and blue-patterned chinaware. The meal matched the richness of the setting: tender roast beef, heaps of potatoes and carrots, pickled herring, sweet red cabbage, fresh peas, and dusty bottles of wine—a Danish meal designed in our honour, or so Reinhardt said. I was permitted one small glass of the wine and it went quickly to my head.

"That's it, boy," Reinhardt said, as if he couldn't be bothered to remember my name. "Don't drink it too fast."

Then he switched his attention back to my parents.

"He is not too young to learn the taste of fine wine, hein?"

He lifted his glass to his guests and gave the Danish toast: "Skoal!"

I ate too much and I believe my father also overindulged in both food and drink. My mother only picked at her food and from what I could tell the commander made a show of enjoying what he was eating, but did not actually eat very much. He did drink, however, but the alcohol did not appear to affect him strongly. He continued his light banter throughout the meal and only turned to more serious conversation when dinner was over. He and my father sat with cups of coffee in front of them, my mother had tea, and I was spooning up a dish of ice cream when Reinhardt changed his tone.

"Herr Finne," he said. "I was pleased when I learned of your appointment to Bornholm. I have read your file and I believe you are well suited for the position."

My father mumbled some thanks.

"Your job will not be an easy one, but I think you will manage it well. Your qualifications from Berlin University, your work with the Party in both Germany and in your homeland, and your dedication to the Führer make you a model Dane for the New Reich. You are in the forefront of your countrymen and you have a chance to prove yourself here on Bornholm."

Reinhardt took a sip of his coffee, as if he needed the time to consider his words. My father sat silent. He must have realized by then that no response was expected of him.

"We are in a unique position here on Bornholm," Reinhardt continued. "Here we are on this island—an island not too large or too small for our purposes—in the middle of the Baltic Sea. The people are all of good Aryan stock. True, they are a mix of Danes and Swedes, not German, but the Führer himself considers you Danes as brothers…and sisters, of course," he added with a smile and a glance towards my mother.

"The Führer says Denmark will be a model for the New Reich, an example for all the new territories to follow. I have been given the privilege and the responsibility of overseeing this one small part of it. Yes, it is a small part, but

I believe it will become very important."

The German commander's voice had changed. He spoke as if he was delivering a carefully rehearsed speech.

"As Denmark will be an example for the Reich, I will make Bornholm an example for Denmark. In the time to come others will look back upon these early years and they will study my efforts here. They will say: 'The Reich was built by men like Reinhardt!'"

The commander pulled himself up short as if he realized he might have said a bit too much. He took another sip of his coffee and focussed on my father.

"You will help me in this," he said. "As editor of the *Bornholmsk Tidendes* you will be my most effective voice on this island. Through you I will speak to the people of Bornholm. However, they will not always know it is I speaking to them!"

Reinhardt laughed at his own joke and my father joined in with a grin and a chuckle. My mother continued sitting in her stony silence. I was still trying to figure out what was funny about what the commander had said when he started speaking again.

"Your job will not always be an easy one," he said to my father. "Not all the people of this island will accept German... how would you put it? Not German rule; that is too harsh a word."

"Perhaps German tutelage?" my father said, speaking a full sentence for the first time that evening.

"Tutelage! Yes, excellent. Already, Herr Finne, you display your worth.

"As I was saying, not all the people of Bornholm will appreciate German tutelage. If their...resistance...becomes too pronounced then I must deal with that, but one of your jobs will be to prevent things from reaching such a point. You must help convince your people that to follow the German way is the proper choice. You must show them through your choice of words, your actions, and your example that a bright future lies with the German Reich."

Reinhardt swirled his remaining coffee, drank it, and then gazed at the bottom of the cup for a moment.

"Oh yes," he said. "You must also produce a good newspaper. I like to be kept informed of what is happening around me."

"Captain Reinhardt," my father said, "I will do all I can to live up to the confidence you show in me."

"Excellent. Excellent," Reinhardt said. Then he looked inquiringly at my father because my father suddenly looked a trifle embarrassed and seemed to have something more to say.

"Yes, what is it?" the German asked, not unkindly.

"Excuse me, Captain. If you would direct me to…."

"Ah, yes, of course."

Reinhardt rang a small silver bell that sat beside his place at the table. The servant appeared and the German commander ordered him to show my father to the washroom. When we were alone with Reinhardt, he turned to my mother, all sign of good nature gone from his face.

"Frau Finne," he asked. "Do you know why your husband was sent here to Bornholm?"

My mother responded warily.

"As you said, Herr Captain, he is a good man for the available position."

Reinhardt smiled briefly, but his smile showed no trace of humour.

"Yes, perhaps, but let me ask the question in a different way: since he is so good, why was he not offered an important position in Copenhagen, or even Berlin?"

My mother had no answer for that. She simply shook her head without speaking. Her eyes never left Reinhardt, but I could see her hands in her lap. She held them tightly clasped together.

"Surely you must have some idea?" Reinhardt said. "No? Well, let me tell you then.

"You are also mentioned in the file I have read, Frau Finne, but the report on you is not so flattering as the one on your husband. It says you not once, but twice refused direct orders to become a member of the Party. It is suspected you do not share your husband's beliefs in any measure and what I have seen of you this evening tends to convince me that the suspicions are correct. You are very poor at hiding your disdain for some of the things I have said."

When my mother spoke I could detect a slight quavering in her voice that I had never heard before. That told me—and it must also have told the commander—that she was very frightened.

"Captain, you must excuse me if my fatigue—it was a tiring journey—has offended you in any way. I certainly have not felt disdain for anything you've said. Quite the contrary is true.

"And as for the times I've turned down the kind invitations to join the party, my reasons were quite clear and they have nothing to do with the party itself. It's just that I've always believed my best place in society is at home, caring for my husband and son. I serve the Party by serving them. Carl will be able to do so much more if he does not need to worry about his home life."

"Indeed?" Reinhardt said. "Yes, I have read your excuses in the file. They are very—how shall I put it?—carefully worded.

"But let me tell you a secret, Frau Finne, and give you a warning: you are a liability to your husband. He was sent here because of you. You are not well liked or trusted in Party circles and the Party believes you will be easier to control on this little island. Unfortunately that means we cannot use your husband to his full potential, but such is life."

Reinhardt shrugged and smiled as he said that, but turned off his false charm immediately.

"Now here is your warning: I will watch you, Frau Finne, so you must never forget that your final duty does lie with the Party, no matter how you choose to exercise it."

I have often wondered why he said those things to my mother in my presence. Did he believe I was too young to understand them? I think that maybe Reinhardt kept me there as a threat because when he was finished speaking he looked at me and smiled.

"You have such a handsome young son, Frau Finne. You'll be sure to take good care of him, hein?"

My mother's face went pale as she looked from the Captain to me. She put an arm around my shoulder and pulled me closer to her, but she didn't say anything more. Just then my father reappeared looking somewhat flustered. He apologized for taking so long, explaining that he'd lost his way somewhere down the long hallway.

"No matter! No matter!" Reinhardt said, once again playing the part of a genial host. "You must all excuse me now: I have business that requires my attention. Please stay and finish your coffee, Herr Finne. It was a pleasure meeting you all. We will surely speak again soon."

With that he was out the door and was instantly replaced by the servant who asked if we desired anything more. My father seemed about to request another drink, but my mother complained of a headache and convinced him it was time to leave.

As we walked back down the hallway to the front door and the waiting car,

I saw Captain Reinhardt one more time. Just as we were passing by one door I could hear a shout of anger from behind it. The door was opened by a harried-looking young German officer who stopped dead when he saw us. Inside the room I glimpsed Reinhardt standing behind a large wooden desk. His face was set in a frightening scowl. His arm was raised and he was pointing a finger out towards the hallway. When we were past the young officer, he closed the door and hurried down the way we had come.

"So your father collaborated with the Nazis?" I asked the prisoner.

"Yes," Finne answered me without looking up. "Yes, he did."

"So, what does that have to do with you killing someone? You want to confess to murder, you say, yet you waste my time with stories about your father. I don't care about your father."

Finne sat up abruptly, as if I'd slapped him. Obviously he had not had much experience with the police. I had to disabuse him of the impression that he could control the flow of this interrogation.

"Who did you kill? How did you kill him? Where? When? Why? These are the questions you must answer. This is the information I need. I am not interested in your family history."

I was standing up by then, leaning over the table towards him. My hands were flat on the wooden surface, my face centimetres away from his.

"I do not care about your Danish King. I do not care that you liked to have dinner with Nazis. Why are you wasting my time? Who did you kill?"

My display of anger sparked something within him. His face turned red— not, I was sure, from fear or embarrassment, but from his own anger. He placed his hands on the table and heaved himself up. The guard at the door moved towards him in alarm, but with a glance I warned him off.

Finne's eyes bored into mine. He was clenching his teeth so hard I could almost hear them crack. The tendons in his neck were stretched as tight as piano wire. He was ready to burst, so I decided to give him a push.

"Say it, Mr. Finne. Are you afraid to tell me?"

To my surprise, and to the apparent relief of the watching officer, my words didn't inflame him. They did the opposite. He suddenly deflated, the air escaping from his lungs in a long sigh. His stance softened and he slowly sat back down in his chair. I followed his example, folding my hands together in front of me. I remained silent and waited a good ten minutes for Finne to speak. When he finally did, he surprised me a second time by ignoring my question. He simply continued with his story. I briefly considered asking it again, but decided to let him talk.

"I've never told anyone about this before, not even my wife. She knew some of it, but I could never bring myself to tell her everything. I was always afraid she wouldn't understand. I was terrified she'd condemn me for the things I did.

"But I was wrong to keep these secrets from her. They were always there between us. Maybe it didn't matter so much most of the time, but I should have told her. She shared her life with me."

Finne's eyes clouded over. He searched for a way to say the painfully obvious.

"She's dead, Inspector. She died last January. At first I just felt grief, overwhelming grief, but when that began to fade my old sense of guilt replaced it. I should have told her everything. I betrayed her by keeping this secret."

He stopped and put his face into his hands. He took a deep breath and when he spoke again he was almost yelling at me.

"I can't keep it secret anymore. No more! But if you want my confession then you have to hear all of it. All of it! If you don't want it my way then I won't tell you anything at all. Why should I? I came here. You didn't come for me. I don't care what you do to me now. I just want to tell my story. If you want to solve a murder then you have to listen to me!"

I studied this foreigner, this Dane. No, Canadian. His history was Danish, but his passport was Canadian. I wondered for a moment why a man would forsake his mother country, but then considered the more pressing question: was it true that he had nothing to lose? Had he already lost it all? Perhaps we were alike in that way. I know what it is like to reach a point of crisis. It hurt, it hurt like hell, but when I emerged from the other side I was ready to start again. I'm still trying to do that, to restart my life. Maybe that's what Finne wanted: to purge himself, to win back hope. Who was I to deny him that?

Also, I had to admit to myself that Finne's story intrigued me. In all my years as a policeman I'd never come across anything like this. I wanted to hear more.

"Okay," I said to him. "Tell me your story."

THREE

"I USED TO climb trees," Finne said after a few minutes.

He was looking at his hands. He held them out like an offering.

"That's when I was young and strong, not like now."

The hands were dry and white, with no trace of ink. They were hands that were accustomed to hard, clean work. Maybe carpentry. Not a farmer. And evidently he had not spent his years making money.

"The wonder of trees is that the old grandmothers get to be eight hundred years old and they're still making babies! Huge, dignified matrons with all their little children sprouting around their skirts!"

He chuckled and then the humour drained from his face.

"I used to be able to climb any tree I set my mind to. Bornholm had some wonderful trees. Sometimes I'd have to scramble up twenty feet before I could reach the first branches, but that didn't bother me. I'd use my arms and legs to clamp my whole body around the trunk and I'd scrape upwards until I could hold onto a branch and rest. I used to love the feeling of accomplishment that gave me. I was a small child and I loved doing something that could startle adults.

"It was because of this that I first encountered the gripping beast. Maybe it wanted me to know who was master. Maybe it wanted to punish me for false pride."

Finne stopped as if to marshal his thoughts. I think he saw I was confused and he wanted to make sure I understood him. What was this beast?

"Lise was proud of Bornholm. She was proud of the island's long, long history. She would tell me of the old battles, the old wars. How we won some. How we lost others.

"When we had the chance she would take me to the old places on the island. The old churches. The old graveyards. The old wharves and smoke-houses. We'd follow the old walls through the forests. We'd trace old foundations in farm fields. And once we climbed the rocky hills in the very centre of the island to reach the old city—just once.

"That's all it's called: the Old City. The crumbling, overgrown walls sit like a crown on the wide crest of a steep-sided hill. Once, hundreds or maybe thousands of years ago, it teamed with human life. People came and went through the city's two great gates, buying and selling and fighting and loving and just living, living as best as they could.

"But when I saw it, no one lived there anymore. No one had lived there for a long, long time: so long ago it seemed like it wasn't even haunted. That's what I thought when I first looked at it—too old even for ghosts. But I learned differently.

"Where men had once built homes for their families between the walls, grass now grew and hollows had filled with brackish water. Where sentries once paced on the top of the walls, bushes and trees sprouted. At one spot on the very crest of the wall an ancient oak dug its roots into the old stonework beneath the turf and lifted its branches to the high blue sky. A beautiful tree. A beautiful tree to look at and to climb.

"I was about four metres up when I made a sound that caught Lise's attention. She was lying in a patch of sunlight near the tree, dozing in the warmth. I was above her and when she opened her eyes she couldn't miss seeing me.

"My feet were dangling in the air. I swung them over the branch and pulled myself upright, reaching for the next branch.

Lise gasped.

"'Mathias!' she shouted. 'What are you doing?'

"I thought it was obvious what I was doing, so I didn't bother answering her. I just looked down and smiled. I considered dropping bits of bark down to tease her, but then decided against it. I thought the moment was perfect as it was. Lise had gotten to her feet by then.

"'Mathias, you little monkey! What are you doing up there? You're going to fall down and hurt yourself.'

"'No, I won't,' I called back. 'I never do.'

"'Come down right now before you get hurt!' she yelled. 'Right now! Do you want me to get into trouble with your mother?'

"'But I want to go higher! I've hardly started!'

"'I don't care! Come down!'

"But I decided to go higher, anyway. I liked Lise, but she wasn't my mother, was she? I suppose I was showing off for her, taking risks I wouldn't have normally have taken. I shouldn't have been thinking of her down on the ground. I should have been looking more carefully at the branch I was grasping.

"But I didn't look at the branch. It was dead—dead and brittle. I was actually looking down, grinning at Lise, when it broke. My grin turned into a gasp when the wood snapped and I felt myself starting to fall. I scrambled for another handhold, but I couldn't find one in time. My feet slipped off the rough bark. It happened so quickly. I heard Lise scream as my body crashed through the twigs and leaves.

"I was luckier than I deserved to be. I was above the slope of the old wall, rather than the top of it, so I didn't hit the ground square on. Instead, my feet hit the angled turf and tore the earth away from the rock and I slid. There was no sudden jar to my body. I scraped down the hard bank, the skin tearing on my hands, and I came to a stop with my cheek hard against the exposed stone. A sharp point was digging into my skin. I lifted my head away and saw a gaping gap-toothed mouth and two round eyes looking back at me. I yelled in fright and jumped back, sliding further down the bank.

"Lise had just reached me and was trying to see if I was hurt.

"'What is it?' I screamed. 'What is it?'

"Startled, Lise looked back up the bank of the wall and gasped.

"'It's the gripping beast,' she said with awe.

"She climbed back up and I followed, forgetting the pain of my scrapes and bruises. She was brushing the dirt away from a large flat stone, exposing an old, intricate carving. I felt embarrassed by having let an old stone frighten me, so I reached to help her clean it off.

"The whole carving was more than two metres from side to side and just as tall. The face was in the middle of it, attached to a small head that was itself stuck on the top of a tiny body. Four long twining limbs surrounded the body in a wild pattern of twists and twirls. They all ended in hands that held whatever they happened to meet: arms, legs, or other hands. I felt those hands could lift off the stone and reached out towards me.

"'What is it?' I asked again, feeling calmer.

"'It's the gripping beast, Mathias,' Lise answered. 'The Vikings carved them. This must be a thousand years old.'

"Lise told me about the beast. I don't know how much she was just making up on the spot, but I remember all of it. I believed all of it. She said I had nothing to fear from this ancient carving—it was just old stone—but she said I had to watch out for the real gripping beast.

"'It's alive today,' she said. 'It lives inside people and it reaches out to bring others into its clutches. It lives inside the war. The Germans are in the grip of the beast. You can tell they aren't sane any more. They are ruled by a madman and they are all becoming mad. The stupid look on the beast's face tells it all. It lives only to draw more people within its grasp and turn them into other gripping beasts. We all have to be careful. We all have to keep out of its reach.'

"I think afterwards Lise was sorry she told me this. I started dreaming of the gripping beast. In the dark nights I fell from the tree and landed on the stone again and again. I saw that gaping mouth and the wide round eyes, but in my dream I couldn't move away. In my dream I couldn't lift myself off the stone. The thing had me and held me. I felt its hands on me, gripping and letting go and then gripping again, harder and firmer. Its touch was cold and rough and dry, and I'd feel numbness spreading across my skin.

"I would scream, but no one heard me. I fought back, but nothing happened. No one could help me.

"The dream went away after a while and I thought that was the end of it, but I was wrong. The dream came back. But it came back when I was awake. The beast finally found me and caught me and held me. I tried to yell, to stop it, but no one heard. I tried to fight back, but it only grew stronger…"

Finne suddenly stopped talking. He looked down at his hands on the table and rubbed the palm of his right with the fingers of the other. He rubbed as if it hurt, as if he was trying to erase an old sore. Then he seemed to realize what he was doing and stopped. He continued his story.

But I'm getting ahead of myself here, aren't I? I'm telling you the end of the story when I should be telling you the beginning. I should be telling you how I met Lise.

My life changed after we moved to the island. It changed far more than I could have foreseen. It changed in ways I only dimly understood.

Once we were on the island and settled into our new house, I felt the effects of my father's decision to take the job with the newspaper almost immediately, although I didn't understand the connection. Children no longer played with me. Mothers, who in other times and places might have smiled at me and given me warm bread to eat, acted as if they could no longer see me. I wondered what I'd done wrong.

For a few days—or maybe weeks—I'd run up to other children and try to make friends, but they'd only run away and jeer at me from a distance. When parents were nearby, they'd pull their children away, scolding them not for their cruelty, I'd think, but for noticing me at all. Those mothers and fathers rarely even looked my way.

They were afraid, you see. They weren't trying to be cruel. They were only trying to protect themselves and their families.

My father was a Dane who worked for the Germans. He was a Nazi. He was seen more and more frequently in the company of high German officials. They were even visiting our house. I was an innocent child, but what did innocence mean in those days? We were at war and my family was helping the enemy.

So I learned how to be alone. I stopped running after the children who might have been my friends. I stopped crying when they taunted me. I stopped wondering. I tried to stop caring.

I grew lonely. My father was rarely home and when he came in he was often in a bad mood, muttering about some job or another and complaining to my mother about little things she'd done wrong. As a result my mother became irritable, too. I could see she wasn't always looking forward to his return in the evenings. A light was going out in her eyes. It would eventually be replaced first with a spark of anger, then by a dull grey mist.

The days would find me crouched alone on the cobbles outside my door, pushing wooden toys over the stones, watching people pass by the end of the lane. The evenings would find me back indoors sitting in silence eating supper with only my mother, or with both my parents. It was just as quiet with the two of them, but the tension was much higher. Later, before bed, I'd pull a book off the shelf and flip through the pages. New books were scarce and I knew my old ones far too well.

In the morning, if it wasn't raining, and sometimes even when it was, I'd be back outside sitting on the step. Day after day it was the same thing. As the spring weather warmed up I grew used to the pain, but I couldn't handle the boredom.

It was on a sunny day that I finally disobeyed my mother and broke through the confines of my parents' lives. She'd forbidden me to go beyond the sight of our front door, limiting my world to the few metres between Butchers Road and the elbow of Soldier Street. I lost interest in my wooden carts and spent more of my time watching people walk past. I'd creep to the end of the street—glancing behind me now and then to see if my mother would call me back—and crouch behind a lamp post, imagining myself well hidden.

Mostly I'd see housewives heading to or from the markets, their cloth bags either rolled up beneath their arms, or weighed down at their sides with their few purchases. There were children I didn't know—some with those same wives, some alone, some in small groups. Since they didn't know me they left me alone, ignoring me completely.

Older kids would go by, too: errand boys who never saw me, girls who would sometimes smile if they caught sight of me behind my post. I'd smile back. I could never resist.

But it was the men who passed who provided the most variety. Office workers dressed in neat suits would stroll sedately by, tipping their hats to each woman they met. Workmen clutching lunch pails or tools walked by in small groups, joking and laughing as they moved from one job to the next.

German soldiers in grey uniforms marched past in double rows or sped by in automobiles and on motorcycles. I didn't see many of them because Butchers Road was not a main thoroughfare.

After a few days the regulars knew me and I knew them. A routine set in. People would walk past and I'd remain. They'd come by again and I'd still be there. I got tired of hiding behind my lamp post.

Then one day a surprise came from behind me. I was at my post in the early afternoon watching people return to work after dinner. My mind was wandering, my attention on nothing in particular.

I heard a loud bang and turned in time to see a young man in dirty blue work clothes run around the corner of my street, his boots slipping on the smooth stones. He gained control of himself, only to trip and sprawl headlong onto the cobbles a couple of metres away. He turned towards me as he scrambled to his feet and I saw blood at the corner of his mouth and a wild look in his eyes.

"Hide!" he croaked and stumbled on, careening around the corner, his boots clacking rapidly on the sidewalk as he sped away. He had come and gone in seconds—and then I saw what he was running from. I ducked around the left-hand wall as two Germans with rifles appeared. They seemed to know where their quarry had gone; they didn't hesitate as they ran to follow. But, in passing, one of them kicked something out of his way. I looked and saw it was one of my toy cars, broken now. I realized it was this that the man had tripped on. Guilt flared inside me. I hurriedly picked up my toy and ran down Butchers Road after the Germans. I don't know what I wanted to achieve— maybe just to say I was sorry.

I didn't have far to go. I darted around a wall and into a larger street in time to see one of the Germans shout "Halt!" and lift his rifle to his shoulder. The fleeing man was a short block away. He checked his stride, his head turning to look. He was groping for something in a deep pocket of his jacket and he pulled out a dark object. There was a crack and the man seemed to trip and fall again, crumpling to the ground. He dropped the object and it hit the stones with a metallic clatter. I could see it was a small gun.

The soldiers had shot the man. Maybe they thought the workman was going to shoot them first. I looked at the broken toy in my hands and I dropped it. I thought that if I hadn't left it in the street he'd still be alive. If I hadn't left it for him to trip over, the soldiers would never have caught up with him—my fault, all my fault.

The Germans walked towards their victim warily, as if they expected him to jump up and attack. One of them kicked the discarded handgun further away from the body. I started to shiver, tears blurring my sight. I felt myself losing control of my grief, all my frustrations pouring out. That's when I felt the hands on my arms, hands pulling me back around the corner to safety. Arms held me as I cried, my wailing muffled against a soft sweater. After what seemed a long while I calmed down, wiped my eyes, and looked up. That's when I first saw Lise.

Suddenly Finne smiled. He smiled with real happiness, the first I'd seen on his face. The years dropped off him. He seemed a younger man full of hope and confidence, a man who knew his place in the world, who was sure of a woman who loved him.

I was entranced. I forgot my fear. I forgot my grief. I forgot the man I saw die in the street. I only saw Lise.

I must have looked pathetic, my face grubby with dirt and tears and now my mouth gaping open as I stared at her in blissful wonder. She laughed and I was lost...

She was beautiful. Hair so long and thick and yellow it ran down her shoulders like liquid sunlight. Eyes so bright blue they were like glimpsing the sky through crossed fingers. Her mouth curved slightly with amusement when she saw my confusion—her lips seemed always ready to break into a full smile. I was lost, sitting there circled by the warmth of her arms.

"My name's Lise," she said. "What's yours?"

"Mathias," I whispered, still in shock.

"Mathias!" she repeated in a stronger voice than mine and with a chuckle. "Well, Mathias, you look a mess! Where do you live?"

I told her. She helped me to my feet, took my hand and we trundled the short distance to my door.

Four

I stopped Finne and called a guard to take him back to his cell. That dirty little room had been his home for two weeks, ever since he appeared at the Petrovka 38 police station and started arguing incomprehensibly with the turnstile guard. He'd never have been allowed inside the station if he hadn't slapped the guard. Even then, he would have rotted, ignored in his cell for much longer, except someone finally understood he wanted to confess to murder.

That changed everything. That's when they called for me. Not that I'm anything special. I was just an officer who spoke English.

Moscow was hot that spring and heat always puts me in a bad mood. I prefer winter. My favorite memories are all of wintertime. I always remember snow wafting down from grey skies when I think back to my childhood. Moscow is a city made for winter.

But now it was hot in Moscow and I was feeling cranky when I first questioned Finne. I didn't want to give him much of my time.

It wasn't long before I was giving him all of it. In my mind he began to represent all I detested about this new world we suddenly found ourselves in. Here was this foreigner from the west. Like all the others, he comes to Moscow with his demands and we have no choice but to listen. What saddens me is they're right. Before Gorbachev, before Perestroika, it would have been different. Before Glasnost I would have been able to deal with them properly. But not now.

Now we are supposed to join with the west and be partners in capitalism. Now we have banks and businessmen. Now we are prostitutes—all of us whores. We have lost our independence. We have lost our pride. We have forgotten the danger of the west and now we must play by their rules.

But this westerner had come to us with his confession. I'd been told to find something to charge him with or to release him. I wanted to make a thorough investigation and charge him with the murder he said he'd committed—I would, at least, do that much for him. If he had indeed committed such a crime then it was my duty to make sure he paid for it. But there were so many problems to solve: this crime was at least fifty years old, he had committed it on an island hundreds of kilometres away from Moscow, and Finne would not even tell me the identity of his victim.

I am a good policeman and so I know that good research makes the foundation for a good case. I knew little of Denmark and nothing of Bornholm that first day, so I looked them up. Denmark is a Scandinavian country on the other side of the Baltic Sea. It is a small land with no serious industrial capacity. Its main exports are butter and fish. As for Bornholm, it's just a Danish island off the south coast of Sweden. From what I could tell it didn't even have butter—just the fish.

What these places had to do with Russia and the Great Patriotic War was harder to discover. I toured the huge, newly built war museum—just the walk from my car to the front doors was long enough to hurt my feet—but found nothing. I saw films of Stalin and Hitler, old rifles and uniforms, maps of campaigns, and panoramic scenes of the great sieges and battles, but nothing about Denmark or Bornholm.

I fought with the crackling phone lines to call one university after another, hoping to find an historian who knew of such things. One, two, three, and then four of them said I was wasting my time. Number five, however, said he knew of a crazy old professor who might be able to help me.

"He's a strange old man," Number Five told me. "But I think he's some kind of authority on Denmark and what we did there in the war. He came around here a couple of years back with a book and he wanted help publishing it. I had a look at it and I think he may even have mentioned this island of yours."

"A book?" I asked. "Did you help him with it? Did he get it published?"

It sounded like just the thing I needed.

"Good Lord, no! If I'd done anything for him I might have ended up in jail. The book was quite dangerous, what little I read of it. No wonder he was having trouble getting it printed. He must have been pretty desperate to go around asking for help like he did. There was nothing I could do for him. He got quite abusive when I told him that."

"Do you know where I can find him?"

"Just a minute. I'll see if I kept his address."

My helper soon returned on the line with the professor's telephone number.

When I called the professor and told him what I wanted, he chuckled—I thought it was out of pleasant surprise—and he said he'd be delighted to help. He'd actually been to Bornholm as a soldier in the months after the war was over, he said. He loved it. The island was like a rest camp for the Red Army troops in Germany. They'd be sent up for a couple of weeks and they'd barter watches and other "acquired" German goods for excellent Danish snaps. The people welcomed them. The children loved them. Never any problems. Nothing important ever happened there.

When I asked, the professor told me I could visit, but not without a hint of hesitation in his voice. It made me wonder if he'd hoped to put me off with all the good things he'd said and was disappointed that I wasn't satisfied. I went around to his place right away.

What I'd taken on the phone to be good humour turned out, in person, to be nervousness. When the historian opened the door to his dingy apartment and saw me, he laughed. It was the same laugh as I had heard on the telephone, but now I saw the restless twitch of his eyes, the insincere smile.

"The police," he said, once he saw my identification. "The police? Why are the police suddenly interested in the war?"

I wondered why was he nervous about that interest. But that wasn't why I was there, so I let the thought sink unexamined into my mind.

"I need background information about this Danish island you were on: why it was important, what we were doing there, what happened before we arrived."

We were standing in the entrance hall, just inside the door. His shoulders were stooped, but he was still a head taller than I was. From that height he looked down, swaying slightly, apparently thinking about my request. His red, watery eyes sat in nests of wrinkles. He looked older than Finne.

"Come," he said and led me into one of the flat's two rooms. He motioned me into an armchair and he sat, bending slowly and carefully, onto the bed. I refrained from placing my hands on the armrests of my chair; they were too grimy for my taste, as was everything else in sight.

"The police," he said again and I realized he was drunk. He had that peculiar sluggishness of mind typical of someone who's sodden with drink. "Why are the police interested in the war?"

I tried again, speaking slowly and clearly, as if to a child.

"You said on the telephone you were on Bornholm with the Red Army. I've been told you've studied the history of this island. When were you there? Why was the Red Army there?"

He ignored me.

"I'm not afraid of the police. I'm not afraid of you. We're a long way past the old days, you know."

Yes, I thought, we are. I could see this going on for some time and I didn't have the patience for it. I fished my wallet from my jacket pocket and counted out five 10,000 rouble notes. Not a lot of money, but as I laid it on the arm of my chair I hoped it would be enough. Expenses didn't cover this sort of thing anymore.

"All I want to know is history," I said. "You're an historian. Tell me."

He looked at me and then looked at the new banknotes. I finally had his attention. The money was probably double his state pension for a month. With rotgut vodka selling at 4,000 roubles a bottle, he didn't really have a choice.

I got my history.

"I landed on Bornholm only a few days after the Germans gave themselves up," the old historian said.

"I won't tell you about the horrors I knew in those years." He chuckled—a dry laugh that turned quickly into a cough. "If you want to know about them you can read them over there!"

He pointed towards a bright plastic bag lying carelessly in a dusty corner. I saw the picture of a pretty blonde girl on the outside. It was one of those lurid plastic bags you see everywhere these days—one of the fruits of capitalism. Moscow's streets are now full of shoppers—young men, old women—displaying photos of scantily clad girls on their groceries. I looked at it with distaste. It was yet another example of our lost pride.

But the historian wasn't referring to the colourful image on the outside. He was talking about the mass of papers stuffed inside.

"You can read them," he repeated, "but no one else will. They say it's too sloppy, that I'm too sloppy!"

I saw his eyes go towards my money again. He stood up and left the room.

I heard the clink of glass from the kitchen and he returned clutching a large bottle of vodka and two cups. He filled both, handed me one, and downed his in three gulps. He sighed happily and refilled it. I put mine on the arm of the chair and it sat there, quietly inviting me to drink it. I hadn't had a drink for more than a year and the temptation was still strong.

"I'd seen horrors," he continued, "so I was not surprised to see the sunken ships in the little harbour. I remember one: a white ferry with a big hole in her hull, lying on her side, still tied to the wharf. We joked about orderly Germans making sure the wreck didn't drift away." He laughed again. "I would have been shocked if there hadn't been any ships there! It had been so long since I had seen a country without war...

"I wasn't surprised to see all the Germans either. The little herring boat I was on—it stank horribly—had disgorged a load of these beaten soldiers at Kolberg before taking my comrades and me on board. In Rønne, where we landed, there were hundreds, maybe thousands, crammed together by the harbour, waiting to be shipped out. I had a look at them; they were without weapons and looked tired and dirty. They just sat and chatted quietly together. They were beaten and looked it.

"As I walked up through the town I could see men were clearing up the debris from a recent bombardment. I learned we had done it and had sunk the ships in the harbour and some more outside.

"It had to be done. The Germans there wouldn't surrender. Our armies were way past the island. They were already at the Elbe River—they were already in Berlin!

"Hitler was dead and Germany had surrendered, yet here was this Nazi commandant on this insignificant little island in the Baltic and he refused to give himself up!

"He was a real Nazi. He had his orders, you see, and nobody had changed them. He had orders to never surrender to the Soviet Union. I suppose if the English had come, or the Americans, he would have cheerfully let himself be locked up—but not us...oh, no! Not us!"

The historian took a long slug of his drink and glared at me as if I was responsible for how some fascist followed his orders.

"Why aren't you drinking with me?" he suddenly demanded.

I told him I was trying to give it up. He grunted, looking from the full cup to me as if he took my abstinence as a rebuke.

"Anyway," the professor continued, "that Nazi wouldn't give himself up and we had to bomb the place and—you know what?—he still wouldn't give up! He still had to wait for his damned orders and they didn't come until hundreds more died. We dropped the bombs, but he was the one who really killed them—not us!"

Anger rose up inside the historian and I saw his hand tremble as he poured more vodka into his cup. I suddenly felt as if I was witnessing a private argument he'd had over and over again—with himself? With someone else? I didn't know and I thought I'd never know.

But there was something else in his manner that told me he was directing some of his anger at me. Perhaps he did not like to drink alone.

"All those dead Germans," he continued, "probably felt cheated in the seconds before death, if they had time to think about it. Either they'd escaped us across the Baltic and felt safe on this little island, or they'd spent the whole war on Bornholm and had had nothing worse than drunken fishermen to deal with. Getting killed by a Soviet bomb just when they were thinking they might see home again must have been quite a shock for them!"

The historian laughed. He loosened up as he got drunk—or, rather, as he got drunker.

"So what did you want to know?" he demanded. "Statistics? In the war there were about 35,000 Danes living on an island forty kilometres long by twenty wide. The island's rocky in the north and the middle, but sandy in the south. It's got two main towns: Rønne and Nexø—ugly names!"

His mood was rapidly changing, becoming more and more belligerent. He was slopping his drink onto his knees as he gestured with increasing agitation.

"The people are fishermen, farmers, and stone-cutters. They know how to work, but they don't know how to suffer!

"We sat on that godforsaken island for nine months, growing lazy and fat. The children loved us, but the grown-ups couldn't wait to get rid of us. We could tell! We could tell!

"What else do you want to know?" he shouted at me, flecks of spittle spraying onto the rug. "What else!"

I decided to leave. I put my cup down on the floor, thanked him quickly and, as he glared at me, I walked down the short hallway and opened the door.

"Wait!" he shouted. I turned just in time to catch the paper-filled plastic bag as he flung it against my chest. I looked at the photo of the near-naked girl and at the typewritten pages packed tightly underneath her. The bag was heavy and I looked up at the historian with surprise.

His left hand held his vodka bottle while his right hand clutched the doorway to support his swaying body. He waved the bottle at me.

"You want to know about the war? You read that, Comrade Policeman! You just read that!"

He lurched back into his bedroom and I left, carefully trudging down the dark stairway. Once again in my car, I tossed the package onto the back seat and sat gazing at the historian's building before starting the engine. As I drove away I wondered why he'd said nothing about what he'd done on the island. It occurred to me his drunken rant didn't quite ring true. I could not spot any obvious lies, but his anger seemed a little forced, as if he was using it to hide something from me. I put the thought away, hoping vaguely that I wouldn't have to meet him again to find out.

FIVE

"THESE DAYS CHILDREN rebel against their elders, don't they?"

Finne and I were seated at the table in the interview room the next morning. I hadn't said anything to him about my independent research. It wasn't his business at this stage of the investigation.

"I heard all about their rebellions: Paris, London, San Francisco. There was even some of that in Toronto—that's where I live, or where I used to live." He paused for a moment. "I guess it was different here in Moscow. No one was allowed to rebel here, were they?"

I could have told him otherwise.

"Lise was a natural rebel. If she was a child today you'd see her in the streets at the front of every demonstration, behind the hottest barricades, her words in the most radical newspapers. She always knew where she was going, what she was doing.

"But I'm daydreaming again. Lise isn't a child today. Besides, she had something real to rebel against. Those French students going against the French government—that was nothing! They wouldn't have lasted five minutes against the Nazis. Lise lasted five years!

"It wasn't children against parents in those days, not for most people, anyway. I guess things were a lot simpler, in a way. If you wanted to rebel it was easy to find a target: he was patrolling the streets in a German uniform. So rebels like Lise didn't fight against their elders; they fought with them against a common enemy.

"Not that Lise actually did any fighting. I don't think so, anyway. We had a quiet war on Bornholm. What we mostly did was watch and remember. That's what Lise taught me to do: watch and remember."

The girl Lise, Finne told me, started to spend much of her free time at his house. During that first visit she introduced herself to Mathias's mother with proper gravity, explaining fully all that had happened to the boy. His mother had no harsh words for him, although he'd expected some for having left the street. She had grateful and welcoming words for Lise. The three sat at the kitchen table, the young Finne with a glass of milk, the other two with cups of tea, while Mathias's mother asked Lise about her parents and her school. When the girl left, mother and son were both smiling on the steps, urging Lise to come back soon.

So she came the following afternoon. Then she started coming two or three times a week after her classes. Soon, it was like she had always been there and would always return.

One day they decided to go visit Herr Finne at his newspaper office. The prisoner said he couldn't remember who first came up with the idea. He said it may have been him; he'd been in the shop on several occasions and its loud, clashing machines excited his senses. It could have been his mother, who probably needed a couple of hours to herself one afternoon. But knowing Lise, Finne said, he thought it was probably her suggestion.

Lise knew the way. Mathias wasn't surprised by this. Why should he be? By that time his adoration of the older girl was unshakable. He found nothing she did or said to be odd or unexplainable.

"Now don't you ask me any questions about what I'm doing while we're in there," Lise told Mathias as they approached the front door of the newspaper office. "Don't say anything to the soldiers, anything at all. Just watch and remember."

The girl knew there would be German soldiers inside the office because there was one outside beside the short stone step leading up to the entrance. He stood with a dull helmet on his head, a rifle slung over his shoulder, and a burning cigarette half-hidden in one hand. He lifted the cigarette to his mouth, took a quick drag, and exhaled the smoke in a rapid stream through clenched teeth. Then he saw he was no longer alone.

He tried to ignore Lise and Mathias. He tried to retain his dignified pose. They came and waited quietly, looking up at him. It was the first time Mathias had seen a guard at his father's door. They knew they needed his permission to enter, but they weren't sure how to get it. Lise took Mathias's hand and they stood perfectly still.

The forgotten cigarette burned down short. The soldier swore: "*Scheiße!*" and dropped the smoking butt. Lise didn't hesitate. She pulled the boy up the steps and through the door, opening and closing it with one smooth motion, before the German could react.

They were inside the newspaper's printing shop. A noise like a frantically beating metal heart poured out through the doors behind a short wooden counter. At this counter was another soldier, an officer—he wore a cap, not a helmet. He turned as Lise pushed the door shut behind her. A look of annoyance sprang into his face and he called to the man they'd left outside.

Lise spoke.

"This is Herr Finne's son. We are here to see Herr Finne, his father—*sein Vater!*"

The guard opened the door behind them, but the officer dismissed him with a flick of his hand. He turned to shout towards the printing shop floor. Carl Finne walked out, wiping his hands on a hopelessly blackened rag, looking curiously towards the German. Then he saw the children and came around the counter.

"Good day, Mathias. Good day, Lise. What are you doing here?" he asked in a puzzled, but not unfriendly way.

"Good day, Herr Finne," Lise answered. "Mathias promised to show me your shop. He's very proud of it!"

Mathias knew he'd never promised anything of the sort, but he said nothing.

"Can we come in and watch?" Lise continued. "We'll keep out of the way."

Mathias's father spoke with the German officer, who grudgingly looked up from some papers he was scribbling on, glanced at the children and nodded. Herr Finne turned back to Lise.

"Well, there's not much to see," he said, "but if you can keep Mathias under control you can go sit by the stacks."

Mathias noticed Lise was quite pleased with the proposition. But the stacks turned out to be, to the boy's disappointment, bales and boxes of printed papers. Nothing at all interesting to him. Mathias would rather have waited by one of the machines. He sat on a box with his hands on his knees and watched the activity taking place a few metres away.

There were four black machines filling the square room like the dots on dice. Three men worked each: one feeding in the paper, the other gathering it out and the third squirting oil into the mechanism and refilling the ink tank. One machine was silent. Its caretakers were setting the letters on the plate, preparing the words for the paper. These men were being watched by a German soldier with a rifle and a man in a suit and tie.

Mathias felt hot. He was dressed for a mild early summer day, but the heat in the print shop lay on him like a blanket. The air stank of chemicals.

The boy looked at Lise, who was sneaking glances at the papers around her, and wondered how she could be comfortable wearing her overcoat. He was about to ask when she saw his intent and looked at him crossly. Mathias shut his mouth, remembering her order.

But that didn't stop the boy from wondering not only about the overcoat, but also about why she wanted to see what was written on all the papers. She peeked at one stack, ignored it, and casually opened the flap of one cardboard box and then another. Mathias, fascinated, stared while he slipped a sheet out of the second box, folded it, and slid it inside her coat. She noticed his stare and whispered at him to look somewhere else.

The boy turned back to the machines. His father had returned and stood, rag in hand, beside the two German-flanked workmen. It was getting crowded in the corner. The workmen were just finishing their preparations. One threw a switch and the printing machine woke up, humming to life.

This caught Lise's attention. From then on she ignored the boxes and bales and concentrated on seeing where the man deposited this machine's products. At first the papers didn't go far. The workman, his hands clean, took a helping from the ever-growing pile of finished copies, squared them off, and laid them on a low, flat cart. He'd done this three times when the sound of ripping paper and clashing metal interrupted the work.

The feeder shut off the power and cleared the jammed paper, tossing scraps into a nearby garbage can. That done, he restarted the press and they finished off the short print run.

The cart was wheeled towards the children and brought to a halt beside them. The young soldier with the rifle eyed them suspiciously—and somewhat stupidly, Mathias thought—as the workmen packed the papers into boxes and sealed them. Lise smiled at the soldier, who blushed and looked away.

Once packed, the papers were wheeled out the back entrance and loaded into the trunk of a large staff car. All the Germans left with them.

Lise acted as if she couldn't have cared less. She turned her smile back towards the print shop, where the workmen were shutting down the remaining machines, one after the other. They ignored the children, finished their work, and left the shop without looking back. Mathias's father, who'd gone out onto the loading dock with the Germans, had not yet returned.

Alone, except for Mathias, Lise leaped up from her seat and darted over to the trash can. She picked through it, keeping some scraps, rejecting others. Those she kept she slipped inside her overcoat where they joined the other stolen items.

"That's it, Mathias. Let's go!"

She first went to the back door, to bid Mathias's father a polite farewell, then she led Mathias out the front door and into the street. They turned right and headed away at a good pace. Lise said nothing, her eyes studying the road before her feet. Mathias trotted beside her.

They went straight for a little while, then veered left and after that, right again. They wound through the cobblestone alleys, across the small thoroughfares, and ended up where three streets met, creating a tiny park at their junction. In it stood a bench and a tree.

The children sat down and Lise, who made no attempt to hide what she was doing, took the papers from inside her coat and folded them together. She tied the bundle tight with a dark blue ribbon that she pulled from her pocket and placed it, not well hidden, under a flat rock beneath the bench.

Then, without more fuss, she got up and Mathias followed her, the two taking a different route than the one they'd come on. Soon Lise had them steered back towards Mathias's house and the boy could no longer contain his questions.

"Lise? Why did you leave that there? What's it for?"

But she wouldn't tell him. All she said was that he must not speak of it to anyone. She made him promise.

Six

"I SAW MY first Russian in 1943," Finne said.

This was two years before the island was liberated, I quickly calculated. How could he have seen a Russian in Nazi-occupied Denmark? He answered my unspoken question rather cryptically.

"I saw him because Lise was watching him."

A worried look came into Finne's eyes, but it quickly passed. He shook his head as if clearing out an old, unwelcome guest.

"It was summer. She got us onto our bicycles early one morning because a mysterious little fly had crashed on the island. She'd been telling me about these things for weeks: how fishermen were talking about tiny airplanes, too small even for a pilot, that were falling into the waters around Bornholm. Since so few people had actually seen one, even at a distance, Lise said you could hardly believe they were real.

"Now there was one on the ground that had crashed in a turnip field not far from the south coast.

"By this time Lise and I did as we liked—or, I should say, Lise did what she liked and she sometimes brought me along. My parents trusted her, leaving me in her care for hours, sometimes overnight. They would ask where we were going and they would always believe the lies Lise told them.

"Not that they were big lies, not most of the time, anyway. If we were going to the forest, she'd say we were going to gather leaves for school. If we were going to the center of town she'd say we were off to see if there was any ice cream for sale.

"She never told them about the men we would sometimes meet in the woods: young Danes, often dirty, tired, and armed, but always friendly. They'd politely thank Lise for the message or the food she brought and then light their cigarettes with slightly trembling matches. I rarely saw the same man twice.

"Lise never told my parents about the bundles of newspapers we'd pick up and drop off in different places around Rønne. We couldn't allow the Germans to see us with the grubby sheets. They were printed secretly in dark cellars. They told the truth, not the Nazi propaganda that was in the other newspapers—in other newspapers like my father's.

"When we returned to my father's office she'd say it was to bring him a cold ale on a hot day, or to pick up some scrap paper to draw on. She never said we only wanted to visit my father so that we could steal discarded papers from trashcans and desks. She never said that.

"So, my parents liked her, adored her, even, and encouraged my friendship with her. Lise liked them, too, it seemed. She spoke politely and cheerfully to them. She was always happy and considerate around them. She always deferred to their decisions. So, when she wanted me to join her on an expedition of some sort she had little difficulty getting their permission.

"That morning we rode for a couple of hours with the wind at our backs. I enjoyed our near-effortless dash down the dirt lanes between the farms. I tried not to think of the ride home against the wind.

"We reached the spot even before the Germans did, but we weren't the first. In fact, there was quite a large crowd by the road, all kinds of people gathered in bunches, chatting together. One Danish policeman was detailed to keep the mob at bay. This he did by giving stern looks to anyone who seemed to be going too far past a certain line only he could see. Another policeman and a man in a civilian suit and tie were using tape measures on a large crumpled metal cylinder—the thing everyone was here to see.

"We got off our bikes at the edge of the crowd and wheeled them in past the little knots of people. When we were near the front, but not right out first and foremost, Lise stopped. I looked around, but nothing caught my attention as strongly as the crashed airplane.

"The little fly looked three or four metres long, what was left of it, and about a metre wide. It had wings, but little of them remained except cracked and blackened stubs. The skin of the machine was an even dull grey, adorned only by the marks 'Vl 83'. Its tail dug a long gash in the earth that pointed south to Germany.

"The two men by the little airplane had put away their tape measures and notebooks and taken out small cameras. They glanced swiftly around, then moved from one position to another, snapping pictures. Everyone watched, but no one said anything until a woman warned: 'Germans!'

"The cameras disappeared and the two photographers waited calmly as a black sedan drove up, followed immediately by an open-backed truck.

"I leaned my bicycle on Lise—she took hold of it automatically—and slipped away to get a clearer view of the crash site. I could sense her amused frown aimed at my back, but I didn't turn to see it."

The Germans, Finne said, took over the site without much ceremony. The commander looked around, issued orders, then marched over to the top Danish policeman.

"How long have you been here?" he demanded.

"An hour, maybe a little longer," answered the uniformed officer.

The German stepped back and surveyed the crowd. The Danes gazed placidly back at him.

"Has anyone taken any photographs?" He turned to the policeman.

"No, I've seen no one," he answered. "These farmers have no cameras."

A few of the farmers, those who were close enough to hear what was said, nodded affably and helpfully, showing their empty hands, mumbling their agreement. "No cameras. No cameras."

The German didn't look convinced, but to prove anything he knew he had to make quite a few arrests. There were more than fifty people, old and young, men and women, standing patiently in the dirt around the crash site. He didn't have the manpower for any such action, nor the inclination.

"Very well," he said. "Just get these people moved further back and keep them out of our way."

The German officer and two others set to work with their own tape measures and cameras. Mathias had already seen this routine, so he looked towards Lise. She had remained with the bicycles, supporting one with each hand, but she wasn't looking at the crashed airplane; she was looking at a man.

He stood about eight metres away from her in the shade of a tree, behind a clump of women. He was a young blonde man who, Mathias thought, looked uncomfortable in his civilian work clothes. The coveralls seemed a bit too short on his legs and arms.

Mathias moved closer, but he worked his way around Lise's back so she wouldn't notice. The man, he saw, remained perfectly still. Like Lise, he was looking not at the wrecked plane, but at another man in the crowd—the suited man who'd assisted the Danish police.

The man in the suit was speaking with the police officer at that moment, but he didn't stay there long. A minute later he nodded farewell and carefully worked his way out through the knots of spectators. The blonde man followed immediately. Lise started and glanced around.

"Mathias!" she called in a loud whisper. She saw him, beckoned him over, and told him to follow her with his bike.

The suited man walked up the turnip field, past several German vehicles that were parked on the road. The path led to a gravel lane that entered the woods. He walked in. The others followed. None of them were noticed.

The lane cut through an evergreen plantation. The bushy green trees rose to five or six metres on either side of the path. The bright sunlight was shining straight down at that hour, bouncing up again off the white, hard-packed stones. The trees gave no shade against the increasing heat.

Once within the trees, the blonde man picked up his pace.

"Jensen!" he called.

Jensen turned suddenly, startled. He stopped and faced around to see who was behind him and Lise found a need to inspect the back tire of her bicycle. Mathias just continued on his way along the lane towards Lise.

The two men met and walked on together, passing out of the evergreens and into a stand of elms. They left the lane and followed a smaller path into a shallow valley. Lise pushed her bicycle to hide it among the pine branches and she called on Mathias to do the same. Unencumbered, they followed up the lane and into the forest, keeping themselves as well hidden as possible.

Gradually Lise and Mathias, by darting from tree to bush, worked their way to where a circle of logs lay as benches around a cold, black fire pit. The two men sat there smoking and talking and occasionally arguing.

"There were two of you with cameras," Mathias heard the young blonde man say. "You don't need both films."

"Of course we do!" the suited man answered. "What if one doesn't turn out? Our chances are better with two. Besides, we're not in the business of selling holiday snaps to the Russians! Why can't you bring your own camera to the party?"

"At least tell me the measurements," the younger man said.

The other agreed and pulled a folded sheet of paper out of an inner pocket. The Russian found a grubbier scrap in his overalls and jotted down the numbers with the stub of a pencil. He finished and tucked the information away. The two men stood up and returned to their discussion, the Russian pacing behind the logs while Jensen remained still.

Mathias couldn't hear all that was said at this point. He listened, not wanting to miss anything, but he only caught disjointed words when the Russian turned back towards him: "rockets," "Germany," and then "next month," and finally two words that sounded like a name.

"...von Braun," said the Russian. "When will he be here?"

"How the devil am I supposed to know that? You think the Germans clear their travel arrangements through me?"

The young man turned and paced away. Mathias, behind Lise's shoulder, shifted his weight and a branch snapped beneath his foot. The man spun on his heel. When he stopped he was pointing a gun through the bushes at Lise.

"Who the hell are you?" he demanded.

Lise stood up. The Russian gaped in astonished recognition.

"Lise! What are you doing here?"

Then he saw Mathias.

"Who's this boy?" he said, pointing with his small handgun.

"He's a friend of mine, Aleks," Lise said. "He's safe."

"Safe?" Aleks exclaimed. "Safe? Look where you've brought him! He's far from safe."

It dawned on Mathias that Lise knew the crash site would attract this Russian. She came to see him, not the little airplane. Where had she met him? How did he know her?

The man spoke Danish well, almost beautifully with his Russian accent. But his Danish had an urbane air about it, a taste of the city, the stamp of Copenhagen. It was clear to Mathias's ears that Aleks may not have been born in Denmark, but he'd spent a good deal of time there.

"Aleks, put the gun away," Lise said.

Aleks looked at his hand in surprise and then apologized, somewhat sheepishly. He put the firearm into a pocket and motioned for the children to come out from behind the bushes. Mathias saw no look of welcome on Jensen's face—only worry.

"I've been careless," Jensen said. "I didn't think these children had any-thing to do with us."

The suited man frowned at Lise and Mathias.

"Who are you?" he asked. "Where do you live?"

The children answered quietly and simply with their names and addresses.

"What are you doing here?"

Neither Lise nor Mathias spoke.

"I think the girl is following me, Jensen," Aleks said. "I met her when I was hiding in the woods north of Rønne. She was sent to bring me food. She's part of your effort."

Aleks looked at the girl as he said this and smiled—a wonderfully bright smile, Mathias noticed with an unease he didn't quite understand. Lise blushed, Mathias realized with shock. He'd never seen anyone make her do that before. Jensen looked from Lise to Aleks and nodded.

"I see. Well, I'd better be going. We'll continue our talk at another time."

He said farewell to the Russian, had a final look at the children, then walked away on the path. Aleks turned to Lise.

"What are you doing here?" he demanded harshly. "What business have you here?"

"We came to see the little fly and then I saw you," Lise lied.

"The little fly? Oh, the rocket! And then you saw me?" Aleks frowned. "Somehow I don't think that's all of it. You know I could have shot you?" he asked crossly.

"You couldn't shoot me, Aleks," Lise said, but she managed to sound con-trite. It was her turn to smile at him.

This disconcerted the young man, who stumbled on his words as he tried to speak. Finally he said, "Don't you believe it!"

Mathias was feeling strangely frantic. Lise seemed to have forgotten that he was there. She was talking with someone who had pointed a gun at them and was now threatening to shoot her! He wasn't sure he liked this mysterious blonde Russian. He was sure he didn't like the way this Aleks and Lise were looking and smiling at each other.

"We have to go," the boy said, breaking the spell.

Lise turned to look at him. She thought a moment before answering. Then she agreed, but with apparent reluctance.

The children collected their bicycles. The Russian walked with them a little way through the forest before saying a quick goodbye and heading off on a crossroad. Lise and Mathias mounted their bikes and started their ride home. Between his laboured breaths Mathias tried to get Lise to talk.

"Who is he?" he asked. "Where's he from? Why's he here?"

"I don't know. I'm not sure," Lise answered. "His name is Aleks."

"You don't know where he's from? You're not sure what he's doing here?"

"I think he's a spy," Lise said and then she wouldn't say any more. They rode the rest of the way back to Rønne without speaking, saving their energy for pedalling against the wind.

SEVEN

OVER THE NEXT few weeks Lise set out to learn all she could about rockets. There wasn't much in the town library, just an old encyclopedia with drawings of Chinese fireworks bursting over the Great Wall. Nothing, Lise complained to Mathias, of any use.

Beyond that there wasn't much she could do. Lise was a sixteen-year-old girl trying to find up-to-date information about military technology in an occupied country. Her instinct for secrecy had grown with each month she worked for the resistance, so she hesitated to come out with direct questions to anyone. She was most honest with Mathias, but all she would tell him was that no one could tell her much of anything. The robot bombs were so new and so unusual that few people knew more than Lise did herself.

The girl started making more visits to the newspaper office. Mathias had learned, long before, that she usually went to the shop when somebody else (somebody he never met) told her to go and look for something. Now he sensed she was going solely for her own purposes.

Both Lise and Mathias were now well known at Carl Finne's office. Sometimes even the sentry on duty recognized them with a smile, although they didn't always go when there were Germans on the premises. The two had started to help out—dusting, sweeping the floor, emptying the trash cans—so the workmen, who liked them anyway, were doubly glad to see them. If Lise took more care over the garbage than someone normally would, they didn't care.

Out of sight, Lise always made sure to examine every piece of paper the journalists and workmen had discarded. Some she kept, but she never seemed satisfied. Her forages through the bundles and boxes produced the same results. She would often find something worth keeping, but it would rarely satisfy her.

"What are you looking for, Lise?" Mathias asked a couple of times.

"Nothing," she would say. "Nothing at all."

But Mathias knew she was lying. He knew she was seeking a specific prize and one day she found it.

It wasn't much. The machines had wrenched and torn this sheet of paper. Ink was smeared over half of it and the surviving text looked distorted and stretched. To make matters worse, in Mathias's mind, the letters were printed in the German gothic script.

"Yes!" Lise exclaimed. "Look!"

She pointed at a name: Wernher von Braun.

"This is when he's coming!"

The paper she held was a routine inspection schedule printed for distribution among the troops or the officers. Wernher von Braun (whoever he was, Mathias thought) was going to be on Bornholm in three days.

They left the shop and headed down the lane. Lise tried to take Mathias home, but the boy wouldn't cooperate. He stood in the middle of a small street, a couple of blocks from his father's workplace, and demanded answers.

"Why do you want to know when he's coming?"

"Oh Mathias," Lise exclaimed. "Don't do this now! We're going to be late!" Mathias's mother wanted him home in time for lunch.

"Is it because you want to see Aleks again?"

Lise crossed her arms and stood looking down at Mathias in consternation. She said nothing. Mathias looked back up at her, enjoying, as always, the sight of her pretty round face framed by her unruly mass of blonde hair, but apprehensive of the anger he seemed to be awakening in her. However, he resolved not to back down. He crossed his arms in imitation of her gesture and repeated his question.

"You want to see Aleks again, don't you? Are you supposed to be doing this?"

Lise's frown didn't go away, but her eyes shifted away from Mathias. She unfolded her arms and stuck her hands in her coat pockets. She faced the boy again.

"Mathias…" she began, then stopped. She took a deep breath. "No, Mathias, I'm not supposed to be doing this. I'd…we'd be in big trouble if anyone found out."

"Then why…?"

Again Lise hesitated. She looked around as if checking for someone who might be listening.

"He's special, Mathias. He's come a long way to help us, all the way from Russia. He's not just running away or hiding or waiting until everything's safe again; he's fighting the war. He's risking his life. He wants to win the war. There's no one else like him here."

"But why do you want to see him again? Do you love him?" Mathias asked the question without fully understanding it. Even so, he suspected he wouldn't like the answer.

Lise's face flushed, but she drew herself up straight.

"Now you're asking silly questions," she scolded, but Mathias knew she was simply avoiding the answer. "It doesn't matter what I feel. This isn't about what I feel."

She looked down, avoiding Mathias's gaze.

"It's about the war," she said to the cobblestones at their feet. "It's about the war…about who's going to win the war."

Mathias took a chance.

"I don't believe you, Lise. I think you like Aleks and that's why you want to see him. I think you like him a lot."

"Okay…yes…okay, I like him…but…" Lise stopped. She seemed to realize she was backing herself into a dead end and her young friend wasn't going to let her out. She looked at Mathias again. Her frown was gone and there was the beginning of a new respect in her attitude.

"Yes, Mathias, I like him. I like him a lot. I want to see him again. I don't know where he's hiding. I think he wants to find this German scientist, so if we find the scientist first, I think we can find Aleks."

Now it was the boy who shifted his eyes away from Lise, who peered down at their feet.

"If you like Aleks so much, what about me? Does that mean you won't like me so much any more?"

Lise's eyes widened as she looked at the boy. She took her hands out of her pockets and put them on his shoulders.

"No, Mathias. No! It doesn't mean that at all. You're my best friend and I'll always love you."

She pulled him into a hug. He uncrossed his arms, slid them around her waist and held her tight.

Lise pulled away a little from her young friend and looked down at him. With one hand on his chin she lifted his face towards her. She bent slightly and kissed his left cheek.

"I kiss you once to tell you I love you, Mathias."

Then she kissed his other cheek.

"And twice means I'll love you for all time."

The boy looked up at her with wonder.

"I mean it, Mathias. I'll always love you. But Aleks...he's different...I don't know how to explain it..."

The two parted. Lise took Mathias's hand and they walked together towards Soldier Street. Mathias said nothing for a while, not knowing whether to be happy or sad. He had one last question running through his head.

"Do I have to like him, too?" he finally asked.

Lise laughed.

"No, I guess not," she said. "But you do have to help him."

"We became spies," Finne told me. The sun was on its way down and it was sending hot rays straight into the interrogation room. Neither of us had eaten anything at noon. Finne showed no inclination to interrupt his narrative and I wasn't hungry. We were drinking tea again to stave off the heat, but I was longing for something cold. I had a vision of a bottle of vodka taken straight out of a freezer, so cold it poured like molasses. I banished the thought and turned my attention back to Finne.

"We became two little spies," he said. "We'd been couriers and newspaper carriers for the resistance, but then we became spies for ourselves—or, rather, for Lise.

"Lise said this Wernher von Braun must be an important man if Aleks was interested in him, if the resistance knew of him, and if the Germans were scheduling him into their inspections. If he was important, she said, that meant he would be staying either at the main hotel down at the harbour or with the German commander. It depended, she said, on just how important he was.

"This was something we couldn't know without actually asking, and something we couldn't ask. The Germans, naturally, would never have told us. They would, in fact, have been seriously curious about why we wanted to know. That was the kind of danger we never even thought of risking. Their control of Bornholm may have been relatively light-handed, but everyone had heard enough stories about the Gestapo to not want to attract their attention. I never got the sight of the man being shot out of my memory.

"Nor could we ask any of our contacts in the resistance. It was hardly a hierarchical organization, but nevertheless it didn't encourage solo efforts. If anyone had found out we were messing around in resistance business—there's no doubt Wernher von Braun and his rockets were very much resistance business—we'd not have been left to run around for very long. If Aleks and Jensen were both interested in von Braun then the resistance was probably planning something. Our activities were likely jeopardizing their plans; I didn't think of that then, but I know it now. I don't doubt Lise realized it at the time. She was too smart not to have known something like that."

Finne turned to look out the window, his eyes squinting into the last of the sun's rays. I looked, too. The sun was a huge red ball half-hidden behind a mesh of branches and leaves. It wasn't sinking below the horizon—nothing so grand. It was slipping behind an old apartment building. For once I couldn't see the dirt and the ugliness; I just saw the beauty of the sun's light. Even knowing those rays were filtering through the city's polluted air didn't dull my appreciation. Then the sun was gone, but it left behind a red glow across the sky.

Finne was still watching, but no longer squinting. I wondered whether I should call a halt to the day's interview. I was now feeling a bit hungry and tired, but I wanted to hear more. Then Finne decided for me; he wanted to talk.

"Lise was smart and she knew what to do: there were two of us and two buildings to watch, so we got one each. Lise chose. I got the hotel. She got the Nazi headquarters. She said it was best that way seeing as a girl shouldn't be seen hanging around a hotel all alone. I think that maybe she also thought the chances were better to see this von Braun with the German commander.

"I may not have been as smart as Lise, but I wasn't stupid. I saw one problem with Lise's plan: I had no idea what Wernher von Braun looked like. If I couldn't ask anyone about him, I asked her, how would I know if he came to the hotel? Lise thought for a while, as if this had never occurred to her, and then she said I'd just have to listen carefully and trust to luck. I was to pay attention to anyone who looked important, any man who arrived with someone else carrying his luggage; anyone who had doors opened for him.

"So I found myself back down near the harbour. It was morning, but not too early. Lise and I had parted after we made our plans the evening before and we didn't bother to meet again. I assumed she was somewhere outside the German headquarters trying to look inconspicuous—a difficult thing for a pretty girl with sun-blonde hair to do.

"It was much easier for me. Not many people notice an eleven-year-old boy who's trying not to attract attention. Maybe when they see one sitting quietly they think it's a miracle he's not causing trouble, so they let well enough alone.

"Dams Hotel overlooked the waterfront. It sat at the intersection of three main streets: one led out of town northwards, another climbed the hill to the main square, and the third went out to the German camp at the edge of Rønne. Anyone who'd come into Rønne by boat or train had to pass by the hotel unless they wanted to find their way through the tiny, poor streets where the fishermen lived. Most people went by the hotel, which is probably why it did good business and why so many Germans stayed there.

"I sat for a couple of hours watching the hotel's front door from a bench beside the railway station across the street. I saw plenty of men in uniforms and business suits going in and out, walking past me, walking away from me, standing in the warm sunlight smoking and chatting together, or climbing into waiting cars and driving off, trailing gasoline exhaust. I had to keep reminding myself why I was there. At first I studied every man carefully, hoping to spot von Braun quickly, but none of them seemed to carry the importance I imagined he would wear like a cloak.

"I saw a little man with round glasses dart out of the way of a couple of officers who strode up to the door. He shuffled towards me and passed into the station, his eyes anxiously scanning the ground in front of his feet, an attaché case clutched tightly to his chest. No, I thought, that couldn't be him.

"I saw a tall man, broad-chested and well-dressed, come out of the train station. He wasn't carrying his own luggage, which was in the hands of an old porter who followed behind. He wasn't even carrying his own attaché case. A young, equally well-dressed man held the case and walked beside him, nodding seriously as he listened to what the older man was saying.

"The trio stopped a few metres away. The tall man pulled a slim gold box from an inside pocket of his jacket, flipped it open and took a cigarette out. Without waiting to be asked the younger man offered him a light. The older man bent slightly, sucking the flame from the silver lighter into his cigarette.

He didn't thank the younger man; he just blew out a stream of smoke through his nostrils and continued talking in German. I heard enough by that time to know he was speaking about money.

"This wasn't von Braun either. This was a businessman. von Braun wouldn't have bits of gold and silver shining from his fingers and cuffs and looped in chains across his chest. von Braun was a scientist. I somehow imagined him to be quieter in his importance.

"Then I saw a black sedan pull up to the hotel. Two men got out of the back. One of them remained standing beside the car, glancing casually around, while the other opened the trunk and took suitcases out.

"I got off the bench and walked closer to get a better look at the man on the sidewalk. He was about my father's age and about my father's size, but his clothing looked newer than anything my father owned. And they had something else in common: a small, round, red, white and black swastika pin. Like my father, this man wore his on his right lapel. Beyond that he wore no other jewellery and someone else was carrying his luggage.

"My heart leaped with excitement. I thought of how proud Lise would be when I told her I'd found von Braun. It must be him, I thought—and then he spoke in Danish, telling the man with the bags to take them into the hotel while he went across the street to buy cigarettes at the station. It couldn't be von Braun, I realized with disappointment. It was just some Danish Nazi. He was more like my father than I'd imagined.

"Soon after that I saw an old man who looked too frail to be important. There was a harassed-looking woman herding six or seven excited teenage girls out of the hotel. Then some Nazi officers laughing with great hoarse whoops, followed by a serious-looking troop of uniformed boys about my age who were obviously little Germans. I felt conspicuously shabby in my scuffed boots and carefully patched shorts, but they ignored me as their leader marched them past.

"By this time it was close to noon and I was getting hungry. I started thinking more about my grumbling stomach than about who was going in or out of the hotel. The scent of food cooking wafted out of the station restaurant. I could picture the boiled potatoes in brown gravy, the roasted beef and steaming red cabbage. I pictured the food heaped on a plate in front of me and imagined how it would taste as I forked it into my mouth.

"Not far from me, only a few metres away, a couple of hotel workers dressed in smudged white aprons set a huge pot on a table and began selling piping-hot red wieners with bread and mustard to passers-by who didn't have the money or the inclination to go indoors. I had no money at all, so I couldn't even buy a wiener. I could just watch the others enjoying them.

"My mother wasn't expecting me for lunch, but I thought of going home anyway to end the torture.

"So, sitting there on the station bench, preoccupied with imagining the taste of the food I could smell, studying the grocery bags more intently than the faces, I almost missed Wernher von Braun. The wieners saved me.

"I was watching the table, watching the kitchen workers fork the long, delicious tubes of meat into folded pieces of cardboard; watching the customers hand a coin or two over, spoon some mustard onto the cardboard, and help themselves to a slice of bread. I watched them dip the wieners into the strong mustard, lift them to their mouths and take satisfying bites out of them. I imagined the bliss the taste was giving them and I wanted some of that for myself.

"I slid off my bench and edged closer to the table. I had nothing planned; I just knew I wanted a wiener.

"What time is it?"

It took me a second to realize Finne had broken off his narrative and asked me a direct question. All the time he was speaking I was trying to take notes. I had a mass of papers in front of me filled with scrawled words, some in English, some in Russian. I didn't watch Finne much when he spoke. I listened to what he was saying and wrote it down as fast as I could, but my comprehension followed a little distance behind like the roar of a jet trailing a kilometre after the plane itself.

"The time?" I said, looking up at Finne stupidly.

"Oh…the time!" I glanced at my watch. "It's ten after nine."

"Ten after nine." Finne muttered more to himself than to me. "Ten after nine. I haven't eaten since breakfast and I'm not hungry. Am I so old that food no longer interests me? Not like when I was a boy. You're still young. Does the thought of food obsess you when you're hungry? Can you think of nothing else?

"Well, I guess you're not that young," he said as I shook my head. "Not as young as I was back then. What am I thinking? You're no child. You're a grown man!

"I was just an eleven-year-old child. It's amazing what you recall once you try to remember. They say you never forget anything, that your brain stores away every clipped fingernail, every kiss, every word read, every wiener hungered for....

"That may be true, but my brain doesn't always give me back my memories when I needed them. I've always been quick to forget—forget names, forget faces, phone numbers, birthdays. That day at the lunch hour I forgot why I was in front of the hotel. I forgot what I was supposed to be doing there. I let the sight and smell of those juicy red wieners hypnotize me. I let my growling stomach—and not my dull brain—direct my legs. That's how weak I was as a child: a few hours without eating and I felt I was starving!

"So I found myself standing beside the table with a small knot of workmen around me buying and eating wieners. I was a short kid, so this commerce went on over my head. I couldn't even see into the pot; the table was up to my chest and I had to look up to see the wieners pass over the rim of their container.

"Business was brisk, so I was ignored for a little while, but then one of the kitchen workers noticed me.

"'You want something?' he asked me.

"I had to say yes. Anything else would have been a lie.

"'Then let me see your money,' he demanded.

"I felt my face flush red with embarrassment. I had no money. I had nothing to show him. I said nothing, not knowing what to say.

"'Do you want to buy or not?' the man asked me. By this time he had both hands on the rim of the pot—it must have cooled down—and he was leaning over it looking down at me. I looked up at him into his iron-grey eyes set over a thin brown moustache and still I said nothing. I saw him as an adult with power and authority, but thinking back I realize he was probably just using me for a bit of mean fun.

"'What's the matter? Can't talk? No money? Well, go away then. Give room to the real customers.'

"There was nothing I would have preferred to do than disappear. I would have, too, except someone spoke up beside me. I heard Danish spoken in a heavy accent—a German accent.

"'The boy wants a wurst? I'll buy him a wurst. Give me two.'

"I looked up, startled and somewhat afraid, but was momentarily relieved to see the man who spoke was not wearing a uniform. The relief didn't last long. People wouldn't see a German soldier offering me a gift, but that didn't mean I wouldn't be guilty of mixing with the enemy. Young as I was, I knew it was wrong to accept gifts from Germans—everyone knew.

"I could see that the kitchen worker knew it, too. I saw a disapproving look flash over his face. It was, after all, not a feeling anyone could advertise to the Germans too openly. Nevertheless, the stranger saw it and understood it. And he must have seen something in my face as well.

"He looked from me to the kitchen worker and back. He had a large rectangular head with a surprisingly innocent face—a face that suddenly frowned.

"'Oh, come now,' he said to the kitchen worker. 'Where's the harm in giving one wurst to a hungry boy? I tell you what: I pay, you give it to him. Or you give it to the dogs. Or you eat it. Or you throw it away. I don't care. I pay, whatever you do.'

"The kitchen workers shrugged and dished out two wieners, giving one to me and one to the German. I didn't dare reach for any bread or mustard and took a bite out of it plain. It didn't taste quite as good as I'd hoped.

"Just then another German walked up to the table. He was a small, thin man wearing a severely plain dark civilian suit. He seemed annoyed, ignoring the wieners and addressing the stranger. '*Doktor von Braun!*' he said and continued on in a staccato of German, pointing to the station and his wristwatch, telling my benefactor they could not be late for a meeting.

"von Braun! My jaws locked on the meat. I stared at the man I'd been looking for all morning, shocked that I'd actually found him. The doctor was disagreeing with the other man about the importance of the meeting until he caught sight of me staring at him. He cut short what he was saying and stared back, obviously surprised by my expression. His angry companion followed his gaze and glared at me, further annoyed. I turned quickly away to resume my chewing.

"I wondered what to do. I'd found him—or he'd found me—what did it matter? I had to tell Lise, but what would I tell her? I still had to figure out if he was staying at the hotel or where he was going.

"The two men finished their argument and the naval officer stamped away. von Braun examined his neglected wiener, dipped it into a dab of mustard and bit off a length. He eyed me and spoke around the food in his mouth.

"'He is my babysitter. He thinks I should eat there,' he said, pointing with his shortened wiener at the station restaurant, 'and not here. I like better to be outside in this nice weather, but I don't always get what I like.'

"He took another bite and chewed away, stuffing a bit of bread into his mouth as he looked around.

"'It's a pretty town you live in. Nice houses. Nice people. My name is Wernher. What is your name?'

"I told him, almost in a whisper, and he nodded his head.

"'Mathias!' he said. 'A good strong name. I'm pleased to meet you, Mathias.'

"He stuck out his hand for me to take—a thing no adult had done for me before. I reached up and took it. He gave my hand one vigorous shake and let go.

"'Well, my young friend, I must go. Perhaps we shall meet again? Yes, perhaps. Farewell!'

"I watched him until he walked through the main doors of the station. Then I turned and ran as fast as I could to find Lise."

EIGHT

I HAD FINNE brought back to his cell. I went down to my car.

I showed my pass to the exit guard, turned right out of the gate and then left onto Petrovka Street. I hate driving. I especially hate it now when I have to fight for room against all these shiny new BMWs and Mercedes. I can never see the drivers through the tinted windows, but the automobiles themselves exude disdain when they pass my ten-year-old Lada. Even when I bought it five years ago I wasn't "King of the Road", but at least the road wasn't so full of serfs like me. Now all the Mafia are driving supercharged western cars and I can't go half their speed. They blow their clean exhaust at me as they elbow past, blaring their deep-throated horns, and I'm left to doddle along in their wake. I hate driving.

The sun had set and the workday was long over for most, but the traffic was still heavy. I wondered where they all were going at this hour. Probably to the new bars and cabarets and restaurants. Places I couldn't afford. Places I'd have trouble entering even if I was on official business, or maybe especially if I was on official business.

Thinking about the restaurants reminded me that I hadn't eaten for hours. I felt tired and hungry, so I stopped at the next metro station I saw.

Most of the sellers had gone home, but a few old women were still sitting beside their overturned cardboard boxes trying to get rid of what they had left. I found what I wanted: a loaf of bread at one box; a square of cheese at another; a couple of bottles of fruit soda at a third. It all set me back 10,000 roubles—the price of a small cup of coffee at one of the new restaurants. I examined a liter of milk sitting alone on a box, but rejected it; chances were it had turned sour and undrinkable.

I'd forgotten to bring a bag along so I clutched my purchases precariously in my arms as I walked back to the car. I levered the door open, sat down, dumped everything into the passenger seat, and drove on home through the dark streets. I arrived, parked, and looked at my groceries. I wished again that I had a bag to carry them in. Then I remembered that, in fact, I did have one.

I opened the door to turn the dome light on and craned around in my seat to reach for the professor's gift, if gift you can call it. I tugged the papers out of the garish plastic bag, left them on the back seat, and stuffed my purchases inside. The blonde girl was no longer flat; instead, my bread and cheese made her bulge in inappropriate places.

A gust of wind blew in through the open door and I heard the papers scatter. Cursing, I swivelled around again to gather the pages back together. Only a few had left the top of the pile, so it just took a second, but that was long enough for me to glance at the first one.

It was cheap, soft, yellow paper, ragged at the corners, grubby with smudged ink and embellished with a stain from the bottom of a coffee cup. The words seemed to have been typed with an old machine: the letter k was crooked and the O was filled in solid. Corrections had been made by X-ing out the mistakes. There was no title and the author hadn't added his name.

Despite my hunger and fatigue, I started to read.

"When I was young I believed in the Revolution. I venerated the wisdom of Comrade Vladimir Ilyich Lenin. I obeyed Comrade Joseph Stalin. I was a good Communist.

"Now I am nothing. I believe in nothing. The Revolution was a lie. Lenin was a fraud. Stalin was a murderer."

I sighed with disgust. The professor had called his work a history, but it looked like just another diatribe against the past. Nothing new. Still, I thought to myself, there may be something interesting in it. I bundled the papers under my arm and brought them and the groceries inside.

I sat down at my kitchen table, popped open one of the bottles I'd bought, tore off chunks of bread and cheese and gorged myself. No feast, but satisfying. After my initial rush to dull my hunger I continued nibbling at crumbs and flipped idly through the manuscript. I drank the soda in large gulps, suppressing a wish that it was vodka instead.

My anticipated boredom turned into a steadily growing interest. I'd been wrong. This wasn't simply a diatribe.

I sampled one page after the other, tasting sentences as I went along. I learned that the professor had been involved with the GRU—the Red Army's intelligence wing—during the Great Patriotic War. He'd run agents into the German-occupied countries; he had an agent on Bornholm. My interest turned into astonishment when I saw, rendered phonetically into the Cyrillic script, the name of Mathias Finne. I cursed my stupidity for having thought so little about the old historian.

"The boy Mathias Finne," I read, "was used by the Danish partisans as a link to the Nazi rocket scientist Wernher von Braun. Somehow the two had become friends, a fact that could not be ignored given the boy's previous connection with the partisans. My agent perceived the opportunity the situation offered and set about exploiting it. We did not want von Braun to go to England."

I flipped the pages back to read more carefully. I skipped the professor's introduction, which simply expanded on his hate for the Communist Party without fully explaining it, and delved into an account of how he went about recruiting agents in the early days of the war. Aleks had been one of them.

Aleks had been born in St. Petersburg. He was the son of an Imperial government official who fled westwards after the Bolsheviks took power. The family settled in Copenhagen and taught their young son to hate the new regime. He would have gone on hating that regime for his whole life, most likely, except for one thing: the war.

Aleks had been taught to hate the Soviet Union, but to love Russia. The professor used that to draw in many of the young exiles he recruited to his spy network. No one could have convinced them to help the Bolsheviks, but Mother Russia herself was in danger. Stalin used this tactic to rouse the country when the Germans invaded. The professor used it on Aleks. Even so, according to the professor's account, the young man was not an easy sell.

"My next subject for recruitment was Aleksander Baklanov, age eighteen. He was very suspicious of me and he demanded how I knew to find him in Stockholm. We were having coffee in the central railway station, hiding among all the legitimate travellers. However, Baklanov made us conspicuous when he shouted at me in his queerly accented Russian.

"'You have been spying on me!' he accused.

"I told him how we had informants among all the exile groups in Europe and that was how I'd known that he and his mother and father were able to cross the narrow strait between Denmark and Sweden when the Germans invaded.

"'You lure me here with lies, telling me you have bad news about my family and you need me to inform my parents. First you lie to me, then you tell me you've been watching me. What do you want from me?'

"I knew I had to be careful how I answered. I didn't want to scare him away with the truth. I knew the kind of language he must have heard in his home and I used it to wind him in.

"'Mother Russia needs all her sons,' I told him. 'You have fled from the Germans to save your life. Why? Are you now content to hide here while your brothers and sisters die?'

"If I thought the young Baklanov was already angry, then I was wrong. His face turned bright red. He banged his fists on the table. More customers turned our way, startled.

"'I have no brothers, no sisters! What kind of nonsense is this? If you think I'm a coward, why don't you say so? You think I owe Russia my life? My parents and I would be dead right now if we hadn't left. You think I now owe my life to the Bolsheviks!'

"I decided it was my turn to show anger.

"'You young fool!' I hissed at him. 'Your head is stuffed full of mud and clay! You think we are murderers? Your parents would have been welcomed into the Revolution! The Revolution is for everyone, even silly young asses like you!'

"I sat back glaring at him, letting him digest the insult. Then, just as he was about to say something, I continued, but in a calmer, reasonable tone.

"'But how could you know this?' I asked. 'You were a child when you left Leningrad. A little child on a great adventure. You only know Russia through other peoples' memories. Those were wonderful times, but troubled, full of misunderstanding. Now our country is in danger and we must forget our differences.'"

The professor had to meet Aleksander Baklanov several times before he was able to convince the young man to work for him. He wove together a mesh of threats and bribes, of promises, insults, and compliments. One minute he said the Red Army didn't really need him, that it was doing him a favour by offering him a role in the war. The next minute he'd turn it around and fan his immature pride with syrupy words about the man's worth and his potential value for the organization. In the end the young man must have been so confused that he didn't know what he was agreeing to. But agree he did.

I looked up from the manuscript and saw that the darkness was leaving the sky. I'd sat and read longer than I'd wanted. It was too late to go to bed, but too early to go to work. I made myself tea, strong and black. I sat back down and began turning the pages once again.

I awoke several hours later. The sun had risen high enough to clear the neighbouring buildings and shone down through the window and into my eyes. I blinked painfully and lifted my head, again painfully, off the slightly crumpled manuscript that had become my pillow. I was late. My tea was cold, but I drank it anyway.

The plastic bad stuffed full with the manuscript attracted whistles from some of my colleagues when I hurried through the station hallways with it clutched under one arm. I ignored the laughing comments they threw at me.

"Hey, Misha! Late night with your girlfriend?"

I'm not sure why I brought the manuscript. I had no intention of showing it to Mathias Finne, or to anyone else. I just couldn't leave it at home. I wanted it safe. I wanted to be able to touch it.

I didn't go straight to the interrogation room. Instead, I asked a duty officer where Finne was and I found out he'd already been taken from his cell and brought upstairs. I'd counted on this. I decided to use the opportunity to have a look at his belongings.

Finne had an uncommon luxury at Petrovka 38: a cell to himself. Of course, his privacy was the only luxury he enjoyed. He had an old, worn mattress on top of a sagging, rusty bed frame. I did not look beneath the impressively tidy blankets, but I assumed the mattress sported some unsavory stains. The blankets themselves were faded and threadbare and the once-white pillow cover had washed out to a sickly grey.

All of Finne's belongings, at least those he was allowed to keep with him, were neatly arranged either in a small shelf at the foot of his bed or on the wooden table he evidently used at a desk. The shelf held some spare prison-issue shirts and trousers. I looked beneath them, but found nothing hidden there. The table held a small number of books: a Russian-English dictionary; a tourist's guide to Moscow; a mostly blank journal that Finne used to record his purchases (not that he was making any these days); and a red-coloured paperback novel.

I picked this last item up and studied the cover. It showed a picture of a man wearing heavy, black-rimmed glasses. A red orb—a planet, I realized—hung in the background.

"Ray Bradbury." I read the author's name aloud to better sound out the English letters. *The Martian Chronicles*.

Martian? I asked myself. Ah...Mars. So the planet was Mars. I flipped through the well-thumbed pages and decided this was a book of speculative fiction. It seemed to be about American imperialists colonizing the red planet. It was not the sort of thing that would have been allowed into the Soviet Union before Glasnost.

I wondered what it told me about Finne. I wondered what any of these few belongings told me about him. I wasn't sure what I'd come looking for, but I had the feeling I didn't find it. I sighed, tossed the paperback onto the table, picked up my plastic bag, and left the cell. As I made my way down the hall, heading for the interrogation room, I heard a guard locking the cell door behind me.

The usual guard was at the door upstairs. Finne was also in his usual spot, with his hands folded in front of him on the table. Only my place was empty, but no one seemed put out by my late arrival. I sat down and dropped the bag on the floor by my feet.

I did not greet anyone and I did not mention to Finne that I had just been in his cell looking at his things. I thought about what he had been telling me and about what I'd read the night before.

"This Aleks," I said. "Is he the man you think you killed?"

Finne searched my eyes, as if he could find the answer inside me. Then he pursed his lips, nodded, and looked away. He answered slowly.

"Yes," he said. "Yes, I am to blame for his death."

I noted that he hadn't quite answered my question.

"What happened, Finne?"

He avoided my question again.

"I know where he's buried. I've seen his grave. There's a big polished headstone in Allinge. There's thirty names on it. I copied them down and had them translated. Every one of them. I found it: A. L. Baklanov—Aleks!"

"Okay, he's buried on the island, but how did you kill him?"

Finne frowned. He clearly didn't want to respond, so he said nothing. I decided to wait him out.

"You have to understand..." Finne said after a while. "You have to understand..."

He said nothing more. He just sat with his hands resting on his knees. He stared past me at the wall. It seemed to me that he'd momentarily lost the drive that had carried him across the Atlantic from his adopted home in Canada, that had taken him to Bornholm, then brought him here to Moscow. That momentum had kept him talking to me for days, telling me why he'd come. Now he'd lost it and I realized I finally had to start doing my job. I needed to know more before I could decide what to do with him.

"Tell me more about Lise," I said. It was the first thought that came into my head. "What was she like?"

"Lise?" Finne echoed, as if he was trying to remember who the girl had been. "I've already told you what she was like."

"Was she really in love with this Aleks?" I asked.

Finne reacted liked I'd slapped him in the face. He jerked his head around and glared at me in anger. He flushed bright red. I wondered again at this depth of emotion. How could he have kept it alive and so strong for fifty years?

"She was only a girl!" he snapped at me. "She was only eighteen when she died!"

"Yes, but was she in love with Aleks?"

The anger faded from Finne's eyes and he looked away.

"Yeah, I think so. She was always talking about him. Always trying to find him. She was good at it, too. Good at finding what she wanted."

"What did you think about that?"

Again Finne went silent, gazing at the wall. I thought he wasn't going to answer my question, but then he took a deep breath.

"She was my best friend," he said. "She was my only friend. I loved holding her hand. I loved her ruffling my hair. I loved sitting beside her when she read to me or told me stories. I loved watching her. She always had trouble keeping all that blonde hair away from her face. Even when she tried tying it back or braiding it, it would somehow escape and creep around to tickle her nose. She'd get this exasperated look and brush it out of the way. When it returned again and again she'd kind of growl at it and try to tie it all back once more. It never worked.

"I'd laugh at the noises she was making. She'd pout at me because I know she was trying to be serious, but I could tell she was really laughing, too.

"When she read to me we'd sit side by side, crammed together into an armchair. I was shorter than she was so I could rest my head against her upper arm and breathe in the scent of her sweater, or if it was summer my cheek would be right against her bare skin. I could see the book as she held it in her lap with both hands, but I'd rarely follow the words on the page. Instead, I drifted on the lovely sensations of her presence—the song in her voice, the warmth and softness of her body, her delicious smell.

"How do you describe a smell? Was it just soap? Was it the natural perfume of her sweat? Did the wind leave traces of the sea and the forest on her skin and clothing?

"Twice, maybe three times in my life since then I've smelled her scent again and it flung me across the world, through the years. Suddenly I'm no longer walking down Queen Street. Suddenly I'm not drinking coffee in a restaurant. Suddenly I'm sitting beside Lise and the light is fading in the room and her voice is bringing the words of H.C. Andersen to life..."

Again I felt like a voyeur spying on Finne's private life. I could see he'd left his small cell and had travelled back to be with the lost girl. I couldn't leave him there.

"Tell me more about your father," I said.

"My father?" Finne said vaguely as if I'd just woken him up. Then he became petulant. "My father? What about my father?"

I'd wondered why Finne had said so little about his parents beyond what had happened the day they landed on the island.

"What was he like?"

"He was a Nazi! Just a Nazi!"

Finne's bitterness was palpable. He grimaced like he had a sour taste in his mouth.

"He was a member of the Party! A collaborator! He worked for the Germans. He made money from the war! People hated him.

"He was a big man in Rønne. He hadn't always been. Before the war he was just a reporter. The fact that he belonged to the Danish Nazi Party didn't matter to anyone. Nobody cared what you belonged to. That changed.

"Because he worked for the Germans he could buy anything he wanted as long as the Germans were still getting it. The best of everything when everything was rationed! Nobody else could get butter. Nobody else could get chocolate.

"No wonder nobody liked him. At first I didn't realize there weren't many other children left who still had chocolate to eat. I never got much, but I always had some, a little bit every week or so. I didn't know how things had changed. Not at first.

"It was Lise who explained it to me. She explained how the Germans wanted to keep all the best things for themselves, so that meant the Danes had to go without. She explained how the friends of the Germans could still get things because they were helping the Germans. It was Lise who helped me understand what my father had become. My father was important only because he worked for the Germans. As long as my father gave the Germans what they wanted and needed—a loyal Dane—they gave him what he wanted, food and prestige."

Finne paused to collect his thoughts.

"When I realized other children weren't getting chocolate any more I tried to share what I had. I tried to give it away, but nobody would take it. I remember going up to a gang of boys standing at a corner near my house. When they saw me coming they nudged each other and looked my way, falling silent. I held out the chocolate in my hands, but I was too shy to say anything. Nothing happened for a moment. Everyone just looked at the palms of my hands, where the large broken chunks of dark baker's chocolate was starting to go soft in the sun.

"I'm sure they were tempted, but none of them took any of it. Instead, without a word, they moved to form a tight circle around me. There were five or six of them and they started poking me with their fingers, harder and harder, chanting 'German, German, go home. German....'

"It confused me. I tried to tell them I wasn't German, that I was Danish just like they were. I tried to talk, but they wouldn't listen. They just kept jabbing me and jabbing me. They knocked the chocolate out of my hands and started kicking my shins. I wasn't talking any more; I was screaming at them to stop. My screams become wordless as the kicks and punches hurt more and more. I tried to get away, but they wouldn't even let me fall down.

"Then one of the boys was yanked away and I heard Lise and my mother yelling at them to leave me alone. Lise pulled me to her and I buried my face in her shoulder to hide my tears. The boys must have run away because my mother shouted after them, telling them their parents would hear from her. They took me home. I didn't eat chocolate for a long time after that."

NINE

FINNE LOOKED FAINTLY amused, as if not eating chocolate was somehow funny. He even laughed, just one short exhalation of breath, almost a grunt. He looked at me and shrugged.

"So what else do you want to know?" he asked.

"von Braun," I said. "I want to know about von Braun."

"He was a nice man," Finne said. "A very nice man. I never met anyone else like him—a genius! He'd talk and I'd understand maybe half of what he said. Half! Maybe a quarter. Maybe an eighth!

"He helped me remember that not all Germans were soldiers. They weren't all Nazis.

"The doctor didn't like the war. He didn't care about soldiery. He loved his rockets, but he didn't want them to kill anyone. He wanted his rockets to take men into space—to fly them to Mars!

"You know he went to the United States after the war. The Americans wanted him. They knew he was a genius. The Americans would never have gotten to the moon if the doctor hadn't helped them.

"The times we met that's what he talked about: rockets to outer space. He was still trying to get his little airplanes to fly from Germany to Bornholm, but in his mind he already had them flying to Mars. He'd say all sorts of things I'd never heard of before. Things about orbits and trajectories. He'd talk about lift and mass and thrust, using common words in new and exciting ways.

"But I was never meant to be a scientist like him. His meaning would float on the surface of my mind and then drift away. All I've kept is a memory of his words and his love for Mars."

I thought of the paperback sitting on the table in Finne's cell. I remembered the man with the glasses and the red planet on the cover. I was finally getting an understanding of Finne: his undying devotion to a dead girl and now this borrowed obsession with a faraway world. Maybe some vital part of him stopped growing during the war.

I had no time to follow this thought. Finne was talking again, describing how he'd left von Braun after their first meeting, found Lise outside the Nazi headquarters, and gave her the news. He described how he went back to the railway station bench the next day to wait for the German and how Lise was also there, hidden out of sight, watching for both von Braun and for Aleks.

When von Braun appeared again at noon—alone this time—the scientist smiled at the boy.

"Ah, so, my young friend, here we are again! Was the wurst so good that you wanted another?"

von Braun laughed pleasantly and Mathias smiled back, still feeling shy, but glad to see the man. The German did, indeed, buy Mathias another wiener and had one himself but this time the boy did not hesitate to take some mustard and eat it the way he liked it. The two sat down on the bench and for about an hour they chatted together in the warm sunlight.

Mathias had never met anyone, not even Lise, who seemed to have so much interest in him and in what he had to say. The scientist's questions about Mathias's father and mother, about his friends, about his life weren't like those he was used to. Mathias didn't feel like he was a child being questioned by an adult. He felt von Braun was treating him as an equal. It was a new experience for the boy. It thrilled him and he found himself wanting to impress his new friend.

"What do you want to do when you are old...when you grow up?" von Braun asked at one point. "Do you want to be a newspaperman like your father is?"

This was something Mathias had never wondered about. Although the war was only three years old, the boy was so young he couldn't seem to remember anything clearly from before. The war was his life. Like almost everyone else he looked to the end of the war, but he never thought to look beyond it.

That was something else Mathias learned from von Braun: that the war wasn't everything. The boy thought for a moment about the scientist's question, but he couldn't find an answer.

"I don't know what I want to do," he said. "What do you think I should do?"

"Me? What do I think?" von Braun exclaimed. "It is not for me to tell you something like that. It is your life, not mine. What do you like doing?"

Mathias frowned at his feet and scuffed them on the cobblestone under the bench. He liked riding his bicycle. He liked walking with Lise. He liked watching ships and boats come in and out of the harbour. But he didn't think those were the types of things von Braun was asking about.

"I like to read," he said finally. "But I'm not very good at it."

von Braun chuckled.

"That's fine!" he said. "You'll get better. Just keep reading. Maybe you'll be a writer or a teacher. What do you think?"

The boy smiled at the man, but he couldn't think of anything to say. The scientist smiled back, satisfied with the silence. He pulled a watch out of a pocket and looked at it.

"Late!" he said. "You have kept me too long, my young friend, and now my babysitter will be angry with me. I must go now."

He stood and offered his hand to the boy. Mathias slid onto his feet, matched the scientist's formal demeanor, and solemnly shook his hand.

"Thank you for an enjoyable hour, Herr Mathias. Shall I see you tomorrow? Yes, I think I shall! Good day to you."

Mathias watched von Braun walk away up the hill past the hotel. Lise appeared beside the boy, surprising him by suddenly tapping his shoulder.

"Let's go," she said. "Hurry!"

Lise and Mathias followed von Braun. They kept as far away from him as they dared, but every time he turned a corner they raced to it to make sure they didn't lose him. They'd run to the corner, peak around it, and then follow their quarry again at a slower pace. von Braun was not difficult to follow. He strolled through the streets like a man enjoying the warm air and sunshine, like a man in no hurry to reach his destination.

Most of the time, except for the brief dashes to the corners, the children didn't have to hurry. While they walked they discussed von Braun.

"He doesn't look like a scientist," Lise said. "At least, that's not how I thought a scientist would look."

Mathias was puzzled. Lise had told him to look for an important-looking man and von Braun looked important to him.

"What do you mean?" the boy asked his friend. "What did you think he would look like?"

"I didn't think he'd be so young," Lise answered.

The scientist didn't look young to Mathias. The boy thought von Braun looked at least thirty years old.

"He's quite handsome, too," the girl added.

Mathias peered at the scientist's back, trying to decide what Lise meant by von Braun being handsome. It wasn't something he thought about before.

"He looks all right, I guess," Mathias said, just to say something.

Lise looked at the boy and smiled, so he figured he'd said the right thing.

von Braun's destination, it turned out, was the German military head-quarters. The headquarters were one of Rønne's upper class homes, taken over at the beginning of the occupation and turned into offices for the naval personnel. It was an old and beautiful building, with heavy beams and posts framing tall windows and plaster walls. A lesser building would have taken on the taint of its occupiers, but this house seemed more like a noble old soldier, held captive against his will. Its nobility diminished the captors.

Several men were standing together, talking at the foot of the steps leading up to the inset front door. Mathias, peering around the last corner, recognized two of them: one was the man von Braun humorously referred to as his babysitter, the man who rudely interrupted the scientist the day he and the boy met; the other Mathias knew to be the commander of the island's occupation forces.

The bitter memory flooded back. Mathias didn't like that face. No softness dulled the sharp lines. Heavy black eyebrows hung over steady blue eyes. His nose jutted out and down like a stabbing knife. Thin, humourless lips barely outlined his tightly clenched mouth. He stood straight and solid, staring fixedly over the roof of a parked automobile. Mathias was sure that no wind was strong enough to knock him down. He said nothing and didn't even seem to notice the babysitter berating von Braun in a high-pitched whine. Mathias wondered if his friend was being yelled at for being late because of their lunchtime meeting.

Finne was no longer sitting up straight. He'd hunched over the table and was resting his elbows on the wooden surface. He laced his fingers together and stared at them as he twiddled them aimlessly.

"Then they got into the car and drove away," he said. "Reinhardt stopped the babysitter's whining with a sharp bark and ordered everyone into the car.

They all did as they were told right away—there was no arguing with this man. The car drove away, leaving us and the smell of gasoline smoke behind.

"We couldn't follow, so we just went home. I could tell Lise was disappointed we couldn't go further because she said nothing at all. I knew that meant she was thinking about what we should do the next time.

"'We'll bring our bikes tomorrow,' she finally said. 'Then maybe we can keep up with him if he drives away again. But maybe we won't need them. Just because he rode in a car today doesn't mean he'll ride in one tomorrow.'

"I thought it would still be hard to follow a car even if we had our bikes. Maybe we could keep up with the slower steam-powered motors the Danes had been using, but not the gasoline cars the Germans had. But I didn't say anything. When Lise made up her mind there was rarely any point in arguing.

"When we went back to the railway square the next day Lise hid out of sight with our two bicycles while I waited on the bench for my scientist friend. I expected his usual happy, smiling greeting, but I was disappointed. He was, of course, still courteous and friendly, saying 'Good day, Mathias' and leading me to the lunch table to buy our usual wieners, but he was not smiling. He looked worried.

"Being so young and inexperienced I didn't know how to ask him what was wrong, so I just worried with him and waited. In a way I didn't want him to tell me. I was afraid his mood had something to do with me, and I was right.

"We sat side by side on the bench and ate silently, concentrating on the food. He ate quicker that day, as if it was just something he wanted to get out of the way so he could move on to more important business.

"'Who was your young friend, Mathias?' he asked while he was brushing crumbs off his pant legs.

"The wiener I was eating suddenly tasted like paste.

"'My friend?' I echoed in a near whisper.

"von Braun looked down at me with a frown.

"'Yes, your friend: the yellow-haired girl. I am not as old as you may think—at least I am not yet blind. When a pretty yellow-haired girl follows me, I see her. I see her especially if she is following me with my friend Mathias Finne. I see it and I wonder why they follow me. Who is she, Mathias?'

Finne looked at me then, taking his troubled eyes away from his hands.

"Have you ever been frightened, Inspector, truly and deeply frightened?"

he asked me, not expecting an answer. "von Braun frightened me. I had almost forgotten he was German. I had almost forgotten he belonged to the enemy. With his wieners and friendly talk I had almost forgotten the man I'd seen shot to death near my home. But von Braun reminded me. With his question he made me remember the war. He made me remember I was in danger and Lise was in danger. I suddenly remembered the game we were playing could kill us; I had seen it happen.

"My first thought was to run, to throw my wiener down and run away from the square as fast as I could go. I almost did, too. von Braun must have seen the fear in my eyes, the sudden tensing of my body. He must have known how hard his question hit me because he immediately softened his tone.

"'Now, now, don't you worry, my boy. Don't worry. If your friend means no harm to me then I mean none to her. I haven't told anyone about your little—what would you say?—your little game. No one knows about this strange thing you and she are doing. No one needs to know. I just want to know who she is.'

"He put his hand on my shoulder—not to hold me there, but to comfort me, I think. He didn't want me to be afraid of him. He wanted me to trust him. I felt the warmth of his hand and looked up into his eyes and the fear drained out of me.

"'She's Lise,' I told him.

"'Lise,' von Braun said, as if tasting the sound. 'Lise—a pretty name for a pretty girl. She is your friend? I mean…she is your girlfriend?'

"I blushed and when he saw that he smiled. I said nothing, but smiled back.

"'Well, perhaps you are too young still for a girlfriend, but I think you like her very much, no?'

"I nodded.

"'Yes, how easy it is to lose your heart to a pretty girl like her. You are together much? Often?'

"I nodded again.

"von Braun looked away from me. He made a sound deep in his throat, something between a hum and a grunt, and he nodded as well.

"'Yes, you are with her often….'

"He glanced around the square and then looked back at me.

"'Is she here now somewhere?' he asked. 'She is waiting here now, is she not? She is watching us, no?'

"I hesitated and then nodded yet again, carefully watching his eyes to see if they would change from being friendly to being…to being something else. They didn't. von Braun glanced around again, as if he was hoping to spot Lise, and then he turned to me.

"'Now, Mathias, this is important and I want you to be absolutely honest. Your girlfriend, is she…is she…' von Braun stopped to search for the precise Danish word, but he couldn't find it. 'Is she with those who are fighting against my people?' Then he found the word. 'Is she with the resistance?'

"The fear started creeping back into my body, stiffening my muscles. It was bad enough that I was even talking to this German. It was bad enough I'd given him Lise's name. Now he wanted me to give him Lise's most dangerous secret. I said nothing; I only stared at him, wishing he wouldn't make me answer.

"'Mathias, you must trust me! As I said, if she means me no harm, I mean her no harm. But I must know!'

"I knew I couldn't tell him, I knew! But I looked at this man sitting beside me and I wanted to be able to tell him anything and everything. I'd known him for only a short time, but in that time I was already seeing him as man I wanted my father to be. I found I had to tell him the truth. I needed to earn his trust. I wanted him to like me.

"'Yes,' I answered, my voice so low von Braun had to bend down to hear me. 'Yes, she is.'

"von Braun straightened up and sighed.

"'*Mein Gott*!' he said. 'This is bad. This is *sehr schlecht*.'

"'But that's not why we wanted to find you,' I exclaimed, my fear having taken a different channel. 'That's not why we're following you! It's got nothing to do with that. It's Aleks Lise really wants, not you. It's Aleks…'

"I stopped, finally realizing I was saying too much.

"'Aleks?' von Braun said. 'Who is Aleks?'

"The scientist was looking at me with alarm.

"'He's a man,' I said. 'A man Lise likes…'

"'But what has this Aleks to do with me?'

"I looked up at von Braun, saw his puzzled frown and I knew what I had to do. I thought if he understood that this wasn't about the war, that it was about Lise liking Aleks, he wouldn't be afraid. I had to convince von Braun that Lise meant him no harm. So I told him everything."

TEN

MATHIAS TOLD VON Braun about cycling out to the turnip field to see the pilotless airplane. He told him about the men with the cameras, about the Germans who came late to the scene, and about the man, Aleks, that Lise found more interesting than the rocket. The boy told the scientist about following the Russian, about overhearing Aleks's demand for the film, and about the discussion concerning von Braun himself.

Mathias told von Braun about Lise searching for papers in his father's office, about staking out the hotel and the Nazi headquarters, and about following von Braun the day before.

When pressed, the boy told the scientist more about his father: how the man came to work for the occupation forces; how his membership in the Danish Nazi Party changed from being a small part of his life to being his main drive. Mathias told von Braun about meeting Lise, about the day he'd seen the two German soldiers chase and shoot the running Dane. He told him about errands Lise had brought him on: surreptitiously scattering underground newspapers throughout the town, running messages between resistance workers, and delivering food to hidden Danes, escaped prisoners, Allied flyers, and even sometimes to foreign spies like the Russian Aleks.

"*Mein Gott*!" von Braun repeated sadly, shaking his head. "*Der Krieg! Der Krieg!*"

The scientist crossed his arms and stared at the ground. His frown deepened and he grunted every now and then as he thought about what he'd just heard. After many minutes ticked away, he turned once again to Mathias.

"I want to meet this young girlfriend of yours," he said to the boy. "I want to meet Lise."

"Meet her?" Mathias said. "You want me to bring her here now?"

"No, no, no, no—that won't do!" von Braun said. "She mustn't be seen with me. I am being watched, my friend. You remember my babysitter? He is not the only one keeping his eyes on me. He is only the most obvious one.

"No, it is perhaps no longer safe for you to be seen with me anymore. It was fine when you were just an innocent little boy, but it seems you are not so innocent after all. No, I must think about this…"

von Braun lapsed again into silence. Mathias's thoughts raced. What had he done? He thought he could trust this man, but could he really? What would Lise say? What would she think? Would she be angry with him? How could she not be angry with him? But what choice had he had? None—that's what he kept telling himself—he had no choice.

"No," von Braun finally said. "I was wrong. We must meet again here, just as we have been meeting. We must not show that anything has changed."

This, Mathias understood well. He had learned not to let a mad dog know he was afraid. He had learned not to let the Germans know he feared them. He had been taught to ignore them. If he pretended the soldiers weren't there, then they wouldn't be able to really see him; they wouldn't be able to know him, to understand him. If he and von Braun pretended no new danger had arisen, then the Nazis wouldn't know they were afraid.

"But I still have to meet your girlfriend Lise," von Braun continued, "and I must meet her without anyone knowing. This must happen in secret. Now, I do not know your town as you know it, my boy. Where is a good place to go? Where can we be secret?"

Mathias thought about all the places he knew. There was the church overlooking the harbour, but too many people might pass by. There was the woods around the old round tower south of the harbour, but that was getting too close to the main German camp on Galloken Moor. There was the harbour itself, the town's squares, the little parks, the winding back streets, but none of them seemed right.

"I don't know," Mathias said. "I don't know any place, but Lise might know!" he added with sudden inspiration. "Lise knows places like that!"

"Yes. All right. Very good," von Braun said. "But I must meet her soon. I cannot stay long on this island. My work here is almost done. Can you meet me here tomorrow again? Then you must tell me where I go to see Lise. This must happen soon."

The scientist stood. He looked at his watch, at the hotel and then at the boy, who had remained seated. As he had done on their previous partings the man held out his hand for Mathias to shake. The boy climbed off the bench and reached for von Braun's palm. His small hand was lost within the scientist's larger one. von Braun smiled.

"We are no longer simple friends, you and I," he said. The boy looked up, not quite comprehending, yet understanding that good had come of his confession. "Now we are partners. Do you know what that means? In these times it means my life is in your hands and your life is in mine. I hope I am worthy. Until tomorrow! Good day!"

With that von Braun let go of Mathias's hand, gave him a quick nod, spun on his heels and walked briskly away towards the hotel. Mathias headed the other direction, hoping to get out of the railway square before the unseen watchers saw Lise come to him. He ran, letting all his pent-up fear and tension speed him across the cobblestones.

Mathias ran past the train station and into the narrow streets lined with the fishermen's tiny houses. He ran even when he heard Lise calling his name behind him. He ran past large aproned women, startling them from their gossip as he darted down through a thin alleyway into the sea breeze.

The main harbour lay off to his left and small wharves jutted out into the water in front of him. He spun right and ran along the sandy shoreline, slowing as his feet sank into the shifting ground. His breath rasped from the exertion, his legs burning with the effort, and he suddenly found the sense of fear was gone. The tension had evaporated. He stopped, flopping down onto the side of a dune. He lay on his back breathing heavily, staring up at the blue sky through a frond of waving grasses. That's where he was when Lise finally caught up with him.

She stood over him looking down without saying anything. She too had run and her breath laboured in her chest. Mathias watched her, letting the sight of his beautiful friend feed his senses. For a moment he forgot the day's events, until Lise spoke and brought them back.

"What's the matter, Mathias? What happened?"

If she had been mad at the boy she was no longer. If his sudden departure from their plans had angered her, she was now only apprehensive.

"Tell me, Mathias," she said when she got no response.

Mathias tried to make himself feel comfortable. He stretched out on the dune, crossed his legs and laced his fingers behind his head, using his hands as a pillow. But it didn't work. He might as well have been sitting on hot coals. He squinted from the bright sunlight behind Lise.

"He saw you," he told Lise. "He saw you yesterday."

The girl started. She hadn't met the scientist and she had no idea what he was like. All she knew was that von Braun was a German and he could be a Nazi.

"What did he say to you?" she asked. "What happened?"

"He wants to meet you in secret," Mathias said. "He wants you to find a secret place. I'm to tell him where tomorrow."

Lise sat down on the sand beside Mathias. She pulled her skirt down over her legs and hugged her knees to her chest. She sat looking out over the sea, idly chewing a strand of her blonde hair as her eyes searched the horizon.

"Why?" she asked her friend. "Why does he want to meet me?"

"I don't know," the boy said, and then he felt a rush of guilt. "I told him about Aleks."

The meaning of what he said took a moment to sink in. Lise blinked when it hit her.

"You what?" she blurted. Her eyes widened and she spun to face Mathias. "How could you? Mathias! Do you know what you've done?"

Mathias sat up, his face bright red.

"I know! I know what I did," he yelled, angry at both himself and Lise who, he felt, had put him in that situation in the first place. "I couldn't help it. I had to tell him."

"But Mathias," her voice rising, "you could get Aleks arrested. You could get him killed! You could get all of us in trouble. Why did you say anything?"

The boy turned petulant.

"This wasn't my idea," he flung back at her. "You wanted me to follow him. You wanted to find Aleks. This is your idea! You're the one who's getting us into trouble."

Mathias scrambled to his feet while he was saying this and he kicked at the dune, spraying Lise with the fine, white sand.

"Stop it, Mathias!" she shouted, holding her hands up to protect her eyes. "Sit down!"

The boy stopped kicking the sand, but he remained standing. He angrily crossed his arms over his small chest, which was heaving as hard as when he'd been running.

Lise brushed the sand off her clothes and avoided looking at her young friend.

"You're right, Mathias. It was my idea. I'm sorry."

Still Mathias said nothing, but he let his arms uncross and dangle at his sides. Lise looked up at him.

"I'm sorry, Mathias. Now please sit down."

This time the boy did as he was asked, returning to his place on the dune.

"Sorry about the sand, Lise. I didn't mean to get you all dirty."

Lise smiled and reached out with one hand to stroke the boy's hair.

"That's all right, Mathias. No harm done."

They sat together for a while looking out to sea. Neither said anything. Both had to digest what had just happened. It was a new experience for them. The boy wondered if things had changed between them, if Lise was really still angry at him and was hiding it. The girl, however, was quiet. Mathias watched her face as she gazed at the ocean waves. When he thought he saw a tinge of fear cross her features, he looked away.

As the girl sat silently, the boy idly dug into the sand in front of him. His fingers easily penetrated the fine, loose grains and he scooped up handfuls to let them sift back onto the dune. One handful contained more than sand. As the grains drained away they left a small red stone behind them.

The stone sat in a remaining bed of sand in Mathias's palm. With the fingers of his other hand he picked it up and brushed the sand away on his leg. The stone had a deep hue, the redness suggesting wine more than blood. It was vaguely rectangular and creased with dark, jagged lines.

Mathias didn't consider the stone beautiful in any way, but he found it invited his touch and he liked the colour, so unlike any he was used to seeing. He thought about giving the stone to Lise, but decided that a girl wouldn't appreciate something like that.

When Lise started to speak, Mathias stuck the stone into a pants pocket.

"There's a pond near the railway tracks that run east out of Rønne," Lise said, still looking out over the water. "It's right near the tracks, but you can't really see it. Once you get down to the water the trees and bushes are so thick you're hidden away. I don't think anybody knows it's there."

"Then how come you know it, Lise?"

"Oh, I guess some people know about it, but not many. Nobody we have to be afraid of. I'll show you where it is and then you can tell the doctor how to get there."

The two walked back into town and fetched their bicycles from where Lise had left them leaning against the wall of the train station. They rode north through the streets and then east, soon entering wooded lanes. When they came to where the narrow-gauged railway crossed the road they dismounted from their bikes and pushed them over the ties. Soon Lise led Mathias off the track, breaking a path through a tangled mass of sharp, grasping raspberry bushes. They hid their bikes beneath these at the bottom of the slope and continued on foot.

It wasn't easy. The ground was slightly marshy and willow stands grew thick around the trunks of the tall poplars. Their shoes were wet by the time they reached the shoreline.

It was a small pond, but the water looked clean and fresh. Rushes and cat's tails blocked the remnants of the summer breeze, creating a bright mirror reflecting the high canopy of leaves. A circle of blue sky at its center turned the pond into a huge, friendly eye.

The boy was enchanted, drawn to the place with a sense of homecoming. He stood quite still, gazing on the scene in wonder as Lise picked her way to a hidden campsite. She noticed the boy had stopped following her and called to him to hurry.

In the thickest part of the bush—thickened, Mathias saw when he came close, with cut and roughly woven branches—a hollow space gave room enough for the two of them to crawl inside and stand up. It contained a small ring of stones blackened by fire, a lean-to made of dark green canvas and branches the length of a man, and a black cooking pot with a lid tied down by thin rope.

"This will do fine," Lise said.

Mathias was puzzled.

"How am I going to get him all the way out here?" he asked.

"Tell him it's the only place."

"Are we allowed to use it?" Mathias countered. "Should we be showing it to anybody?"

"Don't you start talking to me about giving away secrets," Lise responded, stern but not angry.

Mathias didn't answer. He thought the place would do fine.

Finne paused in his narrative. He'd been talking for hours, breaking only once to ask for water. Thereafter he punctuated his sentences with sips from the glass, but he didn't really seem to be enjoying the taste. Each time he drank he crinkled his face as if the liquid was as sour as lemon. It probably was. I wouldn't touch it.

I looked at my watch, noted the lengthening hours, and was about to call a halt to the day when Finne once again interrupted my resolve. I let him continue.

"I came to think of it as our pond—mine and Lise's—but it had been Lise's and Aleks's before I ever went there. Lise said that's where she first met him. That was where he'd been hiding when she came to deliver a small supply of food, only enough to make sure the young Russian didn't starve, but all that was available. I suppose he'd only been on the island a few days when she met him."

Finne paused again, but I had had enough for the day. I stood up, scraping the chair back under the table. I picked up the lurid bag containing the professor's manuscript. I hadn't taken any notes and I cursed myself, thinking that was a good reason to get a proper night's sleep. I'd be less likely to forget things.

Eleven

THE NEXT DAY, armed with my notebook and pen, the interview continued in the interrogation room. The window was open to catch whatever breezes were outside. A guard stood within call. As usual, Finne and I sat with the table between us.

"Did you meet von Braun as arranged?" I asked without any preliminaries.

"Yes," Finne answered promptly.

"What happened?"

Finne said he went to the square at noon. von Braun bought lunch as usual and the two sat down. Mathias told the scientist about the pond.

"But why so far away?" von Braun asked. "Is there no closer place?"

"No," Mathias answered. "Lise says it's the only place."

"All right, but it is far."

The scientist pondered for a moment.

"We cannot be seen going together, but you still must lead me. I cannot be seen to go at all, but neither can I disappear from their sight."

Mathias did not have to ask who "they" were.

"I no longer have anything to do this afternoon. I suspected I would need the time. I have told them I want a few hours free of inspections and conferences. My assistants can do what must be done.

"But that will not free me from my watchers. They will be curious. Or perhaps not. Perhaps I shall be lucky. Who can say?

"You, Mathias, will wait for me at the little inn on the Nexø road. You will not come to me. When you see me you will go to the pond. I will follow you."

The scientist looked at his watch.

"If I do not come in one hour you will go away. Do not wait any longer."

"How will I know when one hour has gone by?" asked Mathias. "I don't have a watch."

von Braun grunted. He looked down at the boy.

"When you think it is one hour, then you go. Do not worry about the exact time. Do you understand?"

Mathias nodded his head.

"Good!" the scientist said. "Now we will stand up and shake hands. You will thank me for the wurst and we will say goodbye. All right?"

"All right," Mathias said and that's what they did, parting at the end of the ritual. Mathias went off towards the inn, wondering how von Braun would get rid of his babysitter.

The inn was an ancient building. A thatched roof topped the low, white-washed walls. The dark, deep-set windows blinked in the sunlight. It wasn't doing much business. The workers would be back to seek refreshment at the end of the day if there was any beer or ale to be had.

Mathias sat and waited and tried to think about how long he was sitting and waiting. He was near the inn, but not right beside it. He was perched on a boulder beneath some trees by the side of the road where he could discretely watch people passing by. He sat and he waited.

When Mathias judged an hour had passed, and just as he was thinking he should wait a little longer to be sure, von Braun appeared walking up a small lane that joined the road. When the boy thought the scientist could not avoid seeing him he got up and walked into the woods at his back. The large trees grew with wide spaces between their trunks, making a stroll over the forest floor as easy as following a trail. He did not go far before the scientist caught up with him.

"Very good, my boy," he said. "It seems we have both done well this afternoon. You have found a remarkably pleasant path and I am free for the moment."

"How did you get free?" Mathias asked as they walked together.

"It was easier than I thought it would be," von Braun said. "I imagined all sorts of hardship. I saw myself climbing steep cliffs and leaping raging rivers to escape being found."

Mathias looked up, his mouth gaping.

"Do we have a raging river here?"

The scientist laughed.

"No, my boy. Not yet, I think!"

"So what did you do?"

"Oh, in the end it was quite simple. I told the nice woman at the front desk of my hotel that I was not to be disturbed. A headache, I said. She told me I shouldn't think so much and that would cure it."

"That's all you did?"

"No…I went up to my room. When I was certain my babysitter thought I had gone into my room I went back down the back stairs and out the back door. No problem at all!"

The scientist pondered something for a second.

"Of course, if someone opens my door and I am not there they may have questions for me."

They reached the railway tracks, followed them for a short distance, and then cut down the bank. The large man couldn't slip as easily through the brambles and willows as the small boy, but he came to the campsite before too many minutes had passed.

Lise was waiting inside, alone. von Braun, stooping beneath the branches, faced her and smiled. He gave her a polite "good day" in his heavily accented Danish. Lise returned his politeness with a brief smile.

"Mathias says your name is Lise. My name, as you know, is Wernher. Thank you for agreeing to see me."

Mathias looked from von Braun to Lise. The scientist had squatted down so he could straighten his neck, but even that position couldn't hide his size. He was simply and neatly dressed, but he looked fit for an office, not for the middle of the woods.

In front of him, still standing, but scouting for a place to sit, the smaller girl looked wild and unruly. Her thick mass of blonde hair escaped chaotically from its restraints. Her clothes were clean, but rumpled, and a stray leaf clung to one shoulder.

Mathias realized he wanted to be like both of them, but he didn't see how that was possible. They were so different, he thought.

von Braun spoke.

"We cannot waste time. This is why I am here: I want you to introduce me to your Russian friend."

Lise didn't look surprised.

"Why should I?" she asked. "How do I know I can trust you? How do I know you won't turn him in?"

"You do not," von Braun answered. "Likewise, I do not know if I can trust you. Mathias I know, but not you. Perhaps it is you who will turn me in."

Lise flared, controlled, but sharp.

"What do you mean?" she demanded. "What do you think I am?"

"You? That I cannot say. What I think: I think you are like me. I am here in secret. I would be in grave danger if my employers found me here. You, too, are here in secret, not only from my people, but from your own. Am I correct?"

Lise met his eyes and nodded.

"That is what I think. It is what I hope. However, I cannot know for certain. Danger comes from many directions. It is seldom seen in time."

"If you do not trust me," Lise countered, "then why did you come here? Why do you talk with me?"

"Ah, but I do trust you," von Braun said. "I trust my friend Mathias here and he trusts you. He has good judgement, this boy."

Mathias blushed, pleased with the unexpected praise. Lise saw the boy's reaction and smiled at her friend. She relaxed a little bit more.

"Why do you want to meet…my Russian friend?" she asked.

"Why do I want to meet your Aleks?" von Braun echoed with a smile. Lise glanced quickly at Mathias, giving him a brief frown for having given away the spy's name.

"I do not want to talk about my motives at this time," the scientist continued more seriously. "Either you agree to help me now, or you do not. If you do not, then I will go away and leave you alone."

"What do you want me to do?" Lise asked, as yet uncommitted.

"I do not know Aleks. I cannot approach him. You can. You wanted to watch me until Aleks appeared, or so Mathias has told me. Please continue to do this very thing. When you see him you must speak with him. Tell him about me. Mathias here—if he agrees—can bring your message to me."

The man and the girl turned towards Mathias. He said nothing for a moment. The boy had never imagined he'd make any of the decisions.

"I'll do it," he said in a voice little more than a squeak.

"Good," von Braun said to him. "Thank you, my boy."

The scientist turned back to the girl.

"Now," he said. "Will you do it?"

"Yes," said Lise. "I'll help you."

Mathias continued to meet von Braun by the railway station, but not every day. Some days he didn't go near the square and von Braun wouldn't find his young friend on the bench. Other days the boy went, but it was the scientist who didn't show up. Lise, on the other hand, stayed within sight of the scientist the whole time. von Braun had given her a rough idea of where he'd be on what days and the girl kept watch.

Lise thought she may have seen Aleks on the very first day, but she couldn't be sure. The man was far away and he didn't stay long. On the second, third, and fourth days she saw nothing. Rain kept her home the fifth day; she couldn't devise a plausible excuse for going out in the downpour. The following day was dryer, but just as unrewarding.

The seventh day started like the others. Lise, looking innocent and pretty, was trying not to attract any attention. She didn't succeed. Young men—some Danish civilians, some German soldiers—couldn't help noticing her as she spoke politely with the station newspaper vendor. She bought a magazine for her mother and idly flipped through the pages while standing by the main entranceway.

She saw von Braun come out of the hotel. He and his companion, a man who looked about thirty years old, the same age as the scientist, were dressed warmly in sweaters and waxed-cloth coats. The day was overcast, but not cool enough to warrant such garb for an overland trip.

The two men crossed the street unhurriedly and entered the square, talking together all the while. Both carried briefcases in their right hands and clutched leather gloves in their left. They passed the railway station going in the direction of the western fishing harbour. Lise waited until someone she thought might be one of the scientist's watchers walked by and then she followed in turn.

They were, indeed, headed towards a boat. The craft was tied up to the old stone wharf past the fishing skiffs. It was sleek, grey, and small, but still large enough to need a lifeboat tied over the stern. It was a fast German boat with a machine gun bolted to the deck in front of the wheelhouse.

As the scientist and his companion neared the boat Lise heard the engines cough to life. Once they were on board, the boat swung away from the wharf and rumbled out past the windbreaks.

Unknown to Lise, Mathias was watching and had seen the boat von Braun boarded. The boy was on top of the wall by the church overlooking the harbour. He could see further than Lise, who was quite a way below the cliff, and he kept his eyes on the gunboat as it headed south.

Mathias then saw Lise turn from her place by the fishing boats and walk towards the street that climbed away from the harbour. Mathias leaned out over the parapet and was about to call to her when she stopped. The girl was looking intently up the hill. He followed her gaze until it ended at the form of a young blonde man waiting among trees at the top. Aleks motioned towards the church and strode to the nearest door. He opened it and entered without hesitation. Mathias knew of another door. He looked to see Lise hurrying up the hill. He left the wall and darted around a corner of the church and slipped inside, the heavy wooden door swinging silently on massive hinges.

The boy was in the base of the squat bell tower and he stayed there, peering around the half-open inner door. The altar was straight ahead and the pulpit was up front, off to his right. Pews marched away in rows on either side of him. Aleks stood alongside the left wall, facing the side door. Lise entered.

The plastered stone walls, several feet thick, closed out the world. The sounds of the harbour below did not enter. The rustle of leaves could not be heard. The sun's gentle light seeped through the tall, deep windows and set a warm glow to the burnished woodwork.

Mathias had been here on several occasions, but only when the pews had been full of respectful citizens celebrating a marriage or mourning a death. He'd never seen the church like this, when the quiet was absolute.

His eyes sought their usual resting places, the oases from the tedium of the service. Near the altar hung the model of a tall-masted ship under full sail. For three hundred years she'd caught the wind in the Rønne church, frozen in her endless journey and, as always, the boy marvelled at the sight. Beyond the ship, in a darker corner of the domed ceiling, a section of blank white plaster had fallen away to reveal a colourful drawing of a tree. Mathias wondered what kind of forest lay sleeping behind the remaining plaster and what kind of beast slumbered beneath the painted leaves.

Lise and Aleks did not look around to take in these sights. They just gazed at each other for a few minutes, trying to make up for the months they'd been apart. Neither spoke nor moved, as if each waited for the other to break the spell first. Finally, Lise spoke.

"Good morning, Aleks."

"Lise! Good morning."

The young Russian couldn't hide his pleasure at seeing Lise.

"What are you doing here, Lise? Why do you follow me?"

"Aren't you glad to see me, Aleks?"

Aleks frowned.

"Always these same games! Are you still a child that this is fun for you?"

The teasing grin left her face. She seemed genuinely contrite.

"No, I am not doing this for fun."

"Then why are you here, Lise? What do you hope to achieve?"

"Aleks, how do you know I wasn't sent here? I did want to see you, but how do you know that's all?"

"Is it?" Aleks asked, both curious and wary. "Were you sent here? Then what are you doing? Why were you sent?"

"Professor von Braun wants to see you," Lise said.

Aleks blinked, taken aback by the sudden statement. Lise always managed to surprise him.

"von Braun? What do you know of von Braun?"

"I spoke with him, Aleks. I met him a few days ago. He says he wants to meet you in secret."

"In secret!" Aleks's voice rose. "I should hope so. What is this about? How does he know about me, Lise?"

Lise fumbled her words. She hesitated.

"Um…I told him."

"You? But why? Why would you tell him?"

Aleks looked away from her and gazed over the pews. Mathias saw the gaze come his way and he shrunk further into the shadows.

"No!" Aleks pronounced, turning back towards Lise. "You didn't tell him! It was that boy at the railway station. I knew I'd seen him before. It was the boy you brought to me in the woods!"

Aleks looked outraged. He struggled with his anger, trying not to yell at the girl.

"First you tell me he is safe! Now you are telling me he is informing to the Germans! What is happening here, Lise? Are we surrounded by soldiers and police right now?"

"No, of course not—"

"Why of course not?" Aleks interrupted. "This town is full of soldiers.

Why shouldn't there be policemen outside right now?"

"Because Braun doesn't want the police, either," she answered.

"Braun, you say! Now he is Braun! How do you know what he wants or doesn't want? He's German, Lise. He is using you!"

"He just wants your help, Aleks."

"Then he wants to use me too! He wants to use all of us. That is what they do."

"That's not true, Aleks. Braun isn't like that."

"He's fooling you!"

"Don't you want to meet him, Aleks? I heard you in the woods after they found his little fly. You know all about him."

"But Lise, what if it is a trap? How can I trust this man?"

Trust—Lise thought about what von Braun had said, that his decision was based on Mathias's judgement. She also trusted Mathias, but that would mean nothing to Aleks.

"He just wants to meet you, Aleks. He wants to talk with you."

"Why?"

"He won't say."

"Won't say? That is ludicrous! I am expected to meet him just like this? And where am I supposed to meet him?"

"At the pond," Lise said. "Where you were hiding. Where we met. I've already shown him the campsite."

"Oh fine! So the Gestapo will know exactly where to wait for me."

"It's safe, Aleks."

"Safe! Oh, like the boy is safe?"

Aleks spun away from the girl and walked quickly towards the back of the church. He dropped into a rear pew and sighed, as if resting weary muscles. Lise moved more slowly to follow. She walked with her face downcast and with her hands linked behind her back. She paced carefully by the rows of seats, reached the end and turned the corner towards Mathias's hiding place. But the girl didn't go that far. She stopped behind Aleks.

To watch them better Mathias had to shift a little bit out into the doorway, out of the shadow. Mathias could see Lise and Aleks from the side, but they could not have seen him unless they turned almost all the way around.

Lise was looking at the back of the Russian's bowed head. Her hands lifted from her sides and landed gently on his shoulders. Aleks turned his head until his cheek rested lightly against her fingers. His eyes were closed and he breathed long and deep.

"Aleks…" Lise said softly, close to the man's ear.

The young Russian opened his eyes and waited expectantly.

"Aleks, did you know we are in my church?"

Aleks lifted his head a little higher and looked puzzled at this change of subject.

Lise slipped her right hand away. Her left hand slid from its resting place across Aleks's shoulders and then down onto the back of the pew. She strolled down the length of it, running her fingers along the wood. They leaped the space across the central aisle and continued their journey on the other side. When Lise reached the corner she did a slow pirouette, gazing at her hand on the wood. She stopped, smiled at Aleks, and then walked up the side aisle past the pulpit. Aleks, mesmerized, watched her all the way.

Lise came to a small pedestal near the front.

"Aleks," she called. She had to speak loudly, but somehow her beautiful voice did not break the essential stillness. "Come see where they christened me!"

The young man obediently stood and followed Lise's path around the pews. The pedestal, dark wood richly carved with branches, leaves and flowers, held an empty silver bowl that was almost two feet across. Lise cradled an imaginary baby in the crook of her left arm and dipped her right palm into the empty bowl. She lightly daubed drops into the air where a small head would have rested.

"I was dressed all in white," she said to Aleks, "and my robe was two or three times longer than I was!"

The girl laughed happily.

"My mother says I cried when the pastor put the water on my forehead. She says I never liked getting wet. I always made a fuss at bath time!"

Lise smiled up at Aleks. The Russian couldn't find anything to say, but he managed to smile back. She took his hand and led him to the central aisle. Without letting go of each other, but without making a show of their contact, the two stood at the sill of the altar room. Light filtered through the small side windows, illuminating the richly coloured cloth that covered the ancient stone.

"One day, this is where I'll be married," Lise said, her voice just barely carrying back to Mathias.

The Russian smiled.

"Perhaps I'll be here, too," he said. Before Lise could reply, he added, "Maybe I'll be the one who cleans up the mess after everyone has gone home."

Lise laughed and squeezed his hand. She swung it playfully.

"No, no, no," she said, her fun forcing the words out too fast. "You can be the pastor! We'll call you Father Aleksander!"

She said the last two words in a false bass voice. Aleks chuckled.

"Me in long black robes! Big beard like this!" He measured with his free hand to the area around his stomach.

Lise laughed gleefully, her voice skipping on waves of happiness. Aleks joined in with her, but when he spoke again his normal seriousness was returning.

"Most likely, Lise, I'll be watching you from one of the back rows there, crammed in behind all your family."

Lise looked towards the back of the church and was silent for a moment. Then she turned again to Aleks and raised her eyes to meet his.

"I know where I want you to be, Aleks."

The words hung in the air—a challenge, an invitation. The young Russian stopped smiling. He took her other hand and held both in front of him. He seemed about to say one thing, but changed his mind and said another.

"I have to go, Lise. We have been here too long."

The girl nodded and let go of his left hand. She started leading him up the aisle away from the altar.

"It's better to go out this way," she said.

Mathias's eyes widened with quick fear. He'd been so involved in what he was seeing and hearing that he'd failed to imagine they might come through his door. He pulled his head into the shadow, considered pushing open the heavy wooden door, but instead grabbed the ladder that climbed up to the belfry. Lise and Aleks moved without haste, but they did not have far to walk. Mathias scrambled up, just pulling his foot off the last high rung before Lise came through the doorway.

"Lise," Aleks said. "I'll meet your Professor von Braun. You have to tell me when."

"How will I find you?" she asked.

"I'll be around."

The Russian opened the door a crack to peer outside. He saw no one.

"Aleks," Lise said, softly.

Aleks turned and they faced each other again, not more than a few centimetres apart. The Russian leaned forward and kissed the girl gently on the lips.

"That is one kiss to tell you I love you, Lise," he said and then he leaned forward again and gave her a second kiss. "Twice is for all time."

Mathias stared down, horrified at the actions of the two lovers. His thoughts reeled. That was what Lise had said to him! Those words belonged to him, Mathias, not to this Aleks. How dare he use them!

Then it occurred to Mathias that the Russian had used them before, that Lise had actually gotten them from Aleks, not the other way around. He suddenly could not bear to see what was happening down below. He abruptly backed away from the open trapdoor.

Mathias never thought about the bell until he actually bumped into it. One step too far and too fast and the boy suddenly nudged the bell hard. It started to swing. When Mathias fumbled in his attempt to stop it he only sent it on its way faster. The clapper, when it hit, rang all the louder.

Down below the Russian gasped and cursed.

"That boy, I'll bet," he said and saw Lise was looking up away from him. Without stopping to think he stepped closer and kissed her mouth a third time, hard. Then Aleks was out the door and away.

Lise heard a shout: "Halt!" Then the sound of running feet. Then a shrill whistle and another: "Halt!"

"Mathias, come down quick!" she called, having no doubt, either, about who was up in the belfry.

The boy scurried down the ladder. Lise grabbed his hand and pulled him into the church. They ran down the central aisle and had only enough time to crouch in front of the pews. The main door opened again and they heard the sound of boots on the stone floor. Almost immediately a German soldier came through the inner door. He walked towards the altar, throwing glances down the pews on either side of him as he passed. Someone had stayed behind in the bell tower. Mathias could hear him climb the ladder to inspect the bell.

Lise gestured for Mathias to follow her. She crept away from the central aisle and crawled around the front corner of the pews. She moved down a few rows and tried to squeeze herself behind one of the pew ends. Mathias was smaller and suspected he could be hidden, but he didn't hold the same hope for Lise.

She realized this, too. She hid as best she could without losing sight of the soldier. When he was one row away, Lise waited until he turned his head to look the other direction and she silently scrambled three rows down.

The soldier reached the end of his walk without spotting them. He paused briefly to admire the rich altar cloth and then turned to leave. When he was two-thirds of the way back down the aisle Lise darted to the door she'd entered, opened it, ushered Mathias through, and closed it quietly behind her. The soldier hadn't noticed.

Lise and Mathias peeked outside and, seeing no one, slipped into the warm air and hurried to lose themselves in the town's streets.

TWELVE

MATHIAS MET WERNHER von Braun at the railway square on two more occasions. On the first, the day after the incident in the church, the boy told him about Aleksander Baklanov's decision. On the second, three days later, Mathias returned to Lise with a date and an hour and a message that he was to have no more involvement in the matter. He was to give Lise the time and then go home and stay safe.

After Lise received the time she also told Mathias to go home and stay out of the way. Lise was still sore about Mathias having followed her and Aleks into the church, even though she'd found out Aleks had escaped capture and was unharmed. Lise didn't want the boy anywhere near, not only because of the trouble he might cause, but also for his own safety.

Mathias never saw Aleks, but he was sure he knew what the Russian's opinion would be on the matter.

Nevertheless, Mathias had his own ideas. He had already decided to get to the pond early, before any of them.

The meeting was set for the night. The day had been clear and bright, but by dusk the sun was hidden behind a low bank of cloud. As the sky darkened, mist crept through the streets of the town.

The boy went to bed at his usual hour. That gave him plenty of time to prepare. He said goodnight to his parents in the sitting room, kissing his father on his rough cheek. Carl Finne was reading the day's newspaper. His father looked up from the print and nodded to his son.

"Good night, Mathias. Sleep well."

His mother followed him up the stairs to receive her kiss in private after she tucked the thick blanket around her son's chin. She had a preoccupied air about her and seemed distracted when Mathias spoke.

"Mother?" the boy ventured.

The woman's face softened as she focussed her attention on her son.

"Yes, Mathias," she said as she brushed hair away from the boy's forehead.

"When you like someone, do they have to like you back?"

His mother smiled.

"Well, it's nice when they do, but it doesn't always happen."

The boy thought about this.

"But why not?" he continued. "Shouldn't they like you?"

"No, Mathias. You can't make people like you. Either they do or they don't."

Mathias looked at his mother without saying anything.

"Are you thinking about Lise, Mathias? You don't have to worry. She likes you. She like you very much."

The boy nodded.

"Good night, Mathias," his mother said and kissed her son's forehead.

She got up and opened the window, readjusting the blackout curtains so no light could escape. She moved to the doorway, carrying the kerosene lamp with her. With the small flame illuminating her in the doorway, she paused.

"Don't worry about Lise, Mathias. Sleep well."

She closed the door, leaving the boy in total blackness. He lay in the dark, cocooned in his warm, soft blanket, and listened to the sounds of the approaching night. Outside it was still dusk. Two or three men and women walked by, chatting as they passed. Once Mathias heard a carthorse clopping down the street.

He listened carefully to what was going on in the rooms below him. He heard his mother descend the stairs. He heard her say something to his father and he heard him respond. No words reached his ears, just the buzz of conversation. They settled down and then the sounds drifted away. He imagined what they were doing: his father would have finished his paper and picked up a book. His mother would be clicking her knitting needles to the beat of the ticking clock.

Mathias got out of bed. He pulled on his pants and shirt over his pajamas, slipped socks onto his feet, and found a sweater in a dresser drawer. He had no shoes. He always took them off at the front door and put them in the hall closet. He had no way of getting to them. He grabbed his slippers from under the bed and put them on instead.

Mathias pushed the curtains out of his way and swung the window open as far as it would go. The roof tiles glistened in the twilight. The fast approaching night coated them with a film of moisture. Mathias crawled out backwards, clutching the sill with both hands. He gingerly reached for a foothold.

The edge of the roof was only a couple of feet away. The sidewalk lay one storey down. Mathias craned his neck and saw what he was looking for: the street light. It was turned off, but the boy could still make out the iron fretwork of the standard. It made a perfect ladder. The only problem was getting to it.

Mathias didn't dare let go of the sill. He couldn't close the curtains. He couldn't shut the window. He could only shift his feet from spot to spot, never quite trusting them on the slick, rounded ceramic tiles. The light standard wasn't right behind him; it was a metre or so to his right and another metre away from the house.

The boy struggled with his nervousness, finally stilling the tension that threatened to send his body into shivers. He let go with his right hand and pushed himself upright with his left. He shifted his weight from one foot to the other on the fragile tiles. He let go, balanced for a second, took one step down the roof towards the light—then his feet started to slide. He panicked and jumped before he could fall.

His hands hit the standard first and clutched where they landed. His knee banged into the iron. He hung for a second, whispering: "Ow, ow, ow, ow, ow...." He climbed down to the sidewalk, limped along the cobbles for a moment and then loped off through the streets towards the northeast of town.

When Mathias reached the railway he didn't cut down off the tracks at the usual spot, but waited until he was a little further down the line. Without a flashlight he had to feel his way through the alders, trusting to his sense of direction and hoping he'd see something of the pond when he came close. He tried hard to move silently, but couldn't. Sticks cracked under his feet. Branches rustled with his clumsy passage. But it didn't matter; there wasn't anyone near to hear him.

Finally he gave up trying to find his way. He'd forgotten the direction of the pond. The labyrinth of interwoven bushes had him turned hopelessly around. He felt the ground for a dry spot and sat down. His feet were wet and cold. His sweater didn't keep the chill out. He sat hoping he wouldn't have to wait long and that he wasn't too far from the campsite to see and hear what was happening.

Lise and Aleks came first—not from the railway tracks, but from the other way around the pond. Mathias didn't see them until they were quite close, and even then all he saw was the brief flicker of a small flashlight. They made little noise. The boy wasn't even sure who it was until they entered the camp hollow and the light shone on Lise's face.

She wasn't far away from the boy. Only about two metres of criss-crossed branches separated her from her young friend. Mathias couldn't see all of her face. He couldn't read her expression. He could only see she was looking up away from the source of the light. Then the bulb snapped off and all three waited again in darkness and silence.

von Braun came alone. His approach was more obvious. He followed the same path he'd taken on his only visit to the site almost a week before. His limited knowledge of the route forced him to use his flashlight continuously to pick his way between the alders. When he finally arrived at the hollow he was out of breath.

Aleks flicked on his flashlight and shined it into von Braun's face. The scientist likewise turned his beam up to reveal the Russian. Aleks gestured to the right with his eyes. The beam swung sideways until it flashed off Lise's hair and rested on her smile. Both lights snapped off.

"You are Aleks, then?" von Braun asked.

"I would ask you not to use my name," the Russian said dryly.

"Yes, of course. Forgive me."

"You asked to meet me. What is it you want?"

"I want to go to Sweden," von Braun said. "Can you help me with that?"

The Russian grunted, but said nothing.

"You are not surprised?" the scientist asked.

"I am not surprised by your request," Aleks said. "Of course, I do not know what you really want."

"It is precisely what I want. That and nothing else. Will you help me or not?"

Again the Russian was silent, as if undecided. His next words, however, hinted he'd already made up his mind.

"You are an important man, Doctor. Your disappearance will be noticed. Sweden is a long way away for you."

"I know all that. I know it will not be easy."

"No, it will not be easy. In fact it will be very difficult. Difficult and dangerous. What do I get out of helping you? Once you are in Sweden where will you go?"

"I will go wherever I am permitted to continue my work. That is all I ask."

"Will you come to Moscow?"

"Yes, I will go to Moscow."

Silence followed that statement, as if Aleks didn't want to dilute its importance with unnecessary words.

"You realize, Doctor, I cannot decide this by myself" the Russian said after a few minutes. "There are many plans to make. I cannot arrange things alone."

"Yes, I realize this," von Braun answered. He paused. "You must arrange things for two people."

"Two? This will not be a tourist excursion, Doctor. We will not have many seats to spare."

"Nevertheless, there will be two of us."

Mathias held his breath. Two? Two of us? Who could that be? The boy thought back to his talks with the scientist. von Braun knew he was unhappy. He knew how much Mathias looked up to him. The boy could not help comparing the German to his own father. Could it be that the scientist felt the same attachment to Mathias? Was Mathias to be the second? Why would the scientist want to take him? Why wouldn't he? He knew the boy was in danger on Bornholm. Maybe he wanted to bring him to safety in Sweden. Maybe von Braun wanted a son like Mathias as much as Mathias wanted a father like von Braun, a father he could like and respect.

Mathias let his breath out slowly and silently, staring at von Braun through the branches. The boy struggled to bring his racing thoughts under control. Of course von Braun wouldn't want to bring a boy along when he fled the Nazis. Why would he? Mathias would only be in the way. But then, who was the second person to be? Maybe the scientist wanted the boy along, maybe he didn't, but Mathias knew he wanted to go. More than anything, Mathias wanted to be with von Braun when he escaped to freedom.

"All right," Aleks said with an ironic twist in his voice. "There will be two of you. What else? Any more demands?"

"Only that we must go Saturday night."

"Saturday night? But that is only three days from now. Why so soon?"

"It is the last night we are on the ocean before we go back to Germany," the scientist answered. "I do not know when we will next return."

The two discussed their plans for the coming night. von Braun's boat would head due west after nightfall to rendezvous with a test rocket fired from Peenemünde. They would already be part-way to Sweden. von Braun told Aleks what the boat looked like and how many men, besides themselves, would be on it.

"You want us to snatch you away from them?" Aleks said. "That is the best plan you have?"

"I believe it will be easier for me to get off the boat than to get off this island. You do not know how close they are watching me here."

"I do know," Aleks answered. "That is why I know it is time for you to go back to your hotel. I do not think we need to meet again."

"Not until Saturday," said von Braun.

"Yes, until Saturday."

With that von Braun picked his way back out to the railway tracks and away. Aleks and Lise waited silently until they were sure the scientist was gone and then they left in the same direction. Mathias couldn't wait as long, but stood up to ease his cold, cramped legs as soon as they were out of earshot. He clawed his way to the hollow and then out to the tracks. No one was in sight when he regained the road, but he thought he heard a gasoline engine start up and drive away into the dark night. The boy stopped and listened, but he heard nothing more. He dismissed the sound and headed home.

"My father was awake when I got there, sitting in the kitchen with all the lights blazing inside the blackout curtains. I knew something was wrong as soon as I came around the corner of Soldier Street. All the houses were black except for ours; on the second floor lamplight peeped around the partially drawn curtains of my window. A patrol would likely see it soon.

"I stared at the light and wondered fearfully what to do. Finally I realized I had no choice. There was no point in sneaking back in. The front door, usually locked at that hour, opened easily when I turned the knob.

"My father's shoes, scuffed and dirty, stood inside the door. My own boots, much cleaner, lay on top of my jacket, which was draped across the seat of the hall chair. It looked to me as if they'd been dropped there when my father entered the house. He'd gone outside after I'd left and he'd gone prepared to find me. I could only hope he hadn't, but the memory of the engine noise returned to my mind. My father didn't have a car, but I still feared it had something to do with him.

"I looked at my feet and decided there was no point to keep wearing my slippers. They were soaking wet and newly ragged. I kicked them off and padded on in my socks, leaving liquid footprints as I went.

"My father sat at the kitchen table. His arms were in front of him, resting on the white cloth, and his fingers were laced together. He was studying those fingers, frowning at them as the thumbs wrestled each other. He didn't look up until I'd spent a good five minutes standing in the doorway.

"I was terrified. I was just a child, remember. I'd left the house in the middle of the night. I'd been gone for I don't know how many hours. My father was angry and he'd never been one to hide his displeasure.

"This time, however, he did nothing. He said nothing. He didn't get up. He just looked me over carefully for a moment and then went back to staring at his thumbs.

"I couldn't summon the strength to leave without his permission and I could sense I hadn't been dismissed. I was rooted to the spot, unable even to speak. I hadn't imagined getting caught and I had no story to tell.

"'Where were you, Mathias?' my father finally asked.

"'Outside,' I said lamely.

"'I know you were outside. Where did you go?'

"'Just around.'

"'Around where?'

"My father was losing his patience, but I was gaining confidence. His questions were leading me to believe he really didn't know where I'd gone. If that was still a secret, I thought, then everything would be fine.

"'Around the town,' I said. 'I was just walking.'

"'Just walking!' He looked at me then. 'Do you know what time it is?'

"'No,' I said, truthful for once.

"My brain started working then. I wondered where my mother was. Why hadn't she appeared as soon as I came in? My father had obviously gone to look for me, but here he was as if he'd expected me just then. I knew it wasn't normal, but I couldn't figure out what it meant. Then my father seemed to make up his mind about something.

"'Sit down,' he said, pointing to the chair opposite him.

"I gingerly walked the few steps over to the table and pulled out the chair as quietly as I could. I felt as if any unnecessary noise might spark my father's anger into full flame. I wanted to avoid that. I climbed onto the chair and sat with my hands in my lap and my eyes cast down onto the tablecloth.

"'Look at me, Mathias.'

"I looked up. My father held his eyes steadily on my face, while the fingers of his right hand rapped steadily on the table top. I simply waited, unable to speak. Tears, born of nervousness and fright, threatened to erupt from my eyes. I fought them back as hard as I could.

"'Listen to me, Mathias. Do you know what you're doing? Do you know what's happening here?'

"I shook my head, more because I didn't understand his questions than because I was trying to answer them. His eyes never left me and he also shook his head—in disgust, it seemed to me.

"'I can't stop this, Mathias. It's bigger than me. Do you understand that? I can't protect you.'

"These words startled me more than anything he'd ever said. My father had never spoken to me like this before, never made an admission like that. Suddenly, he wasn't treating me like a child. It occurred to me that if he couldn't protect me, then he couldn't control me either. What was stopping him? Who was stopping him?

"I still couldn't speak. I couldn't voice my questions. If my father was unable to speak openly about what was happening, how could I?

"'Go to bed,' he finally said and that was it.

"My mother was upstairs. When I came to my room she was closing the window and fussing with the curtain, making sure it did its job. She turned when I entered, sighed when she saw me, and ordered me to get out of my wet clothing. While I was doing this she kept making cross noises. She never addressed me directly, but she made sure I knew they were aimed my way.

"Some of them, however, seemed to be aimed at my father. It made me think I wasn't the only one keeping secrets from my mother. She finished fussing with my clothes. She picked them off the floor where I'd dropped them, folded them, and laid them neatly on a chair. Then she looked at the pile, reconsidered, and picked all the clothes back up again.

"I got into my bed and waited. I didn't know what was coming and I was in no hurry to find out.

"My mother stood with the clothing in her arms for a moment, wondering what to do with them. Then she went to the doorway and placed the pile on the floor of the landing. She came back in, closing the door behind her, and sat down on my bed.

"'Mathias,' she said, speaking rapidly. 'What you did, you must never, ever do it again!'

"'I won't,' I said and meant it. I meant it, but at the same time I couldn't help thinking about the boat and about the trip von Braun would be making in three days.

"My mother took a deep breath. She picked up one of my hands from the cover and cradled it within her own.

"'Mathias,' she said, still angry, but calming down. 'What you did, sneaking out of here, did it have anything to do with Lise?'

"I wasn't sure what to say. I didn't want to lie to her, but there was no way I could tell the truth. If I said anything about Lise then Lise herself would probably find out I'd gone somewhere. She would easily guess where I'd been.

"'No,' I said and hoped she would leave it at that.

"My mother pursed her lips and searched my eyes, trying, no doubt, to find out if I was lying or telling the truth. I tried to hold her gaze, to not look away, thinking that if I didn't then she would have to assume I was telling the truth. I don't suppose I was very successful.

"'Mathias,' she said. 'It is possible to like someone too much. You mustn't let yourself get into trouble just because someone wants you to do something.'

"'All right,' I said, not trusting myself to say more.

"My mother sat for a while longer and continued to study me. Then she also said, 'All right' and nodded. She bent down, kissed my forehead, and wished me good night. She paused on her way out the door, just before she closed it behind her, and looked back at me. I guess she wanted to make sure I would stay in my bed this time. Then she was gone and I was returned to darkness.

"I lay thinking about what had happened that night, but less about the meeting by the pond than about my parents. I had made up my mind to leave, but the thought of actually leaving my mother and father scared me. I was going to miss my mother. Would she understand? I surprised myself when I realized I would also miss my father. But I suppressed the thought. I had made up my mind and it was too late to change it.

"I then remembered Lise and knew I would miss her most of all. But she had Aleks. I believed she would not miss me so much."

Thirteen

Finne could not tell me what happened next. In the few days that followed the meeting in the woods it seems much was happening, but it was outside of the boy's knowledge. He spent the three days at home, seeing no one but his parents. No one came to see him, not even Lise.

The old professor, however, was well aware of what was happening at the time since he had engineered many of the events. That night I went back to my apartment and flipped through the worn yellow pages until I reached the section that dealt with the plans to bring Wernher von Braun across the water to Sweden.

Baklanov was able to communicate with me (the manuscript read) through the means of a small radio given to him by the Danish partisans. It was a remarkable instrument, small enough to fit into a leather brief case, but powerful enough to send a signal as far as Leningrad, if need be. It was just a small steel box packed solid with vacuum tubes, wires and crystals. Baklanov told me he was able to string up the antenna indoors and tap away fairly secure against detection. The Germans didn't have many of their signal-finding vans on the island and they were easy to spot in good time. The Germans, it seems, tried to be clever by disguising their vans as ordinary canvas-covered delivery trucks. Unfortunately for them, however, they forgot that no Danish vehicle would still be employing a gasoline-powered motor. Civilians could not procure petrol. It was all reserved for the occupiers.

At the time of Baklanov's first meeting with Wernher von Braun I was staying in a small hotel near Sweden's southern coast. The Swedes were neutral and they did not inquire too deeply into the affairs of men like me as long as we caused no trouble for the local authorities. Of course, one was not absolutely secure from German agents, who enjoyed a similar freedom of movement, but in this operation we seemed safe.

When I received Baklanov's transmission I was quite surprised. Of course we knew of the rocket tests that were ending off the shores of Bornholm. That was why we had sent Baklanov to the island: not to aid the partisans, but to gain as much information as possible about Germany's newest weapon. He had earlier had a stroke of good fortune when one of the rockets went off its designated course and crash-landed on the island itself. He had been able to secure some details about the rocket's dimensions and its mechanical guidance system. We were thus able to get some idea of the weapon's range and destructive capability.

We were also already aware that Wernher von Braun was on the island at that time. Baklanov, exploiting sources within the partisan movement, had learned of the scientist's arrival. Our orders to Baklanov were to watch von Braun where possible and to take advantage of any unforeseeable opportunities. We contemplated theft of papers, perhaps, and maybe, as a last resort, assassination. We never imagined that Wernher von Braun would seek out our agent and ask to defect to the Soviet Union. That caught us all by surprise.

At first my superiors were sceptical. They did not want to trust a Nazi and they suspected a trap of some sort. I finally convinced them that if it was indeed a trap then we would only risk losing a small number of non-essential agents. On the other hand if Wernher von Braun truly wanted to defect, I told them, we stood to gain a great deal. Not only would we be striking a crippling blow to Germany's war effort, but we would be acquiring a technology that could help us during the war and after. Of course, I had no intention of sacrificing Baklanov, but I had to present the risks as being minimal.

We digested what Baklanov told us. Wernher von Braun was scheduled to conduct a test in the seas to the west of Bornholm, south of Sweden, on Saturday night. He would, Baklanov said, be awaiting some kind of attempt to bring him to Sweden. Baklanov's description of Wernher von Braun's boat was not encouraging. It was fairly small, but it had a crew of five or six and it had a machine gun mounted at the bow. Not an easy craft to take by force if the intention is not to kill everyone on board. I did not, at first, see how we would be able to get Wernher von Braun off that boat and into our possession.

Then I reasoned, if something cannot be done by force one must employ subterfuge. This thought did not solve my problem, but it gave me a path to follow. I sent messages to bring more men from Stockholm and I began to make quiet inquiries about the local availability of boats. I did not have much time.

Back in the interrogation room with Finne the next day I did not yet feel the need to tell him of the manuscript, or about the information I was learning from it. I'm not sure why I wanted to keep it a secret; I just did not have a compelling reason to reveal the professor's history to him. I guess I wanted Finne to tell his story without knowing I could check up on some of his facts. If he made a mistake, or lied to me, the manuscript just might help me know about it.

Still, that left me the task of hiding my knowledge, but it wasn't too difficult. Police are not generally in the business of freely giving out information.

While the Soviet preparations were going on in Sweden, the boy resolved to be on von Braun's boat when it set sail Saturday night.

Mathias was confined to the house. He spent his days in his room thumbing through his books, or gazing out at the sky, mulling over his punishment. To his eleven-year-old mind his condition was intolerable. He didn't want to be stuck indoors. He wanted to be outside where he could see Lise, where he could meet von Braun and tell him he was ready to go. He wanted to tell the scientist that he was in so much trouble he could only be saved by leaving Bornholm.

Lise didn't visit. Mathias couldn't imagine what she was doing and he missed her, but still he was relieved she didn't come calling. The new suspicion his parents felt for him extended over Lise, Mathias knew, because his mother and father were obviously aware of the great influence the girl had over their son.

As well, the boy was worried for his own sake. If Lise visited she would probably be told that Mathias had snuck out of the house late Wednesday night. She wouldn't have to guess where he'd gone. She would know, beyond a doubt, that he'd been to the pond. She would know he'd heard what had been said between Aleks and von Braun. What she would do with her knowledge, Mathias couldn't guess, but he didn't want to find out.

On Saturday night Mathias's escape from the house was simple. He assumed that since he'd gone safely out his window once he'd be able to go out a second time without trouble. He was right. He didn't stop to think why this should be so, why his father wasn't making sure Mathias wouldn't be able to sneak down off the roof a second time.

On that Saturday night Mathias was more prepared than he had been three days earlier. In the moments when his parents seemed to relax their vigilance—when his father was out and his mother was occupied in the kitchen or elsewhere—the boy managed to smuggle a jacket and a pair of shoes into his room. He hid them under the bed and behind a chest of drawers.

That night the small family ate supper in silence. Between mouthfuls of boiled potatoes and gravy, Mathias cast quick glances towards his parents at either side of him. They both seemed absorbed by the meal and did not return his looks. He wondered if they would feel sorry when he was gone. In his resentment over his punishment—he didn't see the confinement as a mild retribution for his action—the boy decided they would be glad to see him go. That thought made him resent them all the more.

With supper over, Mathias was anxious to say good night, go to bed and get out his window, but he didn't want to betray himself with his haste. The days were getting shorter, but the sun was still setting fairly late, so the boy had time. Nevertheless, the minutes ticked by slowly until his mother told him it was time for him to sleep.

Once in bed, once his mother had shut the curtains, kissed his forehead, and closed the door behind her, Mathias got up to leave. He dressed in his favourite pants and shirt, pulled on his socks and shoes, and dug his jacket out from under the bed. Into his pockets he shoved the smooth red stone he'd found on the beach and as many coins as he'd managed to save during his short life. There weren't many, but Mathias wasn't concerned about any need for money.

His shoes gripped the roof tiles better than his slippers had, so on his second trip Mathias didn't have to leap through the air. Instead, he was able to take three steps diagonally down the slope and reach gingerly across the gap to the light standard. He grabbed the metalwork, held on tight, and then swung the rest of his body over and climbed down. When he was on the sidewalk he listened for a moment, but heard nothing. He tiptoed away from the blacked-out sitting room window and then broke into a run when he thought no one could hear him. Few people noticed the small boy running through the twilight streets. He made it to the church quickly and without incident.

He paused at the top of the cliff and looked out over the wall from the same spot he'd stood a week or so earlier. von Braun's boat was tied up at the same place. A few soldiers patrolled the wharves, but otherwise the area was quiet.

The boat was as Mathias remembered it. It was long, sleek, and grey: a craft built for speed. The enclosed bridge stood three quarters of the way up the deck. The gun in front of it was shrouded in a white cloth bag and, most important to Mathias, the lifeboat that dangled over the stern was covered over with a sheet of thick canvas.

The boy trotted down the hill, slowing as he reached the bottom. He watched for patrolling guards and crossed the roadway when none were near. Once in the harbour front, he hid behind some fuel drums to catch his breath and plan his next move. Mathias figured he didn't have much time before von Braun was due to arrive, so he didn't waste any of it. He slunk towards the boat, dodging from the drums to a pile of crates to the side of a small shed, until finally he could crouch within a stone stairway leading down to the waterline. From there he had only a few more feet to go.

Mathias couldn't see anyone on board the boat, but he could hear the engine rumbling idly. A low light glowed on the bridge and he watched this to see if he could detect any movement. There was none. He looked up and down the wharf. All was clear for the moment, so he took his chance.

He darted out of the stairwell to the side of the boat. The craft had drifted away from the dock and Mathias didn't want to jump over the watery gap, so he grabbed a hawser and pulled hard. He was surprised at how easy the large boat moved once it responded to his initial tug. Just as the hull bumped against the dock Mathias heard voices off to his right. He looked in that direction, but couldn't see anything in the gloom. The voices, however, didn't sound far away and they were getting closer.

The boy stepped on board. He balanced on the gunwale for a moment and reached for the metalwork that supported the hanging lifeboat. He climbed up on this until he could grab the stern of the boat. The canvas tarp was stretched tight over the edge. He had to work some rope loose until there was enough room for him to pull himself through. The boat rocked when he put his weight onto it, but he managed to steady it and yank the tarp back over by the time the voices drew alongside.

By now, although Mathias couldn't see out of the lifeboat, he could hear that one of the voices belonged to von Braun. He didn't recognize the other.

Mathias wondered if he should let the scientist know he was there, but then others arrived. A flurry of orders and stamping feet drowned out the conversation. Soon the men were boarding the gunboat. Mathias could feel it shift under the extra weight.

The engines coughed to life. More orders were shouted and then the boat pulled away from the wharf. After a few minutes the gunboat passed the harbour mouth—Mathias could tell because the craft started to roll in the swell. He started to feel nauseous. The boy curled up in the wooden bottom of the lifeboat. He longed for fresh air, but didn't dare stick his head outside the tarp.

Mathias didn't know how long the gunboat sped over the water. It could have been minutes, but it seemed like a long, long time. The boy wasn't actually sick, but his head seemed full of cotton and his stomach rumbled back and forth with the waves. He wasn't paying attention to anything but the movement. He just wanted the rocking to stop.

It never did, but eventually the gunboat slowed down and the pitch lessened. Mathias's head continued to throb gently, but he felt well enough to want to know what was happening. He uncurled himself, stretched his cramped legs, and slowly pushed his head outside.

The moon had risen, illuminating a smooth, undulating seascape. The boat was still underway, but it wasn't going anywhere. Instead, it was inscribing a leisurely circle in the water, keeping in place in the featureless ocean by slowly cruising around an unseen point. Mathias craned his head around to look towards the bridge. Several men were on the narrow deck, a few in uniform, but two in civilian clothes. von Braun was one of the latter. Mathias guessed they were waiting for something to happen. They weren't speaking. They were just looking out over the sea. The civilian with von Braun kept glancing at his watch as if the hands were moving abnormally slow.

Time passed and the boat continued circling. Mathias looked for a chance to alert von Braun to his presence without letting anyone else know he was there. The chance never came. There were always at least a couple of soldiers on the deck and the scientist always stood with the other civilian. After a while the two of them moved towards the stern. Mathias ducked back down. They both leaned against the lifeboat looking forward—Mathias felt the boat tilt slightly against its restraints. He poked his head out and watched their backs, hoping the stranger would go away so he could whisper something to von Braun.

The man looked at his watch again.

"*Jetzt*, Wernher," he said to von Braun. "*Es ist Zeit.*"

The engines shut down as if on cue and the boat slowed even more, drifting silently under the moonlit sky. The two men, indeed all the men on board who weren't otherwise occupied, looked the same direction over the sea. Mathias didn't know for sure if they were looking north or south or west or where, but he guessed Germany lay over the horizon that way. Mathias looked, too.

At first he could see nothing but the sea and stars, with the rising moon off to his left creating a glittering, dancing path of light over the water. Then von Braun's companion pointed into the sky.

"*Da!*" he shouted.

Mathias's eyes searched the blackness and finally he saw it too: a red spark that flickered and disappeared and then reappeared again. It didn't seem to be moving, but it did look like it was getting bigger. Then, as the flickering became steady and the boy could see it was definitely flying straight towards them, but fairly high up, he thought he could hear a low buzzing noise. Before Mathias realized just how fast the thing was moving it had flown quite close overhead and the noise, which had grown considerable, suddenly cut out. von Braun's companion looked at his watch one last time and spoke into the new silence.

"Perfect," he said.

Mathias could no longer see the rocket. He figured it was one like that which had crashed in the turnip field since the flame had vanished when the buzzing ended. He looked for some sign of it, trying to guess where it was, but he couldn't spot it among the stars. Then he heard a whistle that grew and grew. With a stab of fear Mathias thought the thing was going to hit their boat and sink it.

The whistling reached an ear-splitting climax and with a great rush of air the rocket flashed in a steep dive overhead. It plowed into the sea, sending up a huge splash of water. The drops fell like rain. The surface of the ocean heaved and bubbled. Then, some thirty to forty feet beyond where it had hit, the grey cylinder broke surface again, heaving into the air like a dolphin reaching for the sky. It poised aloft for a split second and then tumbled back down, splashing into the water. It finally settled down to bob peacefully in the swell. Mathias thought he could hear some kind of hissing coming from it, but he wasn't sure.

The gunboat's engines started up again and the craft swung around to head for the downed rocket. Hidden behind the noise of the motor von Braun spoke so only his companion could hear. He didn't know Mathias was also within earshot.

"Please God, this is the last, George," he said in German. "Maybe we're finished with bombs. Maybe the Reds will let me take them to the Red Planet. Maybe we can do some real work. What do you think, George? No more Vengeance Rockets?"

George laughed, but Mathias could detect little amusement in the sound.

"Don't count on it, Wernher. There's still a war on, you know. They will want to use us for it."

Mathias wasn't so much listening to the words as noting the relationship between the two men. The were easy with each other. They trusted each other. Mathias could tell they were friends. A frightening thought exploded in his mind. It had always been there, but the boy had suppressed it. The scientist did not want Mathias along on his escape. It had only been wishful thinking. The idea was too big for the boy to digest. He tried to fight a growing sense of fear and panic. What was he going to do now?

The boat had slowed again and it bumped against the floating rocket. From his vantage point, Mathias could not see what was happening down at the water. von Braun and George moved away from him towards the action, presumably to check on their rocket. One man was barking orders. A crane was being unfolded behind the bridge. Mathias watched what he could, but his interest was waning. He was wondering if he'd have to go back to Bornholm. He was worried about what would happen when he got there.

Since everyone else was busy it was Mathias who saw the other boat first. For a few minutes he wasn't sure what he was looking at. It was coming from the north, coming from Sweden. The moonlight flashed off a small triangular sail, the type used on Bornholmsk fishing boats to aid their cranky old motors.

So preoccupied were the Germans in their task of pulling the Vengeance Rocket out of the water that they didn't notice the new boat until it burst into flame with a loud whoosh. Then everybody saw it and heard the screams from the men on board the burning fishing boat. It was less than a kilometre away. Mathias could see one man jump into the water while others were tipping a smaller version of his own lifeboat off the deck.

He looked from that scene to the gunboat. The flames were leaping from the stern of the fishing boat, which had begun to turn and list, and were illuminating the surprised faces of the German soldiers. They'd stopped working with the rocket, probably assuming the new situation would mean new orders.

Those orders came. The engines revved up and started pushing the gunboat carefully towards the fishing boat. By then the burning craft seemed to have been completely abandoned and the lifeboat was crammed with about half a dozen men. Two of them were trying to pull someone out of the water—the man who had jumped in earlier, Mathias thought. When they succeeded in dragging him into the cramped boat, the others began paddling to put distance between themselves and the fire.

They had apparently spotted the gunboat because they were moving towards it. Mathias heard someone shout "Help!" in a Swedish accent and a couple of men were waving their arms.

It took a few minutes for the two boats to meet. As the gunboat swung to starboard to let the lifeboat pull up on the side away from the rocket another "whoosh!" was heard from the fishing boat and the flames jumped higher. Now the whole rear of the craft was burning fiercely. The wheelhouse had caught and the flames were licking up the mast. The stern was sinking, lifting the bow up to the stars.

Two of the German soldiers were helping the fishermen out of their lifeboat, while others stood back watchfully. Mathias noticed a strong stink of fish, but he also saw a blonde man who looked like Aleks.

What happened next happened without warning. Mathias heard a loud bang and one of the soldiers fell backwards over the gunwale, hitting the rocket and splashing into the sea. It took everyone a moment to realize he'd been shot. By the time they did it was too late. A few more shots rang out. Mathias ducked down into his lifeboat and covered his head with his arms, hoping the wooden hull would protect him from the flying bullets. He heard shouting and more shots, some splashes and a painful scream. Then silence. That was finally broken by the sound of von Braun's shocked voice.

"*Mein Gott!*" he said and then he continued in Danish. "This is not what I wanted."

Mathias heard a laugh and then Aleks answered the scientist.

"Not what you wanted? Do you think they would have given you up freely? Do you think we should have asked for you politely? I'm sure that would have worked very well. I'm sure your military friends would have said: 'Yes, please. Take him!'"

The Russian laughed again, but without real humour.

Mathias eased his head back out into the air. von Braun stood with his back to the bridge, looking down. He had a stricken look in his face and his body was wracked with a sudden shudder. He knelt out of the line of Mathias's sight.

"He was just a boy," the scientist said. Mathias wondered who he was talking about. Then it occurred to him. One of the German soldiers. Mathias felt sick.

One of the men who had boarded the gunboat, a tall, thin man in his thirties, spoke in a language Mathias had never heard before, but since Aleks answered in the same language he assumed it was Russian. The two talked back and forth for a couple of minutes before Aleks turned once again to von Braun, who'd stood up to listen to the conversation.

"My superior says you should not be so squeamish," Aleks said. "He says you should have considered your scruples before you asked for our help, not after."

"Tell him I asked you to get me to Sweden, not to kill these men."

Aleks translated the message and received a reply.

"There was no other way," he said dismissively.

Aleks's superior then spoke to the other men on the deck. They started heaving the bodies overboard. Mathias counted three splashes before two men went into the bridge to retrieve a fourth body. They carried the corpse out—Mathias couldn't tell much about it except for the German uniform—and threw it into the sea to join its shipmates. Then the Russians set about finishing the task of hauling the rocket on board.

"This is a fine fish you caught tonight," Aleks said to von Braun. "Or should I say bird? My superior is pleased. You are an excellent prize, but this rocket of yours will save us a lot of work, no?"

The scientist did not answer. Aleks laughed, but to Mathias's ear his laughter sounded strained. The boy had never liked the young Russian. Now he'd begun to fear him. The boy sensed Aleks was holding himself together with difficulty, as if he had shocked himself with his actions and didn't know how to react. His laughter, his bluster, his apparent self-confidence were like a façade Aleks had erected as much to fool himself as others. Mathias wondered how many of the German soldiers Aleks had killed. Maybe all of them, he thought.

The rocket, dangling at the end of the crane, swung out of the water and into the air over the boat. The craft tilted as this was done, but righted itself quickly. The long cylinder was laid crossways on the deck and tied down securely with ropes.

The gunboat's engine, which had been idling ever since the lifeboat had come alongside, now roared back to full power. The gunboat veered sharply and headed north towards Sweden. Mathias curled up again in the bottom of the lifeboat to wait for what might happen next. He hoped it would be landfall on Sweden's shores.

Fourteen

The late night, the heaving swell and the throbbing engines were sending Mathias into a doze, but before long the tempo of the throb changed. He heard a shout out on the deck and felt the gunboat slowing down again. Mathias hoped they had reached Sweden already, but he guessed they were really nowhere near that country. The boy fought with the urge to sink back into the welcoming slumber and he stuck his head carefully outside the tarp once again.

The darkness was leaving the sky. The stars were dimming. The moon had nearly set and the sun was giving warning of its coming on the opposite horizon. It was not yet morning, but the day was not far away.

The sea had not changed. There was still no wind and the surface of the water was a glimmering, swelling mirror. Mathias could not see land any-where.

All the men on board were staring forward, away from the boy. He could not see what they were looking at, what was exciting their comments, their speculative noises. Mathias craned his head one way and then another, trying to look past the bridge without giving himself away. Then the craft rolled on the swell and Mathias saw a boat, a large, grey boat, almost a ship. The swell rolled the gunboat the other way and the boy saw another. Two large boats were waiting ahead for von Braun and the Russians.

The gunboat veered off its course and Mathias got a steady view of both vessels. They were much bigger than the one he was on, much bigger and, Mathias assumed, much faster and deadlier. A light blinked on one of them in a series of long and short flashes. A message of some sort, the boy thought.

No one on the gunboat replied. Instead, the Russians shouted at each other, weapons were checked with snaps and clacks, and von Braun and

George were pushed down through a hatch in the deck. Mathias could not tell if anyone understood the light-message, but it was obvious to him the meeting had not been planned and was definitely unwelcome. He wondered who was on the two boats. He didn't think they were Swedes. In fact, the large boats resembled German craft he'd seen in the Rønne harbour.

Mathias saw a puff of smoke on the foredeck of one of the boats, heard a boom, then a rushing of air, a splash, and an explosion off the front of the gunboat. The blast hurt his ears and the craft heaved in the shock wave. More shouting broke out on deck. The engines roared loud and the gunboat turned sharp to race back the way it had come. Mathias saw sudden puffs of exhaust coming out of the two boats and he knew they were preparing to chase.

No more shots came and the gunboat sped away on an arrow-straight course. The pursuers split apart, angling to each side of the gunboat in an attempt to flank it. They appeared to be going faster than the gunboat and Mathias thought they would soon come level. He worried about what they would do when that happened.

For the first few minutes of the chase Mathias had to keep his head down. The Russians kept looking back and there was a real danger they would spot him. Soon, however, the pursuers were no longer behind and the gazes were aimed outwards. The boy sneaked a glance and when he saw he was safe he stayed up to watch.

As Mathias saw the two boats catch up with the gunboat and begin to draw in towards it he wondered why the Russians were bothering to run. Maybe, he thought with dismay, they'd be better off if they gave up because they didn't seem to have a chance. The gunboat, however, had been saving its strength. One of the pursuers fired another shell into the Russians' path. When the shell exploded, sending up a spume of water, the gunboat veered suddenly and its engine whined louder. Mathias felt the surge of the extra speed and he saw the pursuers dropping back. They seemed to be going as fast as they were able because they made no more attempt to close the distance. They simply held their course.

The sun rose. The bright orange ball lifted over a bank of haze off the portside of the gunboat, sending its light over the glassy ocean. That light reflected off something ahead in the gunboat's path, revealing why the pursuing boats hadn't seemed worried about losing their quarry. Another boat waited for the Russians to the south. Now they were hemmed in on three sides.

The Russians saw the new boat, too. They swung around in a tight curve to run again to the north, hoping to speed through the gap before the Germans closed their net. Four explosions, one after the other, erupted in the water dead ahead. The Russians veered again, turning to the west, only to have to dodge quickly as more shells were lobbed into the water. The boy wondered what it would feel like to die in a blast. Would it hurt? Would he feel anything at all? He slipped back into the darkness of the lifeboat.

By this time the gunboat was reduced to racing in a circle as its three pursuers drew closer and closer, denying escape. Then the engine slowed and shut down. The boy heard the rumbling of larger motors pulling near. An amplified voice yelled in German from close by. The Russians dropped their rifles on the deck. The gunboat was jarred as one of the larger boats pulled alongside and men jumped down.

"*von Braun!*" the boy heard someone shout. "*Wo ist von Braun?*"

There was another flurry of Russian voices, a clang as the hatch cover was thrown off, and more shouts: "*Raus! Raus!*"

Mathias pictured his friend climbing onto the deck. Was he frightened? Was he defiant?

"Ah! *Guten Morgen, Herr Doktor. Guten Morgen, Herr Müller,*" the same voice said. "*Wo gehen Sie hin?*"

Then the voiced laughed.

"You have never liked me, hein, Dr. von Braun? How do you like me now? You are not telling your funny little jokes about me now, are you? It is my turn to be funny, no?"

Again the laugh. Mathias began to think the voice sounded familiar. Still von Braun said nothing, but George Müller spoke up.

"Buchheim, you little shit! What...."

There was the sound of a blow, a cry of pain, and a thump on the deck. Then another blow; another cry of pain.

"Enough!" von Braun said. "Buchheim! Stop this!"

"Stop it? I have barely begun," Buchheim said, clearly enjoying himself. "I have orders not to hurt you. I am not allowed to kill you, but I have no orders concerning your colleague here. I may do with him what I want. One can do what one likes with traitors. Unfortunately you are a traitor with friends in high positions. It would seem you are still more valuable alive than dead. So I must be content by amusing myself with Herr Müller."

"Please do not hurt him any more. It is unnecessary. We will not oppose you."

"Oppose me?" Buchheim laughed. "There was never any question of your opposing me. I only wish to enjoy myself now. This little game is almost over and it has been such fun!"

von Braun did not respond.

"No questions, Herr Doktor? I am surprised at your lack of curiosity," Buchheim continued. "I drop hints, but you do not pick them up. Do you not wish to learn how we found out about your little plan? Do you not want to know why you are not now on your way to Russia?"

"Very well. You clearly wish to gloat. How did you find out?"

Buchheim laughed yet again. Mathias had begun to dread that sound.

"Are you not gracious in defeat? Ah well, never mind, since I am not gracious in victory. Graciousness is so boring. I have a little surprise for you, it seems. Please step this way."

As Buchheim spoke, his voice came closer to Mathias's hiding place. The boy watched in horror as the tarp covering the lifeboat was freed from its fastenings and drawn quickly away. Mathias found himself looking up into the grinning face of von Braun's SS babysitter.

"You did not know you have a stowaway, did you, Herr Doktor?" Buchheim said and smiled.

The scientist appeared at his side and his face dropped in shock when he saw Mathias.

"*Mein Gott!*" he said. "Mathias!"

Mathias, his eyes blurring with tears, forced himself to speak. The words came out in a whisper.

"I'm sorry. I thought…I thought you wanted to take me with you."

"Ah, my boy, my boy," von Braun frowned and shook his head. Then he turned to Buchheim. "What is this farce? You knew he was here. Why have you let this boy endanger his life?"

"Why, we had to discover all your plans, did we not? The boy made his own choices. He proved quite useful to us, but I cannot say I am too concerned for his safety."

"Useful? What do you mean he was useful? What has he done for you?"

"Oh, do not fear, he knew nothing. His stupidity made him useful—your stupidity, too. Do you think we are fools? You must know we have watched

you. Such a lovely sight you and your young friend here: enjoying such innocent meals together, taking such lovely walks through the woods. We are not
without friends ourselves. Your boy here first led us to this one." Buchheim
turned and kicked someone lying on the deck. "And then he led us to this boat.
Very useful indeed."

Buchheim issued orders to a couple of German soldiers, who came over
and roughly pulled Mathias out of the lifeboat. They set him on the deck
beside von Braun and he stood there looking around, blinking in the morning
sunlight. Two Germans stood on one side of the rocket, pointing rifles at the
four Russians who were lying face down on the other. The closest Russian—
the one Buchheim must have kicked—was Aleks. The side of the young man's
face was pressed into the metal deck, but he was still able to watch Mathias.
The boy didn't like the cold look he was getting and he avoided meeting the
Russian's accusing eyes.

On the other side of von Braun, Müller was sitting up holding his stomach. His head was hanging down and he had vomited on the deck beside him.
Buchheim surveyed the scene with evident satisfaction.

"A good day's work and it is not even noon," he said. "I think I will celebrate with some of that first-rate Danish schnapps for lunch. Such civilized
people, these Danes. How about you, Herr Doktor? Oh, I forgot! I believe
you have an appointment with Captain Reinhardt when we return to port. I do
not think he will be in the mood to celebrate with you!"

Buchheim laughed and then walked off to organize matters. He had the
four Russians moved to the larger boat and brought some more German
sailors over to pilot the gunboat back to Bornholm. He left Mathias, von
Braun, and Müller where they were, guarded by an armed soldier. The flotil-
la then swung around to sail towards the rising sun.

Müller remained where he was, nursing his sore stomach. Mathias
slumped down on the deck and cried, his body and mind wracked by remorse
and disappointment. He could not look at von Braun, knowing he had ruined
his friend's great dream. von Braun, however, sat down beside Mathias and
put his arm across the boy's shoulders. He didn't say anything. He just hugged
Mathias to his side.

The boy sobbed once or twice and then his crying ended quietly. He wiped
his eyes with his jacket sleeves and stared down at the deck between his feet.
He still couldn't look at von Braun.

"Do you hate me?" he finally asked the scientist.

"Hate you?" von Braun said with surprise. "No, Mathias, I don't hate you."

Then Mathias looked up.

"But I ruined everything for you. Everything!"

"Ach, no, my boy, you did not. Only the devil himself can ruin everything. You did what you thought best. Maybe you made a mistake, but we all make mistakes."

"But if it wasn't for me you'd be in Sweden by now, wouldn't you?"

"Yes, it is true, I might have been. But only maybe. I think perhaps they would have found out about me in other ways if they had not used you. I have been careless, it seems. I, too, have made mistakes. I am a scientist. I am not good at politics or war. They are very good at both these things."

"What will they do to you now?" Mathias asked. "Will they hurt you?"

von Braun smiled to reassure the boy. He hugged him a bit tighter for a moment.

"No, do not worry, my boy. My babysitter was correct about one thing: I do have powerful friends. And I am too useful to the Nazis for them to discard me. If I was not then I would already be dead. Perhaps we would all be dead. That is why they were so anxious that I not go to Sweden. They will probably just send me back to Peenemünde and put me back to work. I think they will want to keep this incident secret. It would not be good for their propaganda.

"They will trust me less and watch me more. And I will work. I will build them their bombs. I will try to stay alive and I will think of what I may do in future days. You must do the same, I think. We must all do this."

Mathias thought about what von Braun was saying. To him his guilt was overwhelming. He was trying to understand how von Braun could forgive him. He couldn't look past the mess he'd made of the present. von Braun, however, seemed incapable of assigning blame. He was concerned with more important things than a child's lack of judgement.

"Mars," he said to the boy, his voice low and sad. "I only wanted to go to Mars. People say I have space dust in my eyes. Maybe I have. Think of it! Men flying in one of my rockets across the vast emptiness between the planets. Men walking on the surface of the Red Planet. We can do it. I can do it."

von Braun paused and glanced at the soldier who was pointing a rifle at him.

"I can do it," he continued. "I could do it, except I must now give all my gifts to this war. My rockets will be used to kill, not to explore.

"This is an irony, is it not? When I turned my eyes to Mars, Mars looked back at me. Mars is the God of War, did you know?"

Mathias shook his head.

"I am a scientist. I am concerned with the physical realities of life. I see the planet Mars and I know it to be a celestial body. I see it as a destination for my rockets—a destination like Sweden, perhaps?"

von Braun smiled, gazing into the distance. There was no happiness in that smile.

"Perhaps like Sweden, but I hope not. I hope it becomes a real destination. But I was saying: I am a scientist. I am a rational man. When I turned my mind to Mars I thought I would be protected by my rationality, but I was wrong. The old gods are still strong, especially today. Especially in Germany."

The scientist fell silent again, his gaze captured by the approaching shoreline of Bornholm. Mathias looked as well. He thought back to the first time he'd seen this island from the sea, but the bright, beautiful glow of the white beaches and the green hills made little impression on his tired mind. The turmoil of the night's events filled his head.

"We are soon there and we will soon part," von Braun said. Mathias turned to look up at his friend. "I think this will perhaps be the last time we see each other, my boy."

Mathias's eyes widened as he tried to absorb this new, unwelcome fact.

"I have something to give you," the scientist said. "Something for you to keep."

von Braun dug into a pocket and pulled out a walnut-sized cube made of shiny steel. He handed it to Mathias, who took it and turned it to look at all the sides.

"What is it?" the boy asked.

"It is a cube. A perfect cube," von Braun said. "It was a test. When I was a boy, older than you are now, I wanted to be an apprentice in a machine shop. They gave me a lump of steel the size of my two fists together and they said to make them a perfect cube.

"I worked for weeks. I cut. I polished. I cut again. Time after time they measured what I had done and they gave it back to me saying it was not perfect. Do it again, they said. So I did it again and again and my cube got smaller and smaller. Finally it was as you see it now. They measured it and said

I had created a perfect cube. All the edges are equal. I was then permitted to become an apprentice."

von Braun looked at the cube in the boy's hands.

"That was my first test. Passing it allowed me to follow the path that has led me here."

The scientist looked again at the soldier who was guarding them and he chuckled.

"Perhaps this is not the best place to be, but even if I had known I would still have wanted to make my perfect cube. I have done much I am proud of and I hope to do more.

"Life is full of tests, my boy. You will not always know you are being tested and you will not always know if you have passed or failed. But you must always do what you think is best. In the end you are your only judge, even before God."

The scientist's eyes seemed far away, but just for a moment. He soon returned to the present.

"You keep that cube, Mathias. Perhaps when you look upon it you will remember me?"

"I will," Mathias said. He dug quickly into his own pockets and found the red stone he'd picked off the beach. He gave it to von Braun, without saying a word.

"For me?" the scientist asked. "*Danke schön*...thank you very much."

He turned the small stone in his fingers, studying it carefully. His eyes took in the deep red hue and the black creases scarring the smooth, irregular shape.

"How very appropriate," von Braun said, smiling. "A miniature planet Mars to remind me of my friend Mathias. Thank you. I will keep it near."

Finne pushed his chair back, reached into a bulging shirt pocket, and pulled out a shiny metal cube. He placed it on the table between us. I could not tell whether it was a perfect cube, but I had no doubt it was the one made by Wernher von Braun.

"von Braun was right," Finne said. "I never saw him again. I don't know if he ever came back to Bornholm after the war. If he did, it was kept a secret from me.

"After the war – well, everybody knows what happened after the war. He never got to Mars, but he did get the Americans to the moon. I wonder if he was disappointed with his life, but I don't suppose he was. He was not the sort to worry about things like that."

"You lived in Canada," I said to Finne. "That is not so very far from the United States. Did you never think of visiting Dr. von Braun?"

"I thought about it," he answered. "I thought about it. I waited, but the right time never came. Then it was too late. When he died twenty years ago I lost a good friend."

Finne took the cube back and turned it over in his fingers, running the tips over the straight edges.

"When we reached the dock, von Braun only had time to say goodbye to me and then they took him away—to his appointment with the island's commander, no doubt. I was worried about him, but I also had my own problems to deal with.

"My father was waiting for me on the dock, standing with Buchheim. Neither was saying anything. Both were watching me as I was led towards them. My father showed anger; Buchheim displayed great satisfaction.

"'We have much to thank you for, Herr Finne,' Buchheim said. 'Your son does not choose his friends well, but his foolishness has saved us from losing a most important man. We are grateful you came to us. You will find we are generous in our gratitude.'

"Buchheim was not looking at my father as he said this; he was watching me. It was as if he wanted to see my reaction to his words. This man—a small, thin man who usually wore civilian clothes, but on this occasion sported the black SS uniform—was playing with my father and me. He was telling me that my father had informed on me and von Braun. It made sense to me. My father must have followed me the night I'd gone to the pond and he'd seen Aleks or von Braun. I'd escaped from our home so easily the night before because it suited my father's purpose—my father's and the German's.

"Buchheim wanted me to know this. Why? I don't know. Or rather, I cannot be sure. I think perhaps it was just in his nature to sow strife between people. I think he must have enjoyed causing arguments, sparking fights, and setting sons against fathers.

"He succeeded with me. Even now, when I can understand what Buchheim was doing and how he used us for his sadistic pleasure, even now I feel anger at my father for what he did. I am not as good a man as von Braun.

I am not so quick to forgive.

"Buchheim was not finished. He put his hand on the top of my head and smiled down at me like a doting uncle. His touch burned and frightened me. I stood there looking up at him. The fear must have shone on my face. I can only think it pleased him.

"'Such a handsome boy, Herr Finne,' he said. 'You must make sure he does not get into any more trouble. I would not like to think he cannot learn from his mistakes. You will teach him correctness, will you not?'

"He looked at my father, the smile still on his face as if he was talking about rewarding me, not punishing me. My father nodded, but said nothing. He, too, was looking at me, but he was not smiling. I could see his jaw clenched tight and his brow furrowed even tighter. I knew I was in for a bad time.

"Buchheim left us then. My father gripped the back of my neck and steered me away from the waterfront. We did not walk far, however, before our progress was halted. The four Russians, bruised and handcuffed, were also being led away and we had to stop to let them and their guards pass. This time Aleks did not notice me. I believe his vision was too shadowed by pain to see anything around him.

"Although I couldn't move my head to left or right, I could still see beyond the German soldiers and their prisoners. I thought I couldn't feel any worse, but what I saw made my already overwhelming guilt grow even larger and envelop my whole body. My knees weakened and I slumped. My father cursed and pulled me up by the neck.

Lise was watching the scene half-hidden in a small clump of curious bystanders. She looked from Aleks to me and back to Aleks again. The look of anguish and fear in her eyes was so clear to me. She turned and ran. The last I saw of her for many weeks was her bare calves flashing under her skirt. Her long blonde hair flowed in the wind of her passage. I felt alone, so alone."

Fifteen

"When i look back over my life some days seem to last for years," Finne began the next morning. "But some years seem hardly to have happened at all."

Finne took a sip of his tea, blowing on it first to cool it off. An odd gesture, I thought, considering that it wasn't really hot to start with. He looked tired. He looked older than when the interview had begun a few days before.

"I'm almost finished my story in case you want to know how much longer I'll be. There's not too much left to tell. Not too much," he echoed with a hollow laugh. "Just the rest of my life."

I was anxious that he come to the end of his tale. He kept saying he wanted to confess to murder, but as of yet he'd told me nothing that could be considered police business. Not only that, but my superiors were starting to make noise about the time I was taking with this case. So far I'd managed to hold off their demands to bring it to a conclusion, but I didn't know if I would be successful for many more days.

"Most of the next two years after my little boat trip had a kind of numbing sameness to them. I went to school, but had little interest in it and no one seemed to take interest in me. I made no new friends and my teachers hesitated to get too close. I had become a morose child, I suppose, and I made it clear I didn't care about what they were trying to teach me. I didn't fail any courses, but neither did I shine.

"The years that followed were difficult for my small family. Life became an act for all three of us, especially when we were invited to social events hosted by the Germans. My father played the part of the committed Danish Nazi, secure in his beliefs and happy in his role of helping his fellow citizens to see the light. He was good at displaying all the different facets of his role: he was the ideologically pure Aryan, the loving husband who cherished his beautiful wife, and the proud father teaching his son how to become a mature and right-thinking man.

"My mother played the role of the dutiful wife. She would nod and smile to support all her husband said. She would chat with the naval officers, laugh at their jokes and smile at their compliments, flirting with some of the bolder ones, but always making it clear she was loyal to Carl Finne. She was a prize as a guest and gracious as a hostess.

"I was more difficult to fit into a role because some of those occupiers my parents spent time with knew of my involvement in the von Braun affair. If they didn't know all the facts at least they'd heard rumours. At first I wasn't often brought out on display, but gradually the taint attached to me faded somewhat as the old military personnel left and new ones replaced them. To those unaware of my history I was presented as a fine example of Denmark's future, one of the new generation that would walk hand-in-hand with Germany into the new millennium. I gradually took the image of the model son as my own.

"So, in public we presented ourselves as a happy, united family with a secure place in society. The problem was we played that role in an alien society. We were subjugated Danes among Germans, not equals among our own people. The higher we rose with the Germans, the less we were welcome by the Danes. It was that fact that influenced who we really were.

"My father became quicker to anger. I believe he may have concluded he had made a mistake in taking the job on Bornholm. His hoped-for transfer to another newspaper in Copenhagen never came and he may have realized it would never come. Sometimes I thought he blamed us—my mother and me—for being stuck on the island, but at other times he seemed to direct his dissatisfaction towards the Party. However, he could only show that dissatisfaction in small, subtle ways. I began to think he might have started regretting the little swastika pin he used to wear with such pride. I saw it less and less often on his lapel, as if he hoped in this way he could somehow distance himself from the Nazis. But, in truth, it was far too late for that. He'd put himself within their grasp and they quickly took control of all aspects of his life. And, since such was the nature of the beast, he was forced to draw his whole family within its reach.

"The contact sickened us. The sickness was most obvious in my mother.

Deprived of her family and friends in Copenhagen and denied the chance to make new ones on the island, my mother turned to the bottle. She had developed an affection for white wine years before, but now it became a love affair. Somehow she managed to procure a steady supply and soon she was never quite sober.

"She started forgetting glasses of wine in different places around the house, half-hidden and neglected. One day I happened to spot one behind a potted plant in the dining room. Not knowing what it was, I picked up the half-filled glass and tasted the contents. Expecting sweetness, I grimaced at the tart flavour and replaced the glass behind the plant. I walked to the kitchen to ask my mother what it was. She blushed before she answered and that told me more than her words did.

"'It's nothing,' she said. 'Never mind.'

"Even without looking for the glasses I started finding them under the bathroom sink, in cupboards and closets, or behind curtains. Once or twice I caught her sipping from a glass and returning it to its place, but she seemed to lose track of most of them. I got into the habit of emptying them out and cleaning them, hoping my father would not find any.

"When she became truly drunk her attitude towards my father and me changed. Towards my father she became colder, sarcastic even. She would accuse him of things I didn't quite understand, telling him he was inadequate and unfulfilling. At these times my father would either answer back or just wordlessly leave the house.

"My mother would become more emotional and affectionate towards me, but not in a way I liked. It seemed to me that the alcohol was making her sticky sweet. Her displays felt unnatural and I did not welcome them. I knew there was a real love beneath it, but I hated the way the wine made it come out.

"Lise, as I said before, I didn't see for many weeks after she ran from the harbour. When I did finally see her again the meeting was uneventful. She merely stopped by to visit one afternoon while my father was out and we sat together at the kitchen table drinking tea and talking about my schoolwork. It wasn't a topic I chose; she asked and I answered.

"I was shy with Lise and I believe she was shy with me, although maybe not for the same reason. I felt guilty. It was my fault that Aleks had been arrested by the Nazis. I couldn't say I was sorry, because that would have raised the forbidden topic. As we spoke of arithmetic and spelling and geography I felt miserable.

"Gradually, we began to meet regularly again, but never where my father might encounter us together. Lise had apparently managed to escape being connected with Aleks or von Braun, but she was afraid the Germans suspected she was involved in resistance activities. My mother cared less and less about what Lise may have led me into, but we couldn't assume my father would feel the same. It was safer for Lise to stay out of his way.

"So Lise came to the house during the day when my father was at work, or sometimes, more and more often, we would meet at the campsite by the pond in the woods. We had destroyed its secrecy in the summer of 1943. The resistance no longer used the hiding place, which made it ideal for us.

"Lise was considered too dangerous to be used for resistance work. They no longer had her run errands, distribute newspapers, or deliver food and messages. It was assumed the Germans knew her and were keeping an eye on her. No one was certain of this, but lives couldn't be risked.

"Lise knew what had happened that night on the sea without my telling her. She probably learned it from her underground colleagues. How they knew, I can't guess. She was also aware of what happened to Aleks—what happened to him, that is, after he was captured. For a while he was held in the German prison camp on the island, but then he was to have been transferred with the three other Russians to the mainland, to Poland or to Germany itself.

"When Lise told me about this she couldn't hide the fear in her voice. We had all heard rumours about the German concentration camps and while we couldn't believe them all, even the possibility of truth was terrifying.

"Then, about a week after she heard the first news, which was about a year after Aleks was arrested, Lise came to the pond with hope shining from her eyes.

"'He's escaped!' she said breathlessly.

"I didn't have to ask who she meant.

"'Escaped?' I said. 'When? How?'

"'I don't know. All I know is he got away. They never got him to Germany. Only three people were taken off the boat and he wasn't one of them.'

"'Maybe they killed him on board.'

"The words were out of my mouth before I could stop them. I gasped, hoping I hadn't frightened Lise. But it was not a new thought to her. She knew what was at stake.

"'No,' she said. 'There was a big search for him. They didn't know where he was.'

"'But how did he do it? Where did he go?'

"'I don't know, I tell you! What does it matter? He's free! He's alive and he's free!'

"I wasn't so sure, but Lise was so happy that she danced. She knew she could be wrong, but for once she wanted to enjoy herself. What could I do but join in her happiness? She danced! She held her arms over her head and she swung her skirt with joy. She laughed and sang, "'He's free! He's free!'

"I couldn't help laughing, too. Her joy was infectious. She grabbed my hands and swung me around until we could hardly breath. However, I didn't share all her feelings about Aleks. In fact, I felt worried because I knew Aleks held no love for me either. He hated me, for all I knew, and he had good reason. I wondered where he was, what he was doing, and if he would come back to Bornholm.

"Lise said she knew he would return, but the months slipped away and she heard nothing further. She took this as a good sign, reasoning that if he'd been caught again she'd surely have known about it. I wasn't so confident this would be the case, but I didn't want to argue against her feelings. For all I knew she was perfectly right."

The war changed irrevocably in the spring of 1945. The official German-sanctioned newspapers like my father's continued to celebrate German victories and ignore or downplay German defeats, but this didn't fool the Danish civilians. The real news got through. It was announced over the BBC, broadcast from Sweden and reprinted in the illegal underground newspapers.

France was free. Africa was free. Italy and Russia were free. The Nazis were losing ground on all fronts; the Americans, Canadians, and British pushing them from the west and south, the Russians from the east. The Germans may have believed they were still winning the war, but no one else did.

Mathias began to notice more Germans on Bornholm in late March. They were not, however, the same as those who had occupied the island for the past five years. The soldiers he was used to seeing were usually neatly dressed and well fed. These newcomers, though, looked worn and tired and hungry. They never seemed to notice things around them, but would stare listlessly at nothing. Many were wounded; they limped painfully or wore stained bandages around their heads or their arms.

Companies of these soldiers, sometimes with leaders, sometimes without, were always headed westwards. People said how they came off boats in Nexø, the largest town on Bornholm's eastern shore, and cross the island on foot to Rønne. There they would embark again on boats to head south to Germany, perhaps, or further west to the main part of Denmark.

With them came an increasing number of German civilians, women and children, mostly, whose clothes looked like they'd once been expensive, but now appeared torn and dirty. As the numbers of soldiers grew, so too did the number of civilians. Mathias learned a new word: refugee. If Germans were on the run, Danes said amongst themselves, then their end could not be far away.

Mathias was on his own quite a lot in those final days. As his father's worry about his position grew—Carl Finne was, after all, an intelligent man and he could see he'd ultimately chosen a losing side—he spent even more time away from home. His mother, on the other hand, hardly went out any more, withdrawing deeper within herself. Mathias was essentially free to do as he liked by then, new events having relegated his episode with the scientist into irrelevance.

There had been a general confiscation of bicycles in late 1944, but Mathias had managed to save his. The Germans, for reasons of their own—some Danes said they needed them for transportation, but others speculated that they took them to deter saboteurs—stole every bicycle they could lay their hands on and most children were left to travel on foot. Mathias, however, had chance on his side and his bicycle had already been hidden out of sight beside the pond when the round-up took place. He never brought it home again, but left it there and used it sparingly.

So Mathias was still able to wander far afield when the refugees began filtering through the countryside. The soldiers on the move took as straight a line as possible from one port to the other, but the civilians wandered in an almost haphazard fashion, always westwards, but not always due west. They left the main roads to avoid the military traffic. Mathias would come across them in the back lanes, trudging along with blank looks on their faces and heavy bundles slung over their backs. He'd spy on them in the dingy woodland campsites and he saw what little they had to eat: sometimes just some watery soup, sometimes hard hunks of bread.

In his wanderings Mathias noticed something else. The German civilians tended to hold onto what little they had, but the soldiers—more and more of them were travelling without officers—were throwing away things they no longer wanted to carry. At first the boy only saw them discard shovels, helmets, bits of winter clothing, and, once, a radio, but soon they were even tossing their weapons into the ditches.

"One day near the end of April I saw a company of German soldiers coming my way, so I pulled off the road and hid in the bushes to wait for them to pass. By chance I'd picked a spot where the road crossed a little stream. This attracted them—they'd probably been walking all day—so they stopped for a rest and a drink of water.

"There were about a dozen of them. They didn't say much. They just laid down their rifles, sat on the bank, and dipped tin cups into the stream. Once they drank their fill they stretched out. Some lit up ragged cigarettes and smoked. Others just put their hands behind their heads and closed their eyes. One rummaged for something in his backpack.

"The soldier finally pulled out a cloth cap. He took off his helmet, looked at it and cursed it, and then threw it onto the ground. It rolled partway down the bank until it lodged against a stone. The soldier used the cloth cap to wipe sweat off his brow before cramming it onto his head.

"That started an argument. Another of the soldiers objected to throwing the helmet away. The two bickered back and forth for a few minutes with no result until the first tried to make his point by pulling more things out of his pack and tossing them onto the ground. First went a mess kit; then a thick leather-bound book; then binoculars; then a pair of pants and a shirt. Then the soldier upended the pack and shook it. Bits of garbage, a sock, and some shiny bullets fell out. When the pack was empty he threw that away, too, and laughed.

"The second soldier stood up angrily and scolded the first in rising tones. The first said something back in an accent so strong I could not understand him. He kicked his rifle. It skidded down the bank and splashed into the water. He unclipped a leather holster from his belt and showed it mockingly to his angry companion. With an elaborate show of carelessness he tossed it over his shoulder, not watching where it landed. The other soldiers just laughed and the argument ended. After a few more cigarettes were smoked, the company headed on its way.

"I crept out of my hiding place to have a look at the things they'd left behind. I picked up the book and then dropped it again with disgust. The thick black leather of its cover was deeply embossed with a gold swastika. It was Adolf Hitler's *Mein Kampf*. I had no use for the awful thing.

"I kicked aside the discarded clothing to find the binoculars. I tried to look through them, but nothing I did with the knobs would give me a clear sight of anything. When I examined them closer I found out why: one of the large lenses was broken and splintered.

"I tried on the helmet, but it was far too large and sat right over my eyes, blocking my sight. I threw it back to the ground.

"Then I crawled through the bushes until I found the holster the soldier had so carelessly thrown away. I sat cross-legged with the thing in my lap and unclipped the flap. I gingerly slid the gun out, half expecting it to go off from my touch alone.

"The pistol was heavier than I thought it would be. It was a big, square thing—a Luger, I found out later. You see it in all the movies. I could barely hold it steady with one hand as I sighted along the short barrel and made 'pow! pow! pow!' sounds. I felt like pulling the trigger to see what would happen, but I didn't. I was afraid the German soldiers were still near enough to hear it.

"Besides, I didn't even know how to find out if it was loaded or not. I looked at the pistol, saw what looked like the place to put bullets in, but I couldn't figure out how to check if there were any already inside. I just slipped it back into the holster, snapped it shut, and sat with it in my lap.

"What to do with it? Obviously I couldn't bring it home. Where would I put it? There was nowhere I could hide it in the house; even in my room there was always the chance it would be found.

"I didn't want to bring it to the campsite. I didn't want Lise to know I had it and she would likely see it if I tried to hide it at the pond. I guessed she wouldn't be pleased that I found a gun and would probably take it away from me.

"There was no doubt in my mind that I had to keep it. I never even imagined leaving it where I'd found it. I don't know why I wanted that pistol, I just knew I had to have it. Of course, that left me the problem of where to keep it.

"Then I knew.

"I found the soldier's discarded pack, stuffed the holstered pistol into it, and slung it over my back. It was too large for me and it knocked against the seat of my bike when I rode away. I headed northwest, to the woods to the south of Vestermarie. I was looking for an ancient grave I'd discovered on a previous excursion.

"I haven't told you about this place, have I? It was a ship, a stone ship. It lay amongst the trees of the Vestermarie plantation—long and slim and pointed at both ends. A Viking ship for a sea captain dead one thousand years.

"I approached it with the same sense of awe I felt when I first found it. It was not easy to spot. Men had laid the stones down so long ago that the rocks had blended back into the land. The edge was clear, although almost flush with the ground, but the stones filling in the deck were mostly covered over with dirt and leaves. Two fir trees, offspring from the forest around the ship, grew up between the cracks. I imagined that their roots were reaching down to touch the rotting bones of a Viking warrior. I saw his body surrounded in death by the things he knew in life: his gold, his sword and spear, his horses, maybe even his wife.

"All the stones of that great ship, which lay forty metres long and ten wide, were held firm in their places as if mortared there—all the stones, that is, but one. Dead centre, right where the mast would have risen tall and straight to the skies, a large round stone sat loose in the dirt. When I first found it I stood on it and rocked it back and forth. Then I looked for a strong branch to lever the stone out of place, hoping—and fearing—to find an entrance into the burial chamber beneath. I was disappointed. All I found was a small empty hole that didn't lead anywhere at all. But now I had a need for that hole.

"The branch I had used was still there, so I wrenched the stone back out of place. I scooped the hole a little deeper, getting dirt caught up under my fingernails, and stuffed the pack and the gun into the space. When I rolled the stone into its bed it bulged higher than it had before. I pushed the extra earth around it and scattered some old, dry leaves over it. When I stood back I could clearly see I'd disturbed the ship, but I didn't think anyone else would notice what I'd done, especially not in this out of the way forest. I doubted anyone would even come near.

"Over the next few days the number of German military and civilian refugees on Bornholm multiplied dramatically. Soon there were thousands on the island. They were landing quicker than they could leave and their transports always went back for more. They had nowhere to stay and nothing to eat. They were nearly starved and many begged for scraps of food. Some got them; others didn't. They were dirty. They were far from home and they were lost. They were defeated, crushed. They fled because they didn't know what else to do.

"But still the war wasn't over. In fact, the war was coming closer to Bornholm than it ever had before. The Danish island had become part of the eastern front. The Soviet armies had already passed the island on their western march across Germany. Bornholm, it seems, had been momentarily overlooked.

"The waters around our island, however, had not been forgotten. I did not see it myself, but I heard stories about German refugee ships being bombed and sunk off our southern coast. We'd had a quiet war, but suddenly we could hear the awful noise of fighting. The flashing and rumbling on the horizon meant that people were dying. For five years the war had made only brief visits to Bornholm. Now the storm was waiting just off our shores.

"At the same time there was the sense that the war was finally coming to an end. It was like the war was racing with its own demise, trying to consume as much as it could before it lost its strength, before it ground to a halt amidst the wreckage of its passage. We knew peace was on its way. We just hoped destruction wouldn't overrun us first.

"Lise was full of plans. She talked about the peace as if it was already a certainty, as if it wasn't still only a promise. She seemed to know more than I did and could see further than I could. She talked about life returning to normal—something I'd never known, she said. She spoke of the shops offering new clothes, and of others selling truthful books and newspapers, and even of some with butter for sale. Lise was looking forward to walking down the street without having to watch out for German patrols. She wanted to talk freely in public without having to worry if German spies were listening for incautious words. She wanted to be free of fear: fear for me, fear for her family, fear for herself. She said that peace would mean she could be free from worry.

"When the peace actually came it surprised everyone. Even though we'd all been waiting for it, no one expected the form it took. We expected peace to solve our problems and to answer our questions, but it didn't. Peace freed us, but it didn't free us from the Germans. Germany had lost the war, but Germany still held Bornholm.

"The news first came over the radio on May 4. '*Danmark ist frit! Danmark ist frit!*' The announcer's enthusiasm lit bright fires in the hearts of his audience and we could hear the jubilant sounds of celebrations in the streets of

Copenhagen. His words were repeated on all the front pages of the Bornholmsk newspapers the next day, except my fathers, which by then was no longer publishing. But the elation was tinged with worry. We were happy because Denmark was free, but the free Danes seemed to have forgotten about Bornholm. We were not yet free and they did not notice. They did not seem to care.

"But I shouldn't let you think nothing changed—everything changed! The Germans continued to do all they had done before, but now they were powerless, impotent. Their movements were like pantomimes; they became shadowy imitations of real soldiers.

"My mother and I were at home when the announcement came over the radio. And my father, for once, was also home.

"'Denmark is free! Denmark is free!' we heard. I felt joy bubbling up inside me. I looked to my parents. I saw fear in my father's eyes, not a sudden sharp fright, but a profound dread. My mother showed neither joy nor fear. She was watching my father with morbid satisfaction in her eyes, as if she was seeing her unheard warning come true. At first I couldn't tell if she'd been drinking or not, but when her expression softened and she went over to put a hand on my father's shoulder, I suspected she was still sober.

"My joy dried up. I resented my parents, my father most of all. I wanted to celebrate. In all of my thirteen years, the ending to the war was the most momentous thing that had ever happened to me, something I'd waited for for as long as I could remember. To me it promised new life, but to them it promised only darkness and fear.

"In that special hour I needed to be with someone who felt as happy as I did. I slipped out the front door without asking their permission. Either they didn't notice or didn't mind. Neither tried to stop me.

"I ran into the street and was rewarded with the sight of Lise running towards me. Just seeing her restored my good humour. She was breathless and beautiful, a smile lighting her flushed face, a laugh lifting her voice to the sky. I fell in love with her again, as I did every time I saw her.

"'Mathias! Mathias!' she shouted, grabbing my hands and dancing me around on the cobbles. 'Denmark is free! Denmark is free!'

"Those words were on everyone's lips as we ran to the main square. Danes were all over the streets, greeting each other with unfeigned joy. The Germans I saw looked isolated and bewildered, unsure of what was happening. I think they had not yet been told about the war being over, but they could easily see their world had changed. Suddenly they were weak and irrelevant, despite their rifles, despite how powerful they'd been only hours before.

"Soon we began to see Danes with rifles and helmets and Danes in civilian clothing marching in loose patrols. We were seeing something openly on the streets that had been hidden away all through the war: the blue and red resistance armband. The cloth had been torn from the uniforms of our defeated army in the first days of the German occupation. They were hastily sewn together and gloriously adorned with the very symbol of Danish nationhood: a shiny brass disk bearing the three royal lions.

"Until then King Christian was the only man in Denmark able to wear the symbol openly. If anyone else had dared to proudly strap the armband onto his sleeve he would have been arrested the minute he was seen, arrested, probably tortured, possibly killed.

"Now, on that heady day, the blue and red armbands were everywhere. It was the clearest sign I'd seen that the war was over. The Germans were still patrolling the town, but now they were powerless. When we reached the main square I could hardly believe what I saw. Dozens of Danish men and women were helping themselves to rifles and ammunition from wooden crates opened on the cobblestones while German soldiers watched impassively. These weapons had lain hidden for months and years in churches, attics, and farms. All through the war they'd been smuggled over from Sweden. Most had been taken on to Copenhagen, but many had been kept on the island. Now they no longer had to be hidden.

"There was a carnival atmosphere in the main square. The day was a holiday; no one could work in the midst of such events. Bottles of wine, beer, and snaps were passing from hand to hand and mouth to mouth, as if the end of the war automatically brought the end of shortage. Men had their arms across each other's shoulders, merrily singing the old folk songs. Impromptu dancing sprang up at various spots and couples swung around laughing accordion players. Children ran and played tag around the adults. Lise and I dodged from one end of the long square to the other, waltzing briefly at one spot, sampling a bit of wine at another, stuffing our faces full of food at a third. I hadn't been so happy or had so much fun in years.

"But that, of course, couldn't last. If the celebration in the square was a carnival, then it had to have a freak show. It was announced with a scream. A woman appeared, running from a gang of laughing, leering men. She ran awkwardly on stockinged feet, holding her torn dress up to her shoulder. Tears smeared the make-up in black runs down her face. Her head was roughly shaved, the remnants of brown hair sticking in ugly clumps from a reddened scalp. The men chasing her caught her and held her. No one, absolutely no one showed any sympathy towards the girl or tried to help her. The few German soldiers nearby turned away; if they pretended they hadn't seen her, they didn't have to interfere.

"'Who is she, Lise?' I asked, unable to keep the shock out of my voice. 'What are they doing that to her? What did she do?'

"Lise was, to my ear, uncharacteristically dismissive of the girl's troubles. She looked at her with ice in her eyes.

"'She's nothing, Mathias. Don't worry about her.'

"Lise's coldness shocked me as much as the sight of the mistreated girl. I was more used to warmth from Lise, not this hard, biting frost.

"'Why not?' I asked. 'What did she do?'

"'She went to the other side, Mathias. She took Nazis into her bed. She slept with them.'

"'Oh,' I said, inadequately. I knew, of course, that associating with the Germans was a crime, but I hadn't realized what the punishment would look like. I thought about my own friendly associations with von Braun. I thought about my father's professional and social associations. I thought about my mother flirting with the German officers.

"'Lise,' I said. 'I want to go home.'

"Lise looked at me with sudden concern. She glanced back at the woman and then down to me again. I knew she understood me. She always did. We immediately left the square.

"We arrived at my house just in time. Just in time, that is, to see my father being hustled out the front door. He was hatless, his hair ruffled. His tie was askew. His ink-blackened hands bound behind his back. He had two men with the resistance armbands on either side of him, holding his arms. A third followed behind with a handgun pointed at my father's back. More waited in the streets, rifles ready.

"Lise was behind me and she put her hands on my shoulders as if to stop me from going forward to join my father. She needn't have feared. That was the last thing I wanted to do.

"I watched the resistance men pushing my father up into the open bed of a small truck. With his hands tied behind him he had trouble climbing. He looked ridiculous as his legs flayed in the air. One man had to climb up ahead of him and drag him the rest of the way. My father's face was bright red with exertion and humiliation. I, too, was blushing with embarrassment.

"My mother appeared at our front door just then, looking flushed and disheveled as if she'd struggled out of someone's grasp. Several people in the crowd yelled insults at her and someone even spat in her direction. She gave them a confused, unfocussed glance and started towards my father. However, before she could take many steps a couple of men blocked her way. She tried to get past them, but they grabbed her arms and held her fast.

"To my shame I didn't try to help her. I simply watched, stunned and uncertain. I felt Lise's hands tighten on my shoulders as my mother strained against her captors and shouted to my father.

"'Carl! Carl!'

"My father, who was now seated on a bench in the back of the truck, turned when he heard his wife's voice. Anger flashed in his face when he saw what was happening to her, but she wasn't concerned with herself.

"'Mathias!' she called. 'Where is Mathias?'

"My father stood up, momentarily breaking free from the hands that held him. His eyes swept the crowd.

"'Mathias!' he shouted. 'Mathias!'

"Then he spotted me.

"'Mathias!'

"My mother tried to see past her captors to where I was standing and other heads were turning my way. The image of the girl with the torn dress erupted into my mind. I knew these people would consider me as guilty as she was, as guilty as my father. I didn't want what happened to the girl happen to me. I didn't want to be bound and humiliated like my father.

"I panicked. I broke out of Lise's grasp and ran, pushing my way through the crowd. In my headlong rush I careened off a small woman, knocking her over. She cried out in surprise and pain and several other people shouted at me in anger, reaching to catch me. I dodged around and broke free into the empty street behind them. I ran. I didn't stop or turn, even when I heard Lise calling my name over and over."

Sixteen

Finne sat huddled in his chair, his eyes locked on the image from his past. He looked exhausted.

I was tired, too. I left without saying anything to him. I ordered the guard to take the prisoner back to his cell. I went home, dug a bottle of vodka out of a cupboard, found a glass, and placed them both on the kitchen table in front of me. I imagined filling the glass and pouring it down my throat. I imagined the burning sensation and how tears would spring to my eyes. I longed for the initial harshness—the harshness that is quickly followed by a relieving numbness. I wanted both.

I turned the bottle in my hand, studying the cheap label. I had put the bottle in the cupboard months and months ago and this was the first time I'd taken it back out. I had put it there the day my wife left me. She'd been waiting for me to get home from work. She stood in the hall with two packed suitcases on the floor beside her and I had no need to ask what she was doing. I knew she was leaving me. That much I understood. I did not understand why.

"Why?" she echoed after I asked the question. "Why? There's why. You only have to look in your pocket."

She pointed at my right hand, which was protectively cradling a bottle in my large coat pocket. I pulled the bottle out and stupidly looked at the label, as if her reasons were printed on the cheap paper. It took me a second to realize she meant her reasons were inside the bottle.

"That's why I'm leaving you, Misha, because you care more for that bottle than you do for me. I'll bet you were thinking about it all day, thinking about buying it and drinking it."

I lifted my eyes away from the bottle and looked at my wife. I felt resentment, even anger, at what she was saying, but I could not deny her accusation.

I had, in fact, longed for this bottle the whole day at Petrovka 38. I said nothing at all.

"I used to be proud of you, Misha."

She picked up her bags and moved to the door. I hadn't closed it properly so she wrenched it open with her foot. I could see she was flustered and she looked like she might soon start to cry. But before she went out the door she had one more thing to say.

"You won't be lonely, Misha," she shot at me and nodded towards the bottle in my hand. "You've always got that for company."

After she was gone I sat down at the table with the bottle and a glass. I thought about what she'd said, her words running through my head over and over again. I stared at the bottle and I knew if I opened it that my wife would be right. I wanted a drink so much, but I found I wanted her to be wrong even more. It was not a victory, only a delay. I hid the bottle from myself in the back of the cupboard.

Now I had it out again, sitting on the table in front of me. Why did I again have this urge to open it after so many months? Did I no longer care if my wife was right or wrong about me? I realized with relief that I still did. Her opinion meant as much to me as it had the day she left me. So why did I take the bottle out of the cupboard? Was it only to taste the vodka and feel the numbness it brings?

As I stared at the cheap label on the bottle, I thought back over the days I had listened to Finne tell his story. My mind wandered aimlessly from one event to another, piecing fragments and episodes together randomly. My mind went from von Braun's escape attempt to the King riding through Copenhagen, from the woman with the shaved head to the German castigating Finne's mother. I thought about Finne slapping the turnstile guard to get himself arrested. I thought about him reading that book over and over again.

I remembered my attitude towards Finne when he first became my responsibility. My job was to process his case as quickly and efficiently as possible, to solidly establish the guilt he was professing. As a police officer it was not my business to care what happened to Mathias Finne as a person. I realized now that that had changed. He had opened himself up to me and in doing so he'd gotten inside of me. It was no longer enough for me to simply build a case against him that would satisfy the courts. I needed to convince myself that this man was truly guilty of murder. I laughed ruefully when I considered that after all these years it was no longer enough for me to do my job. I had to do it well, even if no one else cared.

But just when I began to care I could not see the way to go. I felt something was hiding in plain view, but I didn't know how to look for it. It's true that Finne still hadn't told me his whole story, so I didn't have all the facts, but I nonetheless felt I was missing something I already possessed.

My thoughts went back to the case, but I looked at the different points more critically. I tried to fit them together: Lise's fisherman father with a shiny metal cube; the lamp post outside of the Finne home with an injured spy escaping from German soldiers; an embittered drunk historian with a boy hiding a gun under a stone. What was I missing?

I focussed again on the vodka bottle's cheap paper label. It was nearly new, but it looked worn and ready to fall off. It was the same brand the old professor had offered me.

I picked up the bottle and twisted the cap, breaking the seal. I removed the top and tossed it towards the garbage can. I missed and it hit the floor, rolling under a side table, but I didn't care. I would not need it. I smelled the strong scent of vodka emanating from the mouth of the bottle and for a second I paused to enjoy the familiar anticipation. Then I stood up, took two steps to the sink, and poured the vodka down the drain. I watched it bubble away and heard it gurgle through the pipes. In less than a minute it was gone and I threw the bottle into the garbage.

The professor, I thought with distaste. Maybe I should go see him again. There was obviously a lot more he could tell me. He was Aleksander Baklanov's superior officer. Was he the man on the gunboat? Had he been arrested? I went to get his grubby old manuscript. The answer, I thought, was likely in here. I flipped through the pages, letting some of them break free and flutter to the floor, and I found what I was seeking.

We were betrayed. Our plan had gone very well. We had eliminated the Germans on the boat and had secured Wernher von Braun safely and we should have been able to reach Sweden again without trouble. But we were betrayed.

They had me with the others lying face down on the cold, wet deck with my hands tied behind my back, but I could see the Germans pull a small boy out of a lifeboat. Baklanov explained to me afterwards—it may have been days or weeks afterwards before we were able to speak together freely, I no longer remember—that the boy had been a constant source of trouble and was possibly collaborating with the Germans. Obviously, it had been a mistake to exploit his connection with the rocket scientist, but I can clearly state I was blameless in this regard. It had not been my decision to do this. Rather, I believe the circumstances had dictated his use. It was very unfortunate.

We were held in a prison camp on the island of Bornholm for several months. The Germans mainly used this camp to hold Danes, but we were kept separate from them and from each other. I spent most of these days in a small dark cell and I was fed very little, usually just some old potatoes in watery soup and some dry bread. I was treated roughly during questioning in the first few weeks, but afterwards I was mostly left alone. Despite this I felt myself misused and I silently cursed my jailers.

After several months the four of us were taken from our cells and brought to the harbour. I looked at Baklanov and the two others for the first time in weeks and wondered if I appeared as bad as they did. All three were thin and pale, with dark blemishes under their eyes. Their clothing was soiled, but their heads, like mine, were shaved to the scalp; the Germans, it seemed, were very particular about lice. Baklanov, I noticed, was missing one of his front teeth. He smiled when he saw me.

I wondered what he had to be happy about and I was soon to find out. I do not know how he did it. There were four of us locked into separate holds on that boat in Rønne, but only three remained when we reached Kolberg. There was quite a commotion when the Germans found Baklanov was missing. They hit us around, but none of us knew anything of his plans. At least none of us told them anything. I do not believe we could have kept any knowledge to ourselves. It is fine to talk of withstanding torture when no one is threatening you, but when the pain actually begins little else seems important.

I suppose they kept looking for Baklanov, but they eventually sent us on our way in the back of a canvas-covered truck. The journey was uncomfortable, so like a fool I looked forward to reaching our destination. That is how I came to Sachsenhausen—if not happy, then at least relieved.

My relief did not last long. There were days I would have preferred death to spending another hour in that camp. It is easy to enter hell, they say, but impossible to leave. I have not seen the inside of Sachsenhausen for more than thirty years, yet I still wake in the night terrified and sobbing. Only my body has escaped.

Of Sachsenhausen I cannot say much. It is not that I wish to keep my experience a secret, but that the horror of the place is buried so deep inside me it can only emerge as nightmares. Whether I am sleeping or awake, the memory of what I saw in that camp seems like a scene out of a madman's worst raving. Yet I know it was real. I know I lived it. I was there and that is what terrifies me most. I lived inside a madman's raving. Sometimes I wonder if I ever left it.

I am repeating myself, describing generalities because I wish to avoid the details. Sometimes I wondered why the Germans didn't just kill us, but then I realized they must have known that living in such a place as Sachsenhausen was about the worst punishment man could conceive. Prisoners ceased to be human in the eyes of our jailers. Brutality is less brutal when practised against mere animals. Death was simply a tool used to dispose of the sick, the weary, and the troublesome. No moral question applied to the taking of a life. One learned not to show illness, to hide fatigue, and to do as one was told. Even in hell one seeks to survive.

I was in the camp for more than a year when they finally emptied it. We could hear rumblings over the eastern horizon. First I thought it was thunder, but then I hoped it was the sound of friendly artillery. I was right. They evacuated Sachsenhausen to prevent us from being liberated.

There were thousands of us, tens of thousands, funnelled out of that gate onto the westward road. The column stretched out ahead of me and, in time, trailed far behind. What a column! A march of the damned. We were not leaving hell, we were bringing it with us, spreading it over all the surface of the earth.

I did not walk alone. Soon after I began I found myself supporting a thin, starving man; he looked seventy, but may have been no older than seventeen. He could not walk unaided, so I helped him. It seemed a natural thing to do. One moment I was trudging along alone, the next moment I was holding the old man up and we are trudging along together. So, I have done some things in my life I can be proud of.

We did not speak, he and I, so I did not discover his name. We had no need to speak. Our only tasks were to sleep when we could, to eat what we could find, to march, and then to sleep again.

On our second morning together, my friend had the misfortune of falling down within eyesight of a German soldier. I tried to help him up, but the soldier prevented me. When he saw that the old man couldn't stand alone, he shot him. He just pulled a pistol from a holster and calmly put a bullet into the back of the man's head. He disposed of a burden. I felt nothing. I looked at the body on the ground and it meant nothing to me. It was just another corpse, perhaps one of hundreds lying in the ditches along that road.

I did not remain alone for long. The old man was replaced by another. He appeared at my side without design and we limped painfully down the road together. My new companion looked much like my old one did. He looked much like the thousands of others around us, much like myself I imagine: dirty striped pants and shirt, a swollen belly, a withered face, arms shrunken to bones.

As the road wound through towns and villages, past lakes, past farms, past small groups of women and children—some of whom just stared at us, some of whom jeered at us, hurling abuse at us—the pain grew. It grew until it eclipsed all else; eclipsed the incomprehensible children; eclipsed the towns and the lakes; eclipsed even the road.

Then, without my noticing, we were liberated somewhere west and north of the camp. One night as we lay asleep in fields by the road, thousands and thousands of us carpeting the ground, our guards disappeared. Since there was no one to drag us to our feet and push us down the road, we simply stayed where we were, too tired too move, too tired to look for food or water, many of us too tired to do anything but die. Sometime later there were other people among us, carefully walking between us, seeing who was dead, feeding who was still alive.

You may ask why I cared so much for life that I fought to survive the camp and the long trek across Germany. What gave me the strength I needed? It was certainly not the meager scraps of food that came my way. What kept me going through those long dark days was the thought, the memory, of Aleksander Baklanov. Why not say it? The state has silently convicted me of so many offences I am innocent of, I may as well confess to one more crime: I loved him. When I felt a hair's-breadth away from death, when I wanted to sleep and not awake, when I wanted to fall by the roadside and let some soldier shoot me, what kept me alive was the memory of his final broken smile. What kept me going was the thought that he had escaped and was alive somewhere, the fervent wish that he had escaped the suffering I'd known. I clung to the hope that I might see him again.

My feelings for him were, by all the standards of our society, an abomination. I tried to fight them, but I could not. I had come to treasure our meetings in Stockholm in the days when I was trying to recruit him. His beauty, his youth, his strength, his impulsiveness, even the spark of his anger: they all spoke to me, called to something deep within me. At first I thought my affection was like that of a father to a son, but soon I had to admit to myself that it was different. It was deeper and sharper. I was in love with the man.

Of course I said nothing to Aleksander. I did nothing to let him know. If anything, I became rougher with him, crueler, more demanding. I did not have the courage to risk rejection. Besides, I had wider issues to concern myself with; we were fighting a war and I could not let my personal affairs interfere with that.

But now the cold cruelty of the Nazis left me empty. Their evil burned white hot through my soul and left me with my life and my love; nothing else was important. I no longer cared for politics or Mother Russia. I only needed to know that Aleksander was alive and well.

When I regained my strength I took to the road once again. Alone this time, leaving the thousands behind me, I turned northeast back to Kolberg. My destination was Bornholm. Somehow I knew that if Aleksander was alive, if I was to find him, I would have to look for him on that island.

The manuscript ended there, finished, but incomplete. I put it down. I was appalled; I was appalled by the fact that the old drunk professor had spent time in one of the Nazi concentration camps. It explained much: his instability, his rage, his hatred. I had never heard of Sachsenhausen, so I thought maybe it wasn't as bad as the more infamous places like Auschwitz or Treblinka. But how does one measure such things? I never knew any of these camps, so I cannot judge if one hellhole was worse than another.

I did not have time to ponder these thoughts endlessly. I had to eat. I had to sleep. And then I had to return to Petrovka 38 to complete my interrogation of Mathias Finne.

"When I ran from my home the next morning," Finne continued, "my feet, as if unguided, brought me to the pond in the woods. Lise found me there quite quickly. She probably didn't even bother to look anywhere else. She knew me very well.

"She found me crouching by the dead fireplace, with my arms wrapped tight around my legs, my chin resting on my knees. I watched as she approached through the willows, but I didn't move or speak. She kneeled beside me and hugged me. She just held me without saying anything for a long while.

"Then we argued.

"'Mathias,' she said. 'You have to go back to town. You can come to my place.'

"'No,' I said. I didn't look at her.

"Lise sighed. She knew how stubborn I could be sometimes.

"'You have to go back.'

"'No,' I repeated. 'I don't want to.'

"'You can't stay here,' she said. 'What will you do here?'

"'I'm not going back.'

"Lise remained silent for a moment.

"'Why not, Mathias?' Why won't you go back?'

"I abruptly pulled away from her, tipping onto the ground and then pushing myself upright.

"'I don't want to!' I yelled shrilly. 'I don't want to!'

"I didn't want to answer her. I was afraid that if I told her my reason for hiding at the pond she would be able to convince me that I was wrong. But I knew better than her. I knew how guilty I was and I didn't want to be arrested like my father. So I said nothing and I didn't give Lise the chance to persuade me to return to Rønne. But she tried anyway.

"'What about your mother, Mathias? She needs you.'

"I didn't want to think about my mother.

"'I'm not going back!' I yelled at Lise. 'Didn't you hear me? I'm not going back!'

"Lise straightened up, her expression hardening. She did not like to be yelled at. With a rush of fresh guilt I knew I'd gone too far, but I couldn't back down. I repeated myself, but calmly and quietly this time.

"'I'm not going back.'

"I sat down beside the cold fireplace. Lise didn't look at me. She had a small stick in her hand and she was idly scratching lines in the dirt. We didn't speak for what seemed a long, long time. Finally, I broke the silence.

"'I'm afraid, Lise,' I said.

"She stopped scratching the dirt and looked up at me. Her eyes were so full of love and concern that I rushed to her and held onto her desperately, as if she could save me from drowning. She hugged me back, pressing my head onto her shoulder.

"'I know, Mathias,' she said, her voice catching. 'I know.'

"We stayed like that for a while, but eventually Lise got up to see what there was in the campsite. The cooking pots were still there, but no food. She did find some tea and brewed it up. By then night was falling. She arranged the blankets under the lean-to and had me lie down beside her. I soon fell asleep like that, cradled in her arms with my back warm against her and her breath softly ruffling my hair.

"I woke up early the next morning, roused by the hunger in my belly. Lise must have already been awake because when I opened my eyes she immediately wished me a good morning. We got up and Lise started talking about having to go back to town. She said she would bring food and other things back. She lingered, and I think she was giving me the chance to change my mind about staying, but I wasn't going to. She didn't raise the topic directly and neither did I.

"So Lise went alone and promised to return. I simply sat in the campsite, looking out over the water. Soon my hunger grew painful. I hadn't eaten since the previous afternoon, but all I could do, if I didn't want to go into Rønne, was to wait for Lise to come back.

"When she appeared a couple of hours later she straightened out a blanket and laid out a loaf of rye bread, pots of butter and jam, hunks of salami and cheese, a bag of tea, and a bottle of milk. She lit the fire and set a kettle on to boil. I ate what I could while she sat and watched me, a slight smile on her face.

"'They are still celebrating,' she said. 'But nobody's really sure what's happening.'

Lise tried to explain to the boy what she'd seen in the town that day. Members of the Danish police were patrolling the streets of Rønne. They were fully armed, uniformed (in that they all wore the resistance armbands), and they assumed full powers of arrest. The official police force was still in existence, but since the Danish government hadn't been reinstated and no one any longer acknowledged the authority of the German occupiers, their position was ambiguous. The police didn't know to whom they should report or from whom they should take their orders, so they took no official role in the new situation.

The German military, however, were still going through the motions of occupying the island. German soldiers still controlled the ports, the train stations, and all the other important facilities on Bornholm and they were also still patrolling the streets. They weren't, however, doing anything about all the Danes who were now carrying rifles. When they met the Danish patrols nothing happened. The two groups of men would simply pass by each other.

"I never thought I'd see anything like that," Lise had said.

There was lots of speculation about just what the Germans were doing. People were saying they were like a dead chicken still running around uselessly after its head had been cut off. Adolf Hitler was dead. The fighting was over. The Nazis had lost the war. In the rest of Denmark the German troops had laid down their arms and British Field Marshal Montgomery was on his way to Copenhagen, but here the Germans were still goose-stepping their way through the streets as if nothing had changed.

People were wondering what it would take for the Germans to give up and get off the island. Most thought the appearance of the British Army was necessary, or, some hoped, the Danish Brigade. Lise said everyone was trying to listen to their radios as much as possible to hear what plans the new provisional government in Copenhagen had for Bornholm, but nobody was able to learn anything.

Meanwhile, there were more and more German refugees flooding onto the island from the east. Soldiers and civilians choked the roadways in their slow scramble to get away from the advancing Russians. Food, already scarce, was becoming almost impossible to find in some towns and villages. People were afraid the refugees might begin looting to survive.

Lise had left Mathias with some books she'd brought along, an extra blanket, some clean clothing, and all the food that hadn't already been eaten.

She came back to the pond the next day with more food and more clothing. While she was preparing a simple meal for herself and the boy, she glanced at Mathias and then spoke, trying to keep her voice light.

"I tried to find your mother, but she wasn't at home."

Mathias didn't say anything.

"I wanted to tell her you were safe."

The boy nodded.

"Did those men take her?" he asked.

"I don't know, Mathias. I tried to find out, but I couldn't."

The boy just stared out over the pond. Lise spoke again.

"My father is coming home tomorrow," she said, her excitement lighting up her face.

"Where has he been?" Mathias asked.

Lise's father was the captain of a large fishing boat. But he was more than that. In private, Lise would sometimes proudly call him a ferry captain, since he did more than fish when he was on the water. Lise was not familiar with all the details, but she knew her father was involved with smuggling between Denmark and neutral Sweden. Sometimes he carried weapons to the resistance in Denmark. Sometimes he carried people back to Sweden.

The fishing, by itself, was dangerous in wartime, but the illegal ferrying of goods and passengers was nearly suicidal. The German's allowed the fishing to take place because people had to eat, but they stopped any smuggling they discovered with brutal swiftness.

Nevertheless, Lise's father, a man I rarely saw, managed to survive five years of occupation. In the last days of the war, however, he went missing after setting out to sea.

"We heard from him last night," Lise said. "He sent us a message. He was in Copenhagen. He helped bring the Danish Brigade home from Sweden. He's a hero, Mathias! Just think, my own father brought liberators home to Denmark. My father is a hero!"

Mathias smiled in response to his friend's enthusiasm. It was the first time the boy had smiled since he'd run away from Rønne. She went on.

"He's coming home tomorrow and he's going to bring chocolate! He said that in his message: chocolate for the children," Lise laughed. "I suppose just this once I can be one of the children again. It's been so long."

Lise paused, but Mathias remained silent. She sighed.

"Oh, Mathias! Please come home with me! Tomorrow we're going to have a celebration for my father. A big lunch! Please come!"

Finne had one hand on the table in front of him and he was lightly scratching the smooth surface. He was silent for a moment, watching his fingers and listening to his nails scrape the wood.

"I wanted to go," he said. "I really did. She was looking at me so imploringly, her sweet eyes so full of concern for me. I wasn't often able to go against her wishes, but this time my fear was stronger. I was no longer quite sure what I was afraid of; I just couldn't go into town. Not yet. When Lise was with me I had all I wanted at the campsite. When she wasn't there I was content to wait for her. Something about the woods and the water soothed me. When I was there I didn't have to think about my mother or my father. I could just immerse myself in the sun, the water, and the wind. I was afraid to leave that.

"Even though I said nothing, Lise saw my resolve to stay. Maybe she saw the tears that were welling up in my eyes. Maybe she sensed my fear. She sighed again.

"'It's all right, Mathias,' she said sadly. 'It's all right. I'll save you some of the lunch and bring it to you.'

"She pulled me to her and hugged me, rocking me slightly. I wrapped my arms around her and rested my head against her shoulder. I closed my eyes and surrendered to her warmth and love. I wanted to stay like that forever.

"But of course I couldn't. She gently disengaged my arms and laid me down in the blankets under the lean-to. She asked me once more if I would be all right where I was. I nodded and she smiled. She said she'd try to come back in the morning for a little while before lunch, but added she probably wouldn't be able to return until after the meal was over.

"Then she hugged me and kissed my cheek. She made her way out of the campsite and I watched her until she disappeared through the thick bushes. I have an image of her. A light sweater, baby blue in colour, covering a cotton dress. The flash of a bare calf in the evening light and, most of all, her thick blonde hair falling over her shoulders, tied back, but escaping wildly from the clasp. Lise turned to glance back at me and then she was gone."

Finne paused.

"That was the last time I saw her alive," he said.

Seventeen

ALL I HAVE left of my life back then is the cube von Braun gave me. It's a miracle I have even that much. I lost von Braun. I lost my father—a large part of him. I almost lost my mother. And finally I lost Lise.

At first all I knew was that she was dead. That became very clear when they pulled me away from the ruins of her house and brought me to the survivors. It wasn't a favour they were doing me. They were treating me like one of the casualties.

They brought me to the hospital, which had escaped damage from the bombardment. Lise's younger sister was there. She didn't look hurt and she was sleeping soundly. For a moment I saw the same horribly injured man I'd seen pulled from the house. I still couldn't tell who it was, but later I learned he was Lise's older brother. I also learned her father lived for one day longer. Lise's mother died when the bomb fell. When Lise's sister woke up she told me what had happened.

The morning had gone much as Lise had hoped. Her father's fishing boat came into the harbour at about ten o'clock. Lise's brother went down to meet him while she stayed home to help her mother prepare the meal. The white cloth on the long table bore an orderly clutter of plates, knives and forks, cups and glasses, pots of mustard and relish, candles and flowers. There was bread and cold, sliced meat and salami. Fresh smoked herring and ripe cheese. Apples and walnuts. Bottles of beer and snaps cooled in the basement. In that time of hardship Lise's mother had laid out a feast.

Lise's father entered the house with a glad shout. It seems the male members of the family had stopped at the bodega for a drink on the way from the harbour. They'd greeted their neighbours with glasses of ale and were in cheery good humour. The captain presented flowers to his wife and hugs and kisses to them all.

There was no delay in sitting down at the table. Beer bottles were opened and fiery, frosty snaps was poured into small glasses. Toasts were drunk to everyone's health. Bread was buttered. Meat and herring fish forked and devoured. More toasts. Laughter. Smiles. Love all around. A happy family at a happy time.

When the meal was almost finished, or, rather, when the eaters needed to take a break and were sipping cups of tea and ersatz coffee before digging into more of the food, the captain's son noticed an oversight. No one had drawn the Danish flag up the pole in the backyard. The flag, a white cross on a red background, was a beloved national symbol that had been denied them throughout the war. But there was nothing to stop them from flying it now.

Lise's mother remembered where she'd stowed the flag away all those years before and she went to bring it out. She wanted to iron it first, but her son dissuaded her, saying the wind would smooth out all the wrinkles. Lise and her father stood looking out the rear window as her brother attached the flag to the rope on the pole and tested the squeaky pulley. He began to run it up into the warm, sunny spring air. Lise's young sister asked permission to leave the table and go outside to play with her friends. Her mother granted it and she ran merrily out the front door and down the street. So, she lived.

The time was twenty-five minutes to one o'clock.

A Russian airplane dropped a bomb straight into Lise's backyard, as if the pilot had been aiming for the flag. It was, of course, pure chance—deadly chance. The bomb left a huge hole where the yard had been and shattered the house into splinters and rubble. The bomb gave no warning. It was a miracle anyone at all survived in that house.

But Lise was dead. If they had her body it was probably somewhere there in the hospital. That stark idea went through my head over and over in those hours following her death. I thought about it incessantly, but without emotion. The horror of it seemed to be hiding away from me, waiting to catch me unawares.

There was horror aplenty elsewhere. The hospital filled with scores of wounded German soldiers and sailors. The Russians had hit the docks with half their payload. Whole areas of the harbour lay ruined and burning.

I never gave the nurses my name. I was still afraid someone would arrest me and lock me up with my father. If anything, that worry became stronger.

Since they didn't know who I was, the nurses didn't know what to do with me. They must have thought I was in shock. However, they were too busy to worry about it, so they just kept me overnight. They were still busy in the morning, so I left the hospital alone. It's possible no one even noticed I was gone.

As I walked away from the grounds and down to the waterfront. I had nowhere else to go; nothing to do. My father was locked up somewhere and for all I knew my mother was, too. At first I didn't even think of looking for them.

One ship, a steel-hulled ferry, lay on her side like a dead whale, a hole the size of a car ripped out of her stern. The names "Bornholm" and "Nexø" just cleared the waterline. A soldier stood on the hull inspecting the damage, peering down into the hole for survivors. Several more soldiers waited on the dock smoking cigarettes.

Further on, a seven-story yellow brick warehouse—it was built right on top of a long wharf under the Rønne church—had been badly hit and it was still smouldering. Half the roof was gone and a third of the walls were crumpled and stained black. German soldiers were picking their way through the tumbled bricks. Searching for bodies, I thought.

Refugees, mostly military, but some civilian, were gathering for the boats that would take them westwards. Beforehand, they'd been a fatigued, but bustling crowd. Now they were quiet, as if they were trying not to attract any more attention. I glanced from side to side when I dared, but no one—not the tired, beaten soldier; not the frightened old woman; not the stunned child—looked back at me. I could stay with them, I thought, and never speak and no one would ever know I wasn't German. With Lise dead, I no longer felt the island was my home. The refugees would eventually be taken away, I thought, and I could go with them. I hurried on before the temptation grew too strong.

The town was in shock. Rubble blocked streets. Few cars were let through to find their way past the ruins. Pedestrians were starting to make their way towards many of the bombed buildings. The doubled patrols kept doing rounds of the town, but they were tight and watchful where before the Danes had been glad and the Germans merely wary.

I returned to Lise's house, or to what was left of it. I stood back from it and hoped none of the men or women who had gathered would see me and recognize me. Neat stacks of bricks had appeared alongside the warehouse walls. Piles of splintered lumber grew nearby. The cobbles were littered with broken shards of roofing tiles. These the workmen and soldiers ignored and their boots gradually ground them into dust.

I didn't know what I was doing there. It's true I had nowhere else to go, but that's not why I set up a vigil over the place where Lise died. Maybe I thought I'd be closer to her there. If so, my hope was in vain. I felt empty, abandoned.

The shattered mess I'd first seen was fading quickly away. A man started to shovel a path through the broken tiles, making room enough for a truck to back in. The driver, and others, heaved the timber and boards into the back so the street could be used for traffic. Later, while men still picked their way through the remaining rubble, a woman and a child came to lay flowers at the edge of the destruction. I didn't know either, but they made me wish I'd brought some flowers along, too.

And then, without surprise, as if I'd been waiting for him without knowing it myself, I saw Aleks. He, too, seemed to be standing vigil. I saw him at a far corner of the back gardens. He hadn't seen me. He wasn't even looking my way. He was staring fixedly at the ruins, his face showing confusion, maybe even indecision. It occurred to me he might not know whether Lise was dead or alive.

I stayed out of his sight, but I kept him in mine. The workmen were no longer interesting to me. The house itself had lost its importance. It was now merely a broken shell with all the life gone. My eyes were pinned to Aleks.

I hated him at that moment. I blamed him for Lise's death. It made sense to me at the time: he was Russian and it was the Russians who killed her. This was the second time he'd taken Lise away from me: first he'd stolen her love and now her life. All the grief I'd been bottling up came pouring out as rage. It burned as I watched Aleks standing by the back wall.

But there was more. I hated Aleks because he'd become the symbol of my own guilt. Only if he was gone could I forget the stupid things I'd done.

He stood in the corner, out of the sunlight, for another half-hour. I couldn't figure out what he was doing there. Surely he wasn't hoping someone would be found under the rubble? He didn't speak to anyone.

Finally he left by climbing over the low wall at his back and cutting through the yard to a parallel street. I took the long way around, running past the ruins and dodging around the nearest corner. I didn't catch up with him. I ran until I glimpsed his blonde head walking under a torn awning and I kept my distance. Aleks did a tour of Rønne, inspecting the damage. He led me back down to the harbour, pausing to gaze at the town's church before look-ing out over the parapet to count the sunken boats and note the milling crowds of German soldiers. For a moment he studied the road out to Galloken Moor, as if pondering whether he should visit the main German camp, but instead he turned away and followed the streets to the center of town.

He went from wrecked house to wrecked house, reading the surviving street signs. He avoided the German patrols, but occasionally spoke with Danish civilians. He made no attempt to hide himself, but neither did he go out of his way to attract attention. I saw he was making an inventory of the destruction. I imagined he was gloating over what his countrymen had achieved.

It was when we were in the square in front of the post office that I heard the sound of airplanes again. There was a roar of high, fast engines approach-ing from the south. Everyone immediately took cover. Soldiers and civilians dived away from the open spaces to the shelter of doorways and trees. Some, who must have considered themselves lucky, were close to the entrance of a German air raid shelter. The heavy steel door shut the bunker tight and eyes peered out the deep gun slits.

A strange woman grabbed my arm and pulled me into her house. I didn't see the point. I didn't think I'd be safe anywhere. It seems Aleks had the same thought. He remained standing out in the center of the square, looking up into the sky. I suddenly envied him, but I fought the feeling. I saw his lack of care as courage, but I tried to dismiss the idea. I didn't want to admire him. I want-ed to nurse my hatred. I didn't want to like him, I wanted to kill him.

Within seconds the planes were overhead—the same silver streaks that had bombed the town the day before. I held my breath and so did the woman behind me. I imagine no one in that square breathed the moment those machines were above us.

There was a burst of yellow and the sky was full of paper. Big flat snowflakes fluttered down onto the streets and buildings. The woman let go of me and I left her without a word of thanks. I never even looked to see her face. All around the square people were emerging from their hiding places, looking out into the light with bemused and relieved smiles on their faces. The papers had fallen so thickly that everyone had dozens within reach. I picked one out of the air as it wafted down towards me and I gazed with incomprehension at the Russian letters. Only one man in the square could read them, I thought. I looked to find Aleks standing by the central flower garden clutching one of the pages with both hands. He read the words, looked at his watch, stuffed the paper into his jacket, and turned to walk north past a line of bookshops.

I hesitated, then followed. Before we had gone too far I suspected Aleks was heading for the pond and by the time he reached the tracks I was certain. I crept quietly behind him and came close enough to see him examining what I'd left in the campsite. I thought he must have landed on the island that same day, otherwise he would have visited the pond already. He ate from the bread Lise had left me and took a swig from my bottle of water. Then he rummaged through the blankets crumpled under the lean-to. He found a sweater, one of Lise's sweaters, and he lifted it to his face and breathed in deep. I could imagine the scent that greeted him because I knew it well.

I drew away and then aimed west towards a point in the Vestermarie plantation. I went on foot since my bicycle was hidden too close to the campsite. I jogged towards the setting sun, hoping to get to the Viking grave before it got dark. Twilight descended before I reached the pine woods. I padded down the dirt lanes, trying not to think of the gloom gathering between the tall, straight trunks. I told myself I had nothing to fear from the old Norse ghosts, but the apprehension remained.

The woods around the burial ship were silent as I made my way through the trees and up onto the gravestones. I rolled the loose rock away from the mast hole and dug out the green canvas bag. It still contained the Luger in the holster. I knew it would be there, but I was still relieved when I saw it. I stuffed the holster under my belt and clutched it to my stomach. I turned to go back to the pond, pausing momentarily in the darkness and listening to the silence, hoping, maybe, to receive a sign. Nothing happened. I was on my own. I went back to find Aleks.

When I came close I pulled the gun out of its holster and tossed the leather case away. I didn't care any longer what noise I was making. The heavy Luger in my hands seemed to remove the need for caution. I stepped through the willows to the campsite with the gun dangling in front of me and the branches rustling behind me. Even so, I took the young Russian by surprise. He'd lit a fire in the stone hearth and he sat staring at it, a cigarette between his fingers. He was so deeply absorbed in his own thoughts he'd let the ash grow more than an inch long.

He finally reacted to the sounds I was making, looking up to peer into the darkness outside the small circle of dim light.

"Lise?" he said, half rising.

Lise? How could he think I was Lise? I moved slowly out of the shadows, raising the pistol as I went. When he saw me clearly the hopeful look vanished from his face.

"Oh, for God's sake," he said. "It would have to be you. What do you want?"

"You killed Lise," I said, aiming the barrel towards him. I tried not to think about how the words sounded nonsensical, even to me.

Aleks wilted when he heard them and I began to doubt even more. He seemed to grow heavier, as if the earth pulled at him harder. He ignored my accusation and he ignored the gun.

"So she is dead," he said. "How did she die?"

It was not going how I wanted. I'd thought the gun would give me unanswerable power, but it wasn't doing anything at all.

"You killed her," I repeated, my voice rising in frustration. "She was at home. You killed her with your bombs."

I could feel my control slipping. I was worried I might start shrieking at him.

"I did not kill her," Aleks said, finally responding. "How could I have killed her? I was not in those airplanes."

My mind rejected the simple logic. I groped for an answer.

"They were Russians! Like you!"

He didn't even bother to respond to that.

"They were your people! Your bombs!"

Still he ignored me.

"You could have stopped it!" I shouted.

That got his attention.

"Stop it?" Aleks laughed bitterly. "You fool. How could I have stopped it?"

Tears began to well into my eyes, blurring my sight. I heard a keening whine emerge from my own throat. I wrestled with the noise and changed it to form words: "No! No! No! No!" I blindly pointed the gun and squeezed the trigger. He grabbed my hands and aimed the gun upward to the sky. The gun went off. The loud bang shocked my ears and the heavy recoil wrenched my arm. I dropped the pistol and fought against Aleks's clutches. My mind raged as I hit and kicked at the Russian. I screamed wordlessly.

"Enough!" Aleks shouted as he tried to pin my flailing fists. "Enough!" he yelled again as he threw me to the ground and held me there. "Enough," he said quietly as I calmed down and started to cry softly.

He let go of me, leaned back and picked up my fallen gun.

"You young fool," he said, opening the clip to check—as I hadn't known how—if any more bullets waited inside. "You stupid child." The clip slipped into Aleks's palm and he thrust it into a pocket.

He weighed the gun in his hand, looking at me with hard eyes.

"I'll bet you don't even know how to use this thing," he said. "Well, let me give you a little lesson. This is what they taught me to do."

He pointed the gun at my head and I involuntarily gasped. I tried to crawl away from him. I tried to convince myself there was no danger. The gun was empty—I had seen him unload it, hadn't I?—but I could not quash the fear he was about to kill me.

"You shoot once to hit and maybe to kill," Aleks said and he pulled the trigger.

The pistol clicked loudly and my body jerked with fright.

"Then you shoot again to make sure he is dead," the Russian said, pulling the trigger a second time.

The empty pistol clicked loudly again, and again my body jerked fearfully in response. I started to cry silently, but my tear-filled eyes didn't leave the gun.

"You want to make sure he is dead so he doesn't come after you," Aleks said. "Once is to stop him. Twice is for all time."

As those familiar words echoed through my head I gradually gained control over my trembling. Aleks snapped the bullet clip back into the pistol and put the gun behind him. He set a kettle full of water onto the fire. It took a while for it to boil, but eventually he placed a cup of tea beside me and sipped on one of his own.

"Now you know what it is like when you point a gun at me," Aleks finally said, speaking gently. "Now stop crying and drink your tea."

I sat up and picked up the drink, cradling the hot cup in my lap.

"You are living here, aren't you?" the Russian asked me unexpectedly.

I looked at him with surprise.

"How did you know?" I asked.

He dug another sweater, one of mine, from out of the blankets and held it up.

"This is too small to fit anyone but you," he said. He threw the garment at me. "What are you doing here? Why aren't you at your home?"

He couldn't know the enormity of the question, the crushing weight of the story he wanted.

"My parents are gone," I said.

Aleks paused briefly in the act of bringing his cup to his lips. He sipped quickly.

"In the raid?" he asked.

"No," I said.

He looked at me more carefully, my silence attracting his attention. His eyes searched my face.

"What happened to them?"

"My father was arrested."

"Arrested," Aleks said in wonder. "Who arrested him?"

I didn't know what to say. If it had been the Germans I could easily have said so. But it wasn't the Germans. It was our neighbours. It was the people in the bakery shops and the fish stalls. They arrested him. How could I explain that without revealing how I was tainted?

"By the freedom fighters," I finally said.

"The partisans? Ahhh...this explains much. It was your father, then, who betrayed us to the Nazis? I always knew you were a dangerous child. You should pick your parents better."

He stopped short, as if suddenly aware that he might have gone too far. He peered at me to gauge my reaction. I just stared back at him. Aleks shook his head. He reached into his jacket and drew out the sheet of yellow paper. As he unfolded it he spoke to me.

"Do you know what this says?"

I shook my head.

"It's an ultimatum. Do you know what that means? It means if the Germans don't surrender the Red Army will drop more bombs."

"When?" I asked.

"Tomorrow at noon."

My mind raced.

"Tomorrow? But people should know. We should tell them."

"They'll know," Aleks said, fanning the yellow paper at me. "They threw out thousands of these. I can't be the only one on this island who reads Russian."

I took the page from Aleks. He gave it willingly. It was cheap printing on cheap paper, just like the one I kept. I gave it back to him and took the food he was offering. I looked closely at this man. My wish to hurt him was gone. My need to hate him was fading away. Lise was dead, so Aleks couldn't steal her from me any more. Besides, he could have hurt me or killed me, but he did neither. He treated me with kindness. After all I'd done to him he treated me with kindness.

This was the first time I'd seen him in almost two years. He had changed. He was thinner, almost gaunt. His hair was dirty and poorly cut. He had new wrinkles on his face. He was missing a tooth at the front of his mouth.

I watched him as he ate. He glanced up now and then to meet my stare, but he didn't let it disturb his meal. When he was finished he got up to leave.

"You'll stay here," he said to me.

"No," I answered. "I want to come with you."

That stopped him.

"You can't," he said. "You don't even know where I'm going."

"Yes, I do. You're going into Rønne. Where else would you be going?"

"All right, so I'm going to Rønne. But you can't come with me. You must stay here."

His accent gave him the tone of a prissy schoolmaster when he was trying to be cross. He'd learned his Danish in higher circles than mine and his voice reflected it.

"I'm not going to stay here," I said. "And you can't make me stay."

Aleks glared at me as he considered this. Obviously he saw I was right and short of knocking me out or tying me up he had no way of keeping me there against my will.

"Okay," he finally said. "But you will do what I tell you. You won't get in my way."

"I won't get in your way," I promised.

He didn't look convinced, but we left together nonetheless. Aleks took the gun.

The town was awake despite the late hour. Every kind of wagon and hand-cart available was in the streets, parked in front of open doorways. People were coming out of their homes with blankets and bundles of clothes. Others were already on their way out of Rønne, carrying what they could on their backs and in their arms.

More papers, white ones this time, were littering the pavement and plastered to walls:

EVACUATION IS ORDERED
Every inhabitant shall leave the
municipality as soon as possible,
and at the latest by 9:00 a.m.

The order went on to detail the evacuation routes, giving a list of belongings people could take, and who was required to stay in town. That last list included electricians, doctors and nurses, and postmen. I wondered why the mail had to be delivered while the town was being bombed.

Clearly, Aleks had been correct and someone else had been able to read the Russian message. No one was taking the chance that the German commander would surrender to the Soviets before the deadline. No one had that kind of faith in Captain Reinhardt.

Aleks hardly paid any attention to what was going on. He passed quickly through the growing crowds with me in his wake. He didn't tell me where we were going, but I soon guessed we were heading toward the Nazi headquarters. We came to the street through an alleyway and were well hidden when we peered around the corner.

Two uniformed guards stood at either side of the main door, their stances perfectly aligned with the building.

"We'll never get in that way," I whispered.

"I never intended to go in that way," Aleks said, stressing the "I". "I just wanted to have a look first."

Other than the two German soldiers the street was empty and quiet. No lights glowed in any of the windows; only the waxing moon illuminated the scene. The Germans were apparently not going to join in the evacuation.

We cut back into the alley and then turned left through an unlocked garden gate. This brought us into the yard that joined corners with the headquarters' grounds. We made our way over the lawn and around flowerbeds to where the walls met. Aleks scrambled up and then paused to look down at me. I was too short to reach the top without help.

"Good," Aleks whispered down. "You stay there."

Then he slipped down the other side and I lost sight of him. I searched frantically around, peering into the darkness, groping with my hands. I found a board and propped it at an angle against the bricks in the corner. By standing on that I was able to reach the top of the wall and pull myself up. But when I looked into the neighbouring yard I couldn't see Aleks anywhere.

I climbed the rest of the way up and over. I dangled above the unseen ground for one second before I let go with the hope I'd land easily and noiselessly. The ground was closer than I thought, so the air rushed out of me in surprise, but I made no other sound. When I crept to the wall of the headquarter building I saw a row of basement windows close to the base. I tried them first and found the second one was open.

It was the coal chute and the cellar room had recently been filled. Unlike the other yards, this one had access to the street and was paved to support wagons. The coal must have been carried to this courtyard instead of being dumped onto the sidewalk out front. Workers had unloaded the cart and shovelled the coal through the ground-level opening. Either someone had forgotten to secure the window, or Aleks had found some way to open it.

The window swung upwards and outwards and it squeaked as I lifted it and crawled in headfirst. I was on hands and knees on the pile of coal chunks that sloped quickly away from the opening. I just had time to wonder why someone would order winter fuel at such a time when I started to slip. The window banged shut behind me and I clattered down the coal pile to the floor.

"God damn it!" Aleks cursed as he grabbed me and held me tight. We froze like that for what seemed like minutes, listening intently for any sound. I heard nothing. Neither did Aleks, but he held me—and his breath—for longer than I thought necessary.

"What the hell do you think you're doing?" he finally demanded in a harsh whisper. "Why must you always foul things up?"

"Nobody heard," I said and left it at that, hoping I was right.

We had several doors to get through, the first in pitch-blackness. It was flimsy, made of slats, and it let us into a chilly, damp passage. We groped along until we came to a set of rough wooden stairs leading upwards. On top, a heavy panelled door swung silently and opened onto an empty, softly lit hall. Once he saw the way was clear, Aleks pulled the pistol out of his belt, but he hesitated, looking from one door to another, unsure of which to choose. I could not help feeling a bit smug when I guessed what he was looking for and pointed at the third door down on the right.

"That's the one," I whispered. "That's Reinhardt's office."

Aleks looked at me with great surprise.

"How do you know that?" he whispered back.

"I've been here before," I answered, but I did not have time to tell him about that supper with the German commander so many years ago.

Aleks walked quietly to the door I had indicated. He paused, as if to let me catch up, and then he opened it and stepped in. I followed as close as I could and was inside when he shut the door again.

We were in a large office. Tall bookshelves on all sides of us were filled with venerable leather-bound volumes. A huge oak desk stood between us and the window. The age-darkened panels facing us were intricately carved with mythical patterns; two of them held intricately winding branches of trees, but the middle panel was filled with the long-reaching limbs of the gripping beast.

I couldn't take my eyes off the thing. It seemed just like the beast carved on the stone in the old city: an animal with a small body and snakes for arms and legs. At the end of each were hands that gripped the nearest limb and held on tight. The beast's face had eyes, but it seemed blind and stupid, unable to escape from its own trap.

Lise had said the war was like a gripping beast. The Germans were just like us, she said. Just people. But at their centre they have a gripping beast, a malicious little animal that reaches out and grasps whatever is close. It reaches further and further, its touch meeting and altering what it encounters. Soon the land was full of gripping, choking beasts. All of Germany, then Czechoslovakia, Poland, and finally Denmark and Bornholm—we were all in the clutches of the gripping beast.

And here it was on a desk in the bureau of a high German officer, the commander of Bornholm's occupation forces, Captain Werner Reinhardt. I knew it wasn't a coincidence. It was a message, a warning—or maybe just an explanation. I turned to see if Aleks had noticed it, but he wasn't looking that way. He had his eyes on Captain Reinhardt. The man was not seated, but stood leaning over a side table heaped with maps. He was facing away from us and had to turn when he heard Aleks's voice.

"Good day, Captain Reinhardt," Aleks said, using the common Danish greeting.

Reinhardt turned quickly, startled, but he did not lose his composure.

"Who are you?" he demanded. "What are you doing in my office?"

Aleks, keeping the gun in his right hand, approached Reinhardt and pulled the yellow ultimatum out of his jacket with his left. He tossed the paper onto the desk.

"I am a representative of the government of the Union of Soviet Socialist Republics," Aleks said. "I demand you surrender to me in compliance with these orders."

Reinhardt looked amused. For a second I even thought he would laugh. Then, suddenly, his face drained of expression. It showed no fear, no anger, not even curiosity. He turned away from Aleks, picked some papers off a shelf, and held them out towards the Russian.

"I have my own orders covering this situation," he said. "I have read them over carefully on several occasions. They are quite explicit. I must not surrender to Russia, only to England. I cannot comply with your so-called ultimatum."

Aleks allowed the barrel of his gun to dip in his astonishment.

"You're mad!" he said, pausing between each of his sentences. "The war is over. Hitler is dead. Berlin has fallen. Your orders mean nothing any more."

Reinhardt ignored the insult. But he was also ignoring the gun. I couldn't understand how something so deadly could be so apparently useless. It had done nothing for me against Aleks and now it was doing nothing for Aleks against Reinhardt.

"Obviously, you do not comprehend the nature of orders," Reinhardt said. "But then you are a Slav…. Your young friend, perhaps he understands better."

The German commander had replaced his order papers on the shelf and opened the drawer of a filing cabinet. He was running his fingers over a line of labels. He selected a file folder, pulled it out, and slid the drawer shut with a metallic crash.

"I believe I know who you are," Reinhardt said, laying the folder on his desk. He opened it and began to read.

"Aleksander Baklanov. Russian, born 1923. Arrested on Bornholm in August 1943 on charges of espionage, sabotage, and kidnapping. We had to keep the matter quiet because of a breach of the Swedish neutrality, as I recall. Also because of the identity of the kidnap victim.

"You escaped in 1944 during your transfer to the mainland. You left one guard dead and another incapacitated. You had been aided in procuring a sharp weapon of some sort. Several officers were reprimanded following that incident."

Reinhardt then gestured towards me.

"I believe I recognize you as well, young man. Your name is mentioned in these files. You were, in fact, instrumental in this man's arrest. And now you are helping him. How curious. You should choose your companions more carefully. These Slavs bear watching. They are not like us, you know."

Reinhardt delved further into the file.

"Ah, yes, of course. Carl Finne's son. How could I have forgotten that? I have not seen your father in several weeks. He is well, I trust?"

He glanced up with a look of innocent inquiry on his face. I nodded without thinking.

"Is he?" Reinhardt said with feigned surprise. "Then he is one of the fortunate ones. All those lovely young women with shaved heads, such a pity! I had imagined your father would have been locked up by now."

"Enough of this," Aleks interrupted.

I had the distinct impression Reinhardt was enjoying the situation. The gun, the spy, me—it all seemed to feed his sense of humour, but it was a humour so dry it would choke the life out of desert grass.

Aleks waved the gun, as if to remind Reinhardt he still held it, and fairly shouted in frustration.

"Stop this! If you don't surrender to me I shall be forced to shoot you!"

"Yes, you are quite good at killing, aren't you?" Reinhardt asked, as if the two were engaged in a purely academic discussion. "Was it you who planned the ambush on the test boat? That was well done. I understand it took my men completely by surprise."

Aleks saw he simply couldn't control this man, but still he hesitated to use the gun. I looked at him and tried to read what was going on in his mind. Why didn't he use the gun?

"Listen, the war is over," Aleks reasoned. "If you surrender now you'll save lives, innocent lives, the lives of your own men. There doesn't have to be more bombing. You can stop it."

Reinhardt waved his hand in the air as if brushing away an irritating insect.

"That means nothing to me. I have my orders and I will follow them until I fulfil them, or until they are changed by the Naval High Command. I have no choice in the matter."

Reinhardt sighed and looked at his watch.

"Now, if you will please excuse me. I am a busy man. I may have lost much of my authority, but that doesn't mean I must tolerate your presence in my office any longer."

He picked up the telephone and barked an order into it. Within a second we heard shouts and the sound of running feet in the hallway. Aleks stepped around the desk and pushed Reinhardt out of his way. He picked up the heavy oak chair and heaved it at the window. The first blow shattered the glass, but left the frame intact. The second blow smashed the wooden bars to bits. He threw the chair outside and jumped over the sill, calling for me to follow.

I looked at Reinhardt and saw he was simply standing back out of the way, watching events with dispassionate amusement. He wasn't going to stop me. I ran to the window and vaulted out as I heard the door behind me burst open. Aleks was waiting. He caught me before I could hurtle onto the cobbles and we ran back the way we came.

Eighteen

Gunshots exploded behind us as we reached the wall. The bullets winged off the bricks to one side. I froze as tiny shards of stone hit me. The nightmare was back. I suddenly saw the young workman again. I saw him trip and fall as the bullets ripped into him.

"Come on!" Aleks yelled from the top of the wall.

He must have known I was frozen in fear. He reached down and grabbed my collar, dragging me upwards.

"Come on!" he repeated.

By then the soldiers had jumped out the window and were running across the courtyard. Unable to shoot us, they were trying to catch us. I finally got myself to move again and I scrambled the rest of the way over the wall. Both Aleks and I dropped down on the other side and we ran. We darted left down the alley and ran flat out for the main square. Here there were lights, not the bright shining globes of peacetime years, but a careful dim glow of hand-held lamps and torches. There were also people, hundreds of people pushing wagons, straining under their own loads, herding gangs of frightened children, moving, always moving. And with them, directing them and guarding them, were men and women from the resistance. In this crowd Aleks and I were safe. Reinhardt's authority no longer reached this far.

There was nothing else for us to do: we joined a stream of refugees heading north. It was a slow, steady march, but not a long one. Some of those around me seemed unaffected by the evacuation; others appeared fearful; still more fretful, but no one was panicky. There was conversation for the first mile or so. I remember a darkly ironic comment about how we'd become like the people in those photographs we'd seen from the eastern countries: the long lines of exhausted families fleeing from horror and wreckage.

Aleks didn't speak to me or to any of the others. He seemed angry and I hesitated to break into his silence, but finally I had to speak. My curiosity demanded the question.

"Why didn't you kill him?" I asked as we walked.

Aleks didn't turn towards me. He just kept his eyes on the dark road in front of his feet. Still, he answered so quickly it occurred to me that he'd been asking himself the same question.

"What would that have solved?" he shot back.

Then he returned to his silence and I didn't have the courage to break it a second time.

After a couple of hours we finally came to a round white church. Many people just passed by, heading to safer points further on, but Aleks and I stopped and entered. Whatever pews or benches had stood in the center of the floor were all cleared away. Bales of hay and straw had been split open and strewn over the flagstones. Families had hollowed out little nests here and there. Small children—wide-eyed with wonder and fear—peeked at us new-comers. Some adults lay sleeping; others were bringing hot food from a small kitchen at the back of the church. Aleks and I each received a bowl of chicken soup, which we ate ravenously along with the large hunk of rye bread we were given to share. When he finished his portion, Aleks wadded his jacket into a pillow and stretched out in the hay.

"I haven't slept in three or four days," he said and before I could ask him where he'd been and what he'd been doing, he was asleep and snoring.

I went to look for more bread and some water to drink with it. I found both without trouble. The tired old pastor was happy to cut a thick slice and pour a glass for me. He tut-tutted as I answered his questions about what I'd seen in town.

"Never," he said with a kind of bemused disapproval, "never did I think such things would happen here in Denmark."

He stood there shaking his head mournfully at me until I started wondering if he was blaming me for the trouble. But then a couple of younger children appeared at his elbow and he turned to see what they wanted. As he was cutting slices for them I went back to my nest.

I sat cross-legged beside Aleks, nibbled at my bread and listened to his noisy breathing. The church was still filling up, but this didn't disturb him. If the bombs has fallen early I don't believe they would have wakened him. We were soon surrounded by men, women, and children who were trying to create little homes for themselves. I laid myself down and stared up at the dim curved ceiling before my eyes closed and I, too, slipped away into sleep.

When I woke up Aleks was gone. Sunlight was shining through the stained-glass windows and people were bustling around with more bread and pots of hot water. Some were washing with it, some were making tea. I asked my neighbours if they knew the time and if they'd seen my companion leave. It was nine o'clock, they said, and my friend had gone out about an hour earlier. I ate and drank and then made an excuse to leave for a few minutes. I slipped outside, out of the crowd, and headed back towards Rønne.

A few Danish refugees were still coming up the road and although some of them called out to me I managed to avoid them. I didn't know that area of the island very well, so I had to stick close to the main road we'd travelled during the night. As I got closer to the town I kept my eyes open for patrols. I was sure they would stop me; neither the Germans nor the Danes would be letting anyone back into Rønne. I did not worry that the Germans would be looking for me because of what happened the night before. The look I saw in Reinhardt's face made me believe he wouldn't be bothered about someone like me at a time like this. He had more important things to occupy his mind.

Entering the outskirts of Rønne was an eerie experience. I've been through the town at night and felt the stillness, but now there was a different quality to it. Previously, in the darkness the quiet was only a mask, because in every house, behind many of the blacked-out windows, people were asleep. On this day, however, I could feel the emptiness. The slapping of my shoes on the cobbles echoed back at me off the walls. The town was empty, the walls seemed to say, and I had no business being there.

I almost agreed with them. I had to fight an urge to turn and run. I wasn't thinking of the bombs that were coming in a couple of hours; I was feeling the strangeness of the evacuated streets.

I did not know where Aleks was, or where he might be going. I wasn't even sure why I wanted to find him. Maybe after losing everyone else—first my father, then my mother, and finally Lise—I attached myself to the first person who showed me kindness. No matter that I knew he was a murderer—hadn't I seen him kill those men on the German boat? No matter that I had blamed him for Lise's death and had wanted to kill him myself. I felt bound to Aleks and could only think of looking to him for the protection and companionship I needed.

Maybe it was because we had both loved and lost Lise. Now that she was dead, and now that I realized I could not truly blame Aleks for her death, I could no longer see the young Russian as a rival for her affections. We both suffered.

My thoughts were interrupted by the sound of men coming from behind. They had not seen me, so I had time to duck into an alleyway and wedge myself into a shadowed corner. If I learned anything from the war it was how to sit still and hide out of sight.

They were five Danish men in civilian clothes and resistance armbands, rifles slung over their shoulders. They were checking doors, knocking at locked ones and opening the others, calling into the empty houses, trying to make sure that they were in fact empty. They weren't at ease. They spoke little and smoked nervously. One of them kept glancing first at his wristwatch and then at the sky, as if he didn't trust what his watch told him and expected the bombers to appear at any second. That got me thinking. I didn't have a watch, could not see a clock, and didn't know how much time I had. I, too, began peering impulsively up past the roofs above me, as if I'd see the planes before I heard their engines.

The patrol passed and I emerged from my hiding place to continue my own search. I picked my streets randomly, first turning right, then left, then right again. I just kept turning corners, watching out for the Russian.

Twice more I encountered patrols and managed to hide myself. One was a Danish patrol of four men and a woman, who acted much like the first, although with less thoroughness. Perhaps they assumed everyone had gone. At any rate, their inspection of the houses was haphazard and incomplete. I guess time was running short and they were heading for safety.

The other patrol was made up of two German soldiers. They did nothing except walk swiftly down the centre of the deserted street. They didn't speak to each other or look around at all. I felt I could have stood on the sidewalk waving my arms at them and they would have ignored me. Oddly enough, I felt sorry for them. These men had been my enemies for so long, but now they seemed pathetic. I didn't think about how different they'd seemed the night before.

Finally my wanderings brought me to Lise's street. I had had no conscious intention of going there, but once I arrived I saw I should have headed there straight away.

Aleks was there. I suppose his own ghosts had forced him to leave the safety of the church and return to the site of Lise's death. When he'd been there the day before he hadn't really known she was dead. Now he could mourn her and mourn their lost future.

I watched him, finally freeing myself of all the resentment I'd felt towards this man I'd considered my rival for Lise. It occurred to me that while I mourned Lise for what had been, Aleks mourned her for what might have been. I saw that his loss was greater than mine.

He was standing to one side of the wreckage, hugging himself with his head bowed. I couldn't really see his face until I approached closer and some sound I made caused him to look up.

Tears were streaming from his reddened eyes. His cheeks were wet and his handsome features were distorted with grief.

"She's dead, Mathias,' he said, as if he'd just realized what the words meant. "Maybe you're right. Maybe I did kill her. Maybe it is my fault. What did I do to save her?"

I stepped closer and he bowed his head again, a sob escaping from his mouth. I didn't know what to do. I couldn't find anything to say. I felt tears welling up in my own eyes.

"No," I finally said. "No."

Aleks seemed to weaken, as if my denial was a final, unendurable blow. His legs buckled and he fell onto his knees—not sobbing, just staring at the ground in front of him. I wiped away my tears and placed my hand on his shoulder, realizing after I did it that I was copying what Lise had done in the church. Aleks didn't respond to my touch.

"I'm sorry," he said, speaking not so much to me as to the ghosts in the rubble. Or maybe he was speaking to Lise. "I can't stop it. I tried. I really tried, but I can't stop it. He won't listen to me. He won't listen…"

Aleks went silent again. I wondered what he was talking about and then I realized he meant the bombs that would soon be falling on the town.

"You could have shot Reinhardt," I said. "That would have stopped it."

Aleks lifted his head and turned towards me. He'd stopped crying, but still looked infinitely sad. It seemed to take him a minute or two to realize it was I who had spoken. He got back to his feet and looked down at me.

"Stop it?" he echoed. "How could that have stopped it? You don't stop killing with more killing. Has this taught you nothing?"

He waved his hand towards the wrecked house. I still didn't really understand what he was talking about. He must have seen the confusion in my face. He grabbed my shoulders and knelt down, pulling me towards him. He held me there hard, my face only centimetres from his own.

"Listen to me, you young idiot. Lise is dead. Do you know why she is dead?"

I shook my head. I had already asked myself that question over and over again, but I never found an answer.

"She's dead because we don't care about life anymore. It's become cheap, worthless. We don't care about ourselves, so we care even less about others. We kill—I kill! But I won't kill anymore!"

He pushed me away roughly and stood up. I stumbled backwards and fell down. I didn't bother trying to stand.

"But it's the war," I said. It seemed very clear to me. The war was supposed to have been over, but it obviously wasn't. And since it wasn't—well, don't people die in war? Wasn't that what it was all about?

I look back now and I see I was fully in the clutches of the beast. The war had taken me into its heart and made me one of its own. I hadn't yet killed, but I saw nothing strange in killing.

I see, too, that Aleks had somehow slipped free from the grip of the beast. He'd been deep inside the war, but Lise's death had shocked him out of it. If anything, Lise's death had sunk me deeper into the gripping beast.

Aleks was looking at me with pity in his eyes. He was about to say something to me, but I was never to hear it. He was just opening his mouth to speak when we heard a shout from down the street. We both turned and saw a Danish patrol coming our way.

"Come on!" Aleks said.

He grabbed my arm and yanked me to my feet and we ran up the street away from the patrol. It was an instinctive action and I never questioned the need to follow him. The Danes in that patrol probably meant us no harm, but both of us only thought to flee authority.

We ran up the street and into the square, turning the corner towards the post office. At that point I noticed two things at once: I saw the clock on the front of the post office showing eleven-fifteen and I heard the sound of airplanes engines growing rapidly louder. We stopped in our tracks.

"Shit!" Aleks said. "They're early!"

He looked at his wristwatch.

"No, god damn it, they're not! Moscow time! They're on fucking Moscow time! They're late!"

The planes were coming fast. We only had seconds. There was a bunker in the middle of the square, but we didn't have time to get to it. We didn't have time to go anywhere.

The noise made me stupid. I stood gaping at the sky, waiting to catch sight of the planes. They were flying so low over the rooftops that their roar deafened me before one actually flashed into my view. That's all I saw, a bright flash, before Aleks knocked me to the ground. I felt his hand on my back between my shoulder blades, pushing me hard down onto the cobbles under a wall.

That same instant the earth buckled up and punched me in the stomach, knocking the wind out of me. Before I had a chance to gasp my ears burst with a terrifying crash. I screamed in terror, but couldn't hear the sound of my voice. Debris hit my back and legs. Then, as the world began to settle down, the smell of dust and smoke crept into my nose. I lay whimpering and coughing, too dazed and frightened to move. Through the ringing in my ears I could hear more blasting further and further away.

I don't know how long I lay there, crying and coughing. It seemed like hours, but it may only have been minutes. The bomb blast itself probably only took seconds, but it felt like it went on and on and on. Once the blast was over my ears rang and my head buzzed. My body hurt in dozens of places. I didn't want to move. I didn't even want to think.

Eventually my thoughts did return and the first thing I wondered was where Aleks's hand was. I could no longer feel its pressure on my back. Then I began to wonder why he wasn't trying to find out if I was unhurt.

Painfully, I moved my arms and started pushing myself up. I felt bits of dirt and rock sliding off me and heard them clatter onto the ground. I turned myself over, sat back against the wall, and looked out over the square.

The small flower garden that had occupied the middle of it was gone. In its place a large hole gaped wide. All the cobblestones were torn up around it. Trees and bushes were stripped of their leaves. The glass had been smashed out of all the windows within sight.

Aleks lay face down beside me. I couldn't tell if he was dead or alive. He was covered in dirt, his shirt and pants were torn, and I could see blood seeping out of his hair. His body must have taken the force of the explosion, protecting me from worse harm.

I gingerly reached out and touched him. He was still warm. This gave me hope, although even if he was dead it would have been too soon for the corpse to grow cold. I brushed the larger pieces of debris off his back and pushed him over.

He groaned when I did this and I started crying with relief. I didn't know what to do. I thought of going for help—maybe that Danish patrol was still nearby—but I didn't want to leave him. Instead, I gently shook his shoulder and whispered his name.

"Aleks! Aleks!"

Whether he heard me and was responding, or whether he was just waking up on his own, I don't know. His eyelids fluttered, opened wide, and then shut tight again against the bright noon sunlight. He groaned again and brought a hand up to rub his forehead. I just crouched beside him and watched, fearful that anything I did would send him back into unconsciousness.

Finally he opened his eyes again, shading them from the sun, and looked towards me. He didn't make any attempt to move.

"Mathias? Are you all right?"

His voice was weak and hoarse. I nodded. He tried to move his left arm, but immediately winced and drew his breath in with a quick hiss through clenched teeth. His already pale face turned white beneath the grime. He lay without moving until the pain subsided.

"I think my arm's broken," he said.

He cradled his left arm and tried to pull himself upright. A curse burst from his lips and he fell back down. He closed his eyes and panted.

"God!" he said. "I think some ribs, too. Help me up!"

With me supporting his back he managed to sit, but I could see it hurt a lot. He rested a few minutes and looked around the square.

"What a mess!" he said. "We've got to get out of here."

"The hospital," I said. "It's not very far away. Maybe I can get help."

"No!" Aleks interrupted. "Not the hospital! We'll go back to the campsite."

"But you're hurt badly. You need a doctor!"

"The campsite!" he repeated. "I'm not supposed to be here. I must not be found. I'll go by myself if you won't help me."

With that he started struggling to his feet, grunting with the effort. He was still holding his left arm snug against his body, so he had trouble pushing himself off the ground. I stood and held his right arm to pull him up.

It was a long way to the pond, longer than it usually was. My head hurt and my leg hurt; my whole body hurt and every step I took was a new and worse ordeal. Aleks leaned his right elbow on my shoulder and I had one arm around his waist to hold us steady together. As time passed he grew weaker and weaker, leaning heavier and heavier against me. We slowed as the pain grew and I became less aware of what was happening around me. My mind focussed on the need to take one more step and then another step. And then one more. Just one more....

I stopped thinking about why we were doing this; where we were going. Even the passage of time lost its meaning, the minutes and hours melding together into a slow surge of pain.

If we encountered anyone during this horrible march I have no recollection of it. People must have been returning to the town, since the bombardment was over, but if anyone saw us, no one stopped us. I can't explain it.

I don't know how long it actually took us to get to the campsite. I don't even remember arriving. I just know I eventually woke up on the ground. It was daylight, but I didn't know what day it was, or whether it was morning or afternoon.

My head still hurt. My body was stiff and sore. One particularly deep cut on my leg was sending a stabbing pain up my calf. I had a terrible thirst. Aleks lay on his back under the lean-to. He was breathing. I assumed he was asleep.

Instead of rummaging around looking for my water bottle I just stumbled out of the campsite and into the pond. I didn't even bother taking off my clothes, just submerged myself in the cool water. It felt and tasted wonderful and it eased my headache. I gulped down as much as I could stand and lay back in the shallows. For a few minutes I was able to escape from my worries and my nagging pains.

When I emerged, my clothes dripping and my socks squelching inside my boots, Aleks was awake. He hadn't moved. He turned his head to watch me approach.

"You idiot," he said.

I looked down at myself and had to agree. My wet shirt was plastered tight to my sparse frame, revealing all my ribs.

"Can't even keep dry."

His voice was not much louder than a whisper, coming out of his mouth with a low, harsh rasp.

"Did you bring me any of that water?" he asked.

I looked around for the bottle until I found it. It was only a quarter-full and the water must have been warm, but it was cleaner than the pond. I held the mouth of the bottle to Aleks's lips and tipped it carefully so that he could take small sips. He finished it off and wanted more, so I had to fill the bottle from the pond after all. The water was brown, but Aleks didn't care.

He was hurt badly, much worse than I was. I had lots of small cuts where my skin had been exposed and I had some bruises, but only the one cut on my leg was bothering me much. Aleks had a broken arm, broken ribs and he had a deep gash on the side of his head. It had stopped bleeding, but he must have lost a lot of blood. His hair was matted thick and he'd even stained the ground beneath his head. I could only assume there were other things wrong with him that I couldn't see.

I knew he needed a doctor and he must have known it, too, but he wouldn't listen to my pleadings. If he'd had the strength he would have yelled at me to shut up, but as it was all he could do was feebly shake his head and repeat: "no, no, no." I shouldn't have listened to him. I should have just gone and got someone to help. How could he have stopped me? He couldn't even sit up by himself. But I didn't go, not for that, anyway. He didn't want anyone to know where he was and I didn't have the strength to oppose him.

So I did what I could by myself. I boiled water and cleaned his wounds as well as I knew how. The one on his head gave me a moment of panic when it started bleeding again, but I stuffed a clean rag into it and stopped the flow. I bound that rag tight around his head and hoped it would hold. It must have hurt him when I was doing this, but he made no sound. Maybe he passed out again during the worst of it.

I couldn't do anything about the ribs, but I knew I should bind his arm with splints. His arm wasn't too bad; it wasn't crooked or anything. I didn't have to snap the bones back into place. I couldn't have handled that. Aleks was feeling more optimistic about his arm. He said maybe the bone wasn't broken after all. Maybe it was just cracked.

We needed food. The little that had been left at the campsite—some stale bread and dry cheese—was soon gone. Aleks wasn't eating much, but I was hungry. We also needed clean clothing and some cloth to dress Aleks's head wound. Just about everything we had was dirty.

So I had no choice but to go back to Rønne. I put it off as long as I could, but on the second day I headed off down the railway tracks. Without money, I had no idea how I would get anything, especially not the one thing Aleks wanted.

Just before leaving I told him where I was going and asked him what I should get. He looked a little better than when we'd arrived, but not much. His voice was strengthening and he answered quickly.

"Vodka," he said.

I didn't go into town on foot. I went and found my bicycle where I'd hidden it and rode down the dirt lanes to Rønne.

Nineteen

My world had changed again. The Germans were gone. The Russians had arrived. The iron grey was replaced by the drab green.

The war was really over this time. We'd been fooled once, but now we were sure. Did I say "we"? Well, maybe I shouldn't include myself. I had lost my trust in such hopes and I still had too many problems in front of me to think of rejoicing. But the people I saw in Rønne seemed to have no such reservations. For them the war had truly come to an end.

Of course, they'd been in the town to witness events that I knew nothing about. After they'd returned from their short exile to the countryside—each one hoping the bombs hadn't struck close to home, but fearing that nothing remained of their houses and belongings—they'd witnessed the arrival of the first of the Soviet troops. They'd seen with their own eyes that the fighting had stopped.

Those first troops were, by all accounts, a scruffy lot. A hard bunch, used to hard fighting. They landed expecting trouble and were surprised when they found none. The Germans were finally ready to surrender; Captain Reinhardt must have gotten his orders after all.

By the time I rode into Rønne the first troops were gone, or at least I saw none of them around. I was tired, sore and hungry and my leg was hurting more and more. The first sign of change that penetrated into my foggy mind was the sound of accordion music being played in the street.

I slowed my bike as I came upon a small crowd of men, women, and children. They were clustered around the source of the music, which I couldn't yet see, and they were swaying and clapping their hands to the exotic, rambunctious beat. It was certainly like no music I'd heard before. It was wilder than Danish or German music. I got off my bicycle and walked it closer so I could see the musician.

He was a short, stout soldier, old, ancient, even, to my young eyes, although he was probably younger than I am now. He was completely absorbed in the music he was making. His body moved with the rhythm like it was channelling the sound emerging from his instrument. His gaze flashed across his audience, but it was as if he wasn't really looking at them. He didn't see they were there until he ended his piece with a flourish and then he smiled shyly at the listeners. They clapped and laughed in appreciation. He said a few words in the language I'd heard only once before on the German gunboat.

He was Russian, but not a Russian like Aleks. He was not tall or blonde. Nor was he like those who had ambushed von Braun's boat. They were slim and athletic. This one made me think of someone who worked the earth: a farmer or a peasant.

As I rode away from him—he'd started into another tune—I woke up to the changes around me. I saw the Soviet soldiers drive by in trucks and cars. I saw them eyeing the contents of shop windows and heard them attempting to speak with local Danes. They seemed hungry for the meagre goods in our depleted shops and for acceptance and friendship.

And they got it. I noticed the townspeople had welcomed their liberators without reservation. The bombings weren't forgotten, but they were forgiven—war is war, after all, people were saying. They blamed Reinhardt. They didn't blame the Russians. I didn't know what to think. It was too big a question for me to decide just then.

I had, however, decided where to go first. The thought frightened me, but I knew I had no choice. If I wanted clothing and food I had to go home.

The house seemed as I'd left it, but no one was there and the door was locked. I didn't mind. Unable to go through the front door, I simply climbed the lamp standard to get up onto the roof. I had no trouble walking up the shingles or breaking into the window of my bedroom. If anyone saw me or heard me, no one gave the alarm.

I'd been in my room only a few days before. All was as I'd left it, but it seemed to me so much time had passed that there were no real traces of me left behind. But these were just fevered perceptions and I had no difficulty finding a rucksack and some clothing to stuff into it. I discarded the dirty clothes I was wearing and put on a fresh shirt and a clean pair of pants. Then I crossed the landing and went into my parents' bedroom to find something for Aleks to wear. I wasn't picky. I just grabbed one of my father's sweaters and one of his shirts and a pair of his trousers and pushed them into my sack. Then I went back out onto the landing and down the stairs.

In the kitchen I found some rye bread that wasn't too stale. I found some cookies, some tea, a couple of bottles of beer, smoked bacon, a hunk of cheese, tinned fruit, a few wrinkled apples, and a pot of raspberry jam. I ate a slice of bread with jam and one of the apples, and then stuffed the rest into my pack. I hoisted this onto my back. It was heavy, but I figured I could manage it. I staggered slightly as I went out the front door, feeling weaker than I thought I should. My bike was where I'd left it, but I didn't bother to mount. The effort didn't seem worthwhile. I just grabbed the handlebars and pushed on up the street.

I had one last item on my list before I could return to the pond: vodka. It was by far the most difficult to procure, but I had an idea. With so many Russians in town there must be at least one bottle of their national drink somewhere. I headed for the main square, reasoning that that's where I'd find the greatest number of our newest occupiers.

I was right. There was a party going on. Guitar and accordion music and singing and dancing were happening in half a dozen spots around the large square. Danes were mixing with Russians in a way they never would have done with the Germans. These were our allies, our liberators. Our occupiers, yes, but not our enemies. Children ran about playing in the crowds while girls and women linked arms and danced with men—both Russian and Danish. Other men sat apart singing and laughing and drinking from bottles of beer and snaps and—I hoped—vodka.

I slowly wheeled my bike between the mobs, trying not to hit anyone with my handlebars or pedals. I looked from one drinker to another, pausing to read the names on the bottles. When I saw Danish words I passed on. Then I spotted it: a bottle three-quarters full of a clear liquid. A cheap label was stuck crooked on the side of it. The words, the letters even, were incomprehensible. This, I thought, must be vodka.

I'd found it, but how would I get it? I had no money, nothing this soldier could want. Then, as I leaned on my bike, I got an idea.

I approached the man and tapped him on the shoulder—he was sitting on a chair in a circle of men. He turned towards me.

"Vodka?" I asked, pointing at the bottle.

He looked confused for a second and then his face cleared. He looked at the bottle and then smiled, nodding his head.

"*Da!*" he said. "*Vodka. Da!*"

Then he laughed, although I couldn't tell what was funny.

I pointed at my bike and then at him.

"Bicycle. You," I said.

I pointed at the bottle and then at myself.

"Vodka," I said, trying to copy his thick accent. "Me."

His confusion returned and he snorted. He looked at me and then at my bike. He sneered and laughed. He'd understood.

"*Nyet!*" he said and pushed me away.

I fell backwards, landing on my full pack. My bicycle clattered to the stones. Anger flared in me as I scrambled painfully to my feet. Without thinking I grabbed the bottle out of his hands and ran with it, sticking my thumb down the mouth to stop any of the precious liquid from spilling out.

With a roar the soldier jumped up and leaped after me. I was running as fast as I could, but it was like I was thrashing through knee-deep water. I managed three or four steps, but every time my right foot hit the ground pain shot up my calf and slowed me even more. I felt the Russian soldier grab my pack. I toppled over onto my face, cradling the bottle in my arms so it wouldn't smash against the cobbles. The soldier yanked on my hair and twisted my head up. He had his weight on my back and he was yelling angrily into my upturned face. His alcoholic breath stank and flecks of spittle hit my cheeks. I gagged with nausea. The pain from my leg, my back, and my scalp all merged together, blacking out clear thought.

Then another voice entered the fray and the soldier stopped yelling at me. A few more words and he let go of my hair and got off my back. I rolled onto my side and pulled my legs up, curling around the bottle and closing my eyes.

The argument went on over my head and I couldn't ignore it. I struggled to open my eyes and see the man who had interfered on my behalf. He looked thin and weak, as if he'd had little to eat for a very long time. The soldier could have flattened him with one hit—and I thought he was about to do just that—but my rescuer growled a few words at him and the danger passed quickly away. The soldier's anger was replaced by a look of resentful fear. He backed away to rejoin his waiting comrades and he said nothing more.

My rescuer? I thought so at first, but then I looked more closely at him. He looked familiar somehow, but I didn't know why. Then he turned his eyes towards me and the memory jumped out: I'd last seen this man on the German gunboat just after he'd helped Aleks kill five men.

I think he'd already recognized me. I thought he must have known how I was involved in his capture. My fear and nausea returned.

He grabbed my shirt collar and hoisted me to my feet. He poked into my pack, examining the food and clothing and then he took the bottle from my hands. He lifted it to his nose, sniffed and nodded. He pointed at the bottle and peered intently into my eyes; I was frightened by a hint of madness I sensed lurking behind them.

"Baklanov," he said. "*Da?*"

I didn't answer. I wasn't sure what he meant. Then I remembered: Baklanov. That's what Reinhardt had called Aleks. This Russian was asking me if the vodka was for Aleks. He'd guessed! Still I said nothing.

He leaned closer. His nose almost touched mine.

"Baklanov," he repeated, his voice gaining a harder edge. "*Nyet?*"

I gave up. My meagre strength had just about left me. I nodded, biting my lower lip.

"Baklanov," he said yet again, gesturing in the wrong direction.

Clearly he wanted me to lead him to where Aleks lay hidden. I didn't trust him and I couldn't know whether Aleks would welcome or dread a visit from this man. I thought back to the gunboat and remembered how Aleks had taken orders from him. I decided any decision I made could be the wrong one. I pointed in the true direction of the pond and the gaunt Russian smiled. He gestured for me to lead the way and he followed as I limped through the noisy crowds.

I used to love going to that pond in the woods. It used to be a quiet sanctuary made all the more special because I shared it with Lise. When my feet used to head that way I would carry the anticipation of joy along with me, sure that I would be welcomed by the trees and the pond and often by Lise herself.

Now I carried this heavy weight on my back and my feet were dragged slower with a sharpening pain that wormed up my right leg. Fear both followed me and waited ahead. All I wanted was to curl into a ball and lose myself in the refuge of sleep, but all I could do was creep forward one step at a time and the only haven I could find lay in a cloud of feverish, muddled thought.

Aleks was asleep when we finally reached the campsite. Asleep? Well, he wasn't awake. I suspect his appearance had more to do with unconsciousness than with restful slumber. He was making low groaning noises as he breathed. His face was flushed red and covered with a film of sweat. He looked as bad as I felt. I sensed he was on the edge of a cliff—one push and he would fall.

I sat down on the ground and leaned back on the pack, too tired to take it off. The thin Russian pulled a handkerchief out of his pocket and knelt beside Aleks. He gently wiped the perspiration off Aleks's face and laid his hand on his forehead in the way that my mother used to check my temperature. He shook his head sadly, not liking what he discovered.

Then he unwrapped the bandage I had wound around Aleks's head and he examined the bloody gash. He turned and gestured towards me, the first notice he'd taken of me since we arrived. When I failed to understand his meaning he became impatient and got up to take my pack away from me. He dumped the contents onto the ground and picked out one of my clean flannel shirts. He doused this with some of the vodka and used it to wipe Aleks's wound.

The sting of the alcohol brought Aleks quickly awake. He wrenched his eyes open with a grunt and fixed them on the thin Russian's face. Then, after a moment of bewilderment, he relaxed.

"Dimitri!" he said.

His voice was weak, but clear. The sound held surprise. If it didn't convey outright joy, at least I heard no animosity. I, too, relaxed, satisfied that I hadn't brought danger into the camp. I'd forgotten that the gripping beast smiles, always smiles.

They spoke slowly and quietly together while the Russian, this Dimitri, finished cleaning Aleks's wound and bound it tight again. I watched as he examined the splint I'd made for Aleks's broken arm and as he touched the other smaller injuries my friend had suffered. I noticed that his touches weren't entirely like those of a doctor or a nurse. Some were almost caresses.

I couldn't understand what they were saying to each other in Russian. Several times they seemed to be talking about me, but I could only guess they were discussing my role in their affairs. I blushed, knowing they had little reason to appreciate that role, but neither one noticed.

Dimitri held the vodka bottle to Aleks's lips, held his head up and let him sip. Aleks coughed, but I could tell he liked the taste. Then Dimitri took a swig. He breathed with satisfaction and then held the bottle back up to his mouth. A large amount of the liquid gurgled down his throat. Aleks protested, reaching for the bottle. Dimitri gave it to him. Together they finished it off and Dimitri tossed the bottle a couple of feet away. It clinked against something hard when it landed. The sound drew my attention and I saw my gun—now Aleks's gun—half hidden in the bushes.

The two Russians continued talking, but I noticed a change in the tone of their conversation. Dimitri, it seemed to me, had grown shy and his words had taken on a plaintive air. One of his hands was resting on Aleks's good arm, not moving, just remaining where it was. Aleks was frowning, as if he was suddenly unable to comprehend what was being said. Then he laughed and shook off Dimitri's hand. He pushed the older man away—not roughly, almost playfully. He was acting like he was sharing a joke.

But it was evidently no joke for Dimitri. He paused for a second, his large eyes blinking rapidly, and then he touched Aleks again with his left hand and gestured to himself with his right. He was pleading, arguing as if with a recalcitrant but loved child.

Aleks was losing his patience. He tried to interrupt Dimitri, but Dimitri's voice just rose louder, becoming a whine at times. Aleks couldn't do much; he was weak from his injuries and still unable to sit up by himself. Yet he was trying to reason with this man, to stop whatever it was he was doing and saying. He was trying to push him away; trying to get the older man's hand off his arm. It was almost funny to see: Aleks was waving his good arm and Dimitri was trying to keep his hand on it and all the while he was talking and talking and talking.

Suddenly, Aleks swung his arm and hit Dimitri backhanded across the face. The blow couldn't have been hard, but it stopped him talking. Dimitri sat back and held his hand to his reddening cheek. Then Aleks spoke, spitting his words at Dimitri. I don't know what he was saying, but I could tell they were hitting harder than his hand had done.

For a moment Dimitri acted like he still thought it was a mere misunderstanding and he leaned forward. Maybe he thought he could still persuade Aleks about whatever it was they were arguing about. I don't know. All I saw was that he gave Aleks a chance to hit him again. Aleks was no longer in the mood to listen. His words were coming out fast and sharp. I wondered if the vodka had given him more strength.

I could tell the insults were sinking in; Dimitri lost his air of misunder-stood innocence and flushed with hurt and anger. He began yelling back at Aleks and the air beside the pond filled with their shouts. I added to the uproar by screaming: "Stop it! Stop it!" But neither of them heard me, or if they did, they ignored me. I became frightened and backed away until my hand touched the empty vodka bottle. I grasped it impulsively.

Aleks was struggling to sit upright, all the while cursing the older man. Dimitri was shaking his head and he held both hands out to stop him. At first his hands were only on Aleks's shoulders, as if he just wanted to hold him down. Aleks fought against him. His face radiated disgust as he spat insults at the man.

Then one of Dimitri's hands went to Aleks's throat. The other moved to cover Aleks's mouth. It was as if Dimitri couldn't bear what he was hearing and he wanted to shut the sound off at the source.

I watched horrified as Aleks's eyes widened with sudden fright. He clawed at Dimitri's hand, but he couldn't match the man's strength. I screamed again and threw the bottle blindly. It hit Dimitri on the side of his head. He yelled hoarsely, let go of Aleks, and turned my way. I'd enraged him even further. The madness I'd glimpsed back in the square was now shone bright from his eyes. It was no longer hidden. It was in full control.

Dimitri made a move in my direction, but Aleks, gasping, grabbed at him with his injured arm—the pain must have been horrific—and swung at him with his other fist. Dimitri punched out, hitting Aleks square in the face and knocking him back to the ground. He yelled incoherently and fell on Aleks, both his hands tight around the young man's throat.

I was sobbing. Through my tears I had this vision of long, thin limbs reaching and gripping and crushing. I had to stop it. I had to kill this beast.

I don't remember picking the gun up, but there it was in my hands. I clicked it open, as I had seen Aleks do, and found that it contained bullets. Without conscious thought, as if my hands were in someone else's control, I found myself pointing the barrel at Dimitri. I yelled and yelled, but he didn't stop what he was doing to Aleks. I squeezed the trigger and the weapon exploded in my hands. As the recoil knocked me back, numbing my right arm, I saw Dimitri spinning away from Aleks, blood spraying across the young Russian and the surrounding bushes.

I got up, my right arm hanging uselessly at my side. Aleks's mouth and eyes were all wide open, but he wasn't breathing. He saw nothing. I tried to pick up the gun again, but my hand would not do what I wanted it to do. I wasn't thinking clearly and a scrap of a sentence kept going through my head: twice is…twice is…

Twice is what? Time seemed to slow down enough for me to think about this, but I could not figure out the answer. Again I tried to pick up the pistol, but it just kept slipping from my useless fingers.

Dimitri was still alive. He lay on his back. His breath gurgled in his throat. The left side of his chest was a mass of torn and bleeding flesh. I saw him die. His eyes closed and the air rushed out of his lungs.

With that the compulsion to pick up the gun left me and the broken words fled from my mind. I collapsed onto my hands and knees and threw up into the dirt. Then there was nothing more.

Twenty

"THAT'S IT," FINNE said. "That's my confession. That's who I killed, this Dimitri. I killed him. I saw him die. I've lived with this all my life. Now I don't want it anymore."

I said nothing. I just stared at him. He looked up at me and then back down at his hands on the table. He was lacing his fingers together, then untangling them over and over again. He seemed to think I was waiting for him to say more.

"Well, perhaps that's not quite all of it," he continued. "But the rest isn't really all that important."

He lifted his eyes to me again.

"Go on," I said.

"I never went back to the pond," he said. "In fact, I don't even remember how I left it. I must have walked away through the woods and into the town, but I've no memory of that. I've got pictures in my head of people looking at me strangely and of someone reaching for me, but they're not clear at all. I just know someone found me somewhere and took me to the hospital.

"When I woke up the first thing I saw was my father's worried face. He was sitting beside my hospital bed holding my good hand, clutching it and stroking it. He said nothing. He gazed at me with the beginnings of hope in his eyes.

"'Father?'

"I don't know if I actually spoke loud enough for him to hear, but he could at least see me trying to move my lips.

"'Mathias,' he said. 'Don't talk. Don't talk. Just rest. Please just rest.'

"And then he started crying. He didn't look away. He wasn't embarrassed. He just gazed at me and wept quietly. And of course I started crying, too.

"My mother was in another ward. The arrest of my father and my sudden disappearance sent her into a frenzy that made her fight against the men holding her outside our home. Her captors dragged her into the house and pinned her down until her rage collapsed. I'm glad I didn't see it happen, but I've always wondered if I could have prevented it by not running.

"After my mother calmed down she sank into a deep depression and they took her to the hospital where she remained for many weeks, even after she saw me and my father again. I had assumed the sight of me would rouse her out of the depths, but of course I was wrong. I didn't yet understand how small blows can accumulate in the mind until the strain is just too much to bear. The final blow that snaps the spring of rationality isn't always the real cause of madness.

"Gradually my mother put herself back together. Deprived of the false refuge of alcohol, she was forced to look at her life and come to terms with it. She never became what she had been, but she began to play more of a role in our lives.

"The resistance had let my father go. They still called him a collaborator, but they could not find an actual crime to convict him. Making money from the Germans wasn't an offence. If it had been then half the island would have been in prison.

"He'd gone home, but he couldn't find me there. He asked around, but those neighbours who were willing to speak with him couldn't tell him anything. There'd been some sightings of me, but nothing definite. He went to the hospital and to his wife and searched through the other wards, but I wasn't there yet. Then a day or two later I was brought in and a nurse sent word to my father that they'd just admitted an unidentified boy.

"He returned to the hospital and there he found me in one of the public wards. I was unconscious, apparently suffering from a concussion. I had blood poisoning from an infected wound on my ankle. I was running a high fever and my right arm was sprained. But I would recover, the doctor told him.

"Eventually they let my father take me home and a little while afterwards my mother joined us. We kept to ourselves in that lonely house. The animosity between us had evaporated, but warmth never really filled the space it left behind. We learned to live together—together and by ourselves. My father wasn't welcome in the community any more and I had no will to go back out into that world. Exactly what my mother thought, I don't know, but she didn't go out much, either.

"Finally my father sold the house. We left Bornholm. First we went to Copenhagen, but even in that big city he wasn't able to win the anonymity he sought. He'd never been an important man, but there was always someone who recognized him and reminded him about his past. So we left Denmark. We sailed across the sea to Canada and we made new lives for ourselves there.

"I can't speak for my parents, but in time I was able to forget, or, at least, to not always think about what had happened. A new language, a new school, and, yes, new friends. My mind was occupied in learning so many new things. I was able to concentrate on the future rather than the past."

Finne paused and shrugged.

"That's really it, then. That's all of it."

But that wasn't enough for me. Not nearly enough. Finne had started this and now he wanted to end it, but I couldn't let him.

"If that's it, then why are you here?" I asked him, unable to keep the edge off my voice. "If you'd managed to forget, then why did you come to tell me this story? Why this confession? Why dig up all these old things? Why not leave them buried?"

Finne looked up, startled by my tone. In our days together he'd come to see me as a confidante. I was someone who could take his burden away from him. He thought I was here to help him. I had seen it happen before during long interrogations.

But I wasn't his friend. I was a policeman.

"Well..." he began, searching for his words. "Well, it's like I told you before: my wife died. I'd kept this a secret from her. I don't want this secret anymore."

I snorted as derisively as I could.

"So why not go talk to a friend?" I asked. "Why not visit a psychiatrist or confess to a priest? Why come all the way over here and take up valuable police time? Or why not just write us a letter: Dear Soviet policeman, I've been a very bad boy.... What makes you think your old crimes are so important to us?"

I watched as the anger sparked to life in Finne's eyes. He evidently did not like being made fun of.

"I do not care if they're important to you," he said, his voice edged with flint. "I did not come here for you. I came for myself."

Finne paused and the anger faded from his eyes and his words.

"And for Dimitri. I came for Dimitri. Doesn't my victim deserve to have his death avenged? He's lain in his grave for fifty years and for fifty years I've said nothing. If you could ask him, don't you think he would want me to pay for my crime?"

An interesting question, I thought, but I did not attempt to answer it. Instead, I pressed him again.

"But why this urgency? You said yourself your crime is fifty years old. Why couldn't you wait a little longer to confess? Why did you demand to be arrested and assault our guard?"

"But I told you!" Finne was shouting now, his anger having returned. "My wife died! And then this guilt, this horrible feeling of guilt. It came back and it grew!"

Again Finne paused and when next he spoke his voice was quieter.

"And the nightmares returned. They went away years ago when I met my wife, but they came back when she died and left me alone. I dream of it all jumbled together: the gun in my hand; the gripping beast; Aleks dead with his eyes wide open; the earth heaving and punching me; Dimitri covered in blood but still moving. I hear Lise calling to me, but I can't dig down to find her…hands—the gripping beast, I think—keep pulling me away. Reinhardt laughing. My father and mother shaved bald and the scissors coming for me. And the gripping beast again. Always the gripping beast. Sometimes it's Dimitri. Sometimes it's me.

"I have not slept well for weeks, maybe months, ever since my wife died. I'm sorry I hit that guard and I hope I didn't hurt him, but I was not thinking clearly.

"I'm better now. Do you know I haven't dreamed since I came here and started talking to you? The nightmares have gone away again. That's how I know I did the right thing."

Finne shook his head.

"But I know that's not enough. I committed a crime. I committed murder and I should pay for it. And it was such a useless crime! Aleks was already dead, don't you see? Killing Dimitri made no difference. If I'd shot sooner maybe Aleks would still be alive. But I didn't. I waited. I didn't save anyone. Two men are dead because of me—two men!

"I couldn't get that out of my head. Aleks himself said killing doesn't save anything. And he knew. He'd already killed.

"So here I am. I'm a murderer. I killed a Russian, one of your people. I want to pay for that. I want peace."

Finne was studying me intently. He was obviously puzzled by my lack of response. What did he want? I guess he expected me to call for the manacles and have him thrown into the dungeons. He obviously wanted to know why this interview wasn't finished. But I wasn't ready to tell him what I knew.

I got up from the table and walked to the door. I spoke with the guard there, issuing two sets of orders and passing him the key to my automobile. He went off to relay my instructions to others. I closed the door and sat back down.

"How do you know you killed this man you call Dimitri?" I asked Finne.

He looked at me blankly.

"But I told you," he said. "I shot him. I saw him die."

"Is that all?"

"All? No, wait…there is more! I told you, didn't I? I went back to Bornholm this spring—my first time in almost fifty years. I thought I could confront my ghosts. I did, too. I confronted them, but they only grew stronger.

"There's a graveyard in Allinge, on the north point of the island. It's where the Soviets buried their war dead. There's a tall obelisk set in a flower garden surrounded by coloured gravel. A large pink headstone faces the obelisk. That stone has thirty names carved into it in Russian. Above them it says in Danish: 'To the Soviet Soldiers who fell in the fight against Fascism.'

"Those thirty names, I couldn't read them, but I copied them all down on paper and I brought them to somebody who could read them. The translation was clear. Baklanov was there. And so, I think, was Dimitri. I could not be sure, but a local historian told me at least three of the dead had the first initial "D". One of them must have been the man I shot. If Aleks is there, Dimitri must be there too."

Someone knocked at the door of the interrogation room and I went to answer. It was an officer carrying the professor's manuscript in its lurid plastic bag. I'd left it in my car. He handed the bundle over with a smirk and gave me back my key. I closed the door on him without comment and returned to the table.

"Do you know what this is?" I asked Finne as I dropped the manuscript in front of him.

Obviously he didn't and he shook his head.

"It's a memoir," I said. "It was written by an acquaintance of Aleksander Baklanov, by his controller, to be precise. You are mentioned quite prominently in there."

Finne didn't know what to make of this. He pulled the papers out of the bag and flipped through them. He couldn't read them, of course, any more than he could have read the words on the stone over the mass grave.

"What does it say about me?" he asked.

"It confirms most of what you told me and it says you were quite disruptive to Soviet plans. The author suspected you may have collaborated willingly with the Nazis."

"That's not true!" Finne's face flushed with anger. "I never did!"

"I believe you," I said. "I merely repeat what is written there."

I thought it was time to have one final glass of tea with Finne. As I ordered it up I could see Finne frowning at the manuscript. When the guard left, Finne could not restrain himself any longer.

"What is this?" he demanded. "What are you doing? What else does that thing say?"

I pondered which question to answer and allowed the arrival of the tea to distract me. I poured the tea myself, giving one glass to Finne and sipping from another before speaking.

"What I am doing is waiting," I said, knowing, but not caring, that this would not calm him down. I was taking a perverse pleasure in upsetting him. "I advise you to do the same and enjoy your tea. We won't have to wait long."

"But what are we waiting for?"

"Why, the answer to your last question."

Finne looked at me like I was babbling, but he seemed to resign himself to waiting. Neither of us spoke for several minutes.

The silence was finally broken by a ruckus in the hallway. A man was yelling hoarsely and evidently struggling against his guards. The noise came closer and someone knocked at the door. I called for them to enter. The door swung open and two uniformed police bundled the professor into the room. He was drunk, unshaven, and swearing. He saw me and he spat onto the floor in my direction.

"You!" he said in Russian. "I knew you would be a problem."

I turned to Finne.

"This gentleman," I told him, "is the author of that manuscript."

Ignoring Finne's questioning look, I stood up and spoke with the officers who were holding onto the historian.

"Remove his handcuffs," I ordered.

They hesitated, obviously thinking I was making a mistake.

"Do it!" I shouted.

The professor calmed down somewhat. He rubbed his wrists and eyed me suspiciously.

"No trouble," I warned him. "Now, take off your shirt."

The two policemen glanced at each other. The inspector has finally cracked, they must have been thinking. I ignored them.

The professor, on the other hand, looked at his manuscript on the table and he seemed to understand. The suspicion didn't leave his face, but he pulled his shirt tails out of his pants and started undoing the buttons.

I studied Finne as this was happening. He, of course, had no idea about what was being said and his confusion showed. He seemed embarrassed to be watching the professor undress. Then, as the shirt came off, Finne's embarrassment changed into a deep surprise.

He stood up and pointed at the professor. He looked at me with shock.

"What is this?" he gasped. "Who is this?"

I looked at the professor and saw what I had suspected would be there. The left side of his chest was disfigured with a curving, puckered scar, as if a large calibre bullet had torn away the flesh and left him bleeding profusely. He must have healed slowly and painfully.

"Haven't you guessed?" I asked Finne. "You wanted me to ask your victim if you should pay for your crimes. Well, you can ask him yourself."

Finne stepped towards the professor. I could sense his lifelong beliefs fight against the evidence before his eyes. He looked at the gaunt face. He looked at the long, thin arms. He looked at the ugly scar. Then he stepped back from the professor and looked at me.

"Dimitri?" he asked, almost hoping I would deny it.

I didn't deny it.

I think the professor may have already guessed who Finne was, but he asked anyway.

"This man was the little boy who shot you," I told him. "He has just told me a most interesting story."

Dimitri nodded and asked me if he could put his shirt back on. I told him he could. When he was done he asked if he could sit down. I pointed at a chair by the table. Then he asked for a cigarette. I gestured to one of the guards. He wasn't pleased, but he gave the prisoner one from his pack. Marlboros. He also had to light it for him. The two policemen stood close behind the professor. They thought they knew a dangerous man, even if I didn't.

Finne had sat down again and was gazing at Dimitri in stunned silence. I had just shattered a lifetime's belief. He wasn't sure how to react.

I, too, sat down. I still had questions, but they were for the professor.

"Why did you kill Aleksander Baklanov?"

Dimitri regarded me through his soft, teary eyes. I looked for the hint of madness Finne had glimpsed all those many years ago. I thought I detected something, but it may only have been my imagination.

I think the madness was gone. My guess was that it had been born in the horror of the Nazi concentration camp. It flared to maturity on Bornholm, brought to full life by the disdainful rejection he got from Baklanov. That was my guess.

I also guessed that it had eventually faded out with the passage of years. Or maybe his crime, the murder of the man he loved, had shocked him back to sanity. Or maybe it was Mathias Finne's bullet that had killed it.

At any rate, what the arresting officers considered dangerous madness I saw as harmless, drunken bluster. I was right, because my direct question deflated Dimitri as suddenly as if he was a balloon I'd pricked with a pin.

"I didn't mean to," he said. "I didn't mean to kill him. I really didn't."

The guards glanced at each other again. I couldn't help hoping there was some respect for me in their silent communication. It's not often you get someone to confess to murder so easily.

"Tell me what happened," I said. "Tell me what the argument was about."

I already had some idea what the answer would be. Hadn't I read the unfinished manuscript? But I wanted to hear him say it.

"He laughed at me," he said. "I told him how I felt and he laughed at me."

A deep sadness still clung to his words.

"You told him you were in love with him?"

"Yes! Yes, I did. I told him about Sachsenhausen. I told him how horrible it was. I told him how his memory kept me alive."

Dimitri paused. His hand shook as he held the cigarette to his lips and drew in a lungful of smoke.

"He thought I was joking. He thought I was crazy. I tried to tell him I didn't want anything from him. I tried to tell him I only wanted to let him know how I felt; that I understood if he didn't return my love. I just wanted to tell him. That's all. Just to let him know how much I owed him. He kept me alive.

"But he got angry with me. He told me to stop pawing at him. I wasn't pawing him! He was hurt. I was trying to help him.

"I wanted to bring him back to Moscow with me, but he would not even consider it. I tried telling him I could help him. I could make him an important man, but he would not believe me. He did not want to leave the west and he did not trust what I was telling him.

"And then he called me names. He said I was disgusting. A pervert! Unclean! I'm not a pervert! He wouldn't listen. I tried to explain, but he wouldn't listen.

"Then he hit me! Why did he hit me? He was getting too excited. It wasn't good for him. I had to calm him down. He was sick. I was trying to calm him down.

"Then the boy hit me with something. I got angry! And Aleksander, he told me not to touch the boy. What did he think I was? I wasn't going to do anything to that boy. He said such ugly things. I had to make him shut up! I had to make him shut up!"

The professor's agitation lifted him out of his chair, but his guards forced him back down. Finne was watching in horror. He couldn't comprehend the words, but I'm sure he understood what was happening. Maybe he, too, was reliving the past.

Dimitri calmed down. The weight of the guards' hands on his shoulders must have brought him back to the present.

"I don't remember anything else. Really, I don't. I didn't even know I'd been shot until they told me when I woke up days later. One of our patrols found me and patched me up. Somehow I lived.

"Then they told me Aleksander was dead. They said we must have been ambushed by Germans, maybe renegades. They believed it. They'd expected trouble somewhere, so they believed it."

I couldn't help asking him:"Did you know on this Danish island there is a tombstone that may have your name on it?"

Dimitri laughed. For the first time I think I saw him genuinely amused.

"No, I did not know this. How fitting! How fitting! I've been dead since the war and I didn't know it. This explains much!"

He laughed again, long and loud.

"I might have been dead," he said more seriously. "For all the work I've been able to do I might as well have been dead."

He shook his head and scowled. All traces of his humour had passed.

"Did you know our dear Comrade Stalin thought it was a crime to have been taken prisoner by the Germans in the war? Of course you did. This is no secret any more. There are very few secrets any more.

"I was a good Communist. I sacrificed much for the Revolution. I was ready to give my life for Mother Russia. But did that matter? Not at all! The only thing that mattered was Sachsenhausen!

"You arrest me. You bring me here. What do you want? Do you want to punish me for killing Baklanov? You think you can punish me any more than I've already been punished? How can you do better than fifty wasted years? They wouldn't give me a job. They would not publish me. I was lucky not to have been sent to another camp. So lucky!

"Besides, you're too late. You just told me: I'm already dead! The state has already killed me off. What more can you do?"

The laughter returned. I couldn't stand to hear it. The humour had leached out of it and the drunken bluster returned to fill it up. I gestured to the guards to take him away. They'd lock him up somewhere and maybe he would get a trial, but maybe not. Probably they would just let the old man go. Fifty years is a long time to wait after a crime has been committed.

I didn't care what they did with him. My superiors wanted charges laid and they would get their charges laid. Maybe they wouldn't be against the man they intended, but what did that matter to me? I was finished with it. I'd done my job.

But I still had to deal with Mathias Finne.

"What now?" he asked me.

"You're free to go."

"Yes, but what now?"

It was my turn to get angry.

"What do you want from me? Why do you think this is my concern? You are free to go. Go!"

My last word was a shout. I stood up and pointed at the door. Finne recoiled, but remained seated. I couldn't help despising him at that moment—a grown man unable to think for himself.

"But...but is there nothing you want from me?" he ventured timidly. "I came here...I thought I'd killed...I wanted to...I wanted to confess...I thought—"

I interrupted him brutally.

"Yes, you came here to confess to murder. What gave you the right? That was fifty years ago. In a few years you'd all be dead anyway. You could have all died in peace. But no! What could it matter any more?"

"But it was murder. At least, I thought it was murder—"

"Yes, murder! But not murder; you should have come here to confess to suicide. You've condemned yourself, obsessed with this crime that wasn't a crime. You've been dead fifty years, just like Dimitri, and now you want us to bury you!"

"That's not true!" Finne shouted. He stood suddenly, his chair scraping backwards. He leaned over the table at me to yell into my face. His chest was heaving with anger as he spat his words out.

"That's not true! I haven't wasted my life. I've had a good life. You know nothing about my life!"

I answered him quietly and calmly. I'd raised his anger and made him speak for himself. Now I just wanted to get rid of him.

"Then why are you still here?" I asked.

He searched my eyes deeply, as if seeking the purpose of my question. His anger faded and he sat back down. He stared off to the side for a few minutes before speaking. I felt tired, but I didn't rush him.

"I wanted to kill the beast," he finally said. "Somehow I knew I hadn't killed the beast. I thought Dimitri was dead, but it seemed to me the beast still lived...here!"

He hammered once on his chest with his fist.

"And here!"

Then, with the heel of his hand, he clouted his forehead—once, just once. He buried his face in his hands and ran his fingers hard down over his skin, as if scraping something away.

"You were right. It was like my life had ended that day by the pond. It ended in the war. First von Braun lit a spark in me and I doused it with treachery. He tried to light it again, but he couldn't. And I had so many dreams about

Lise and then she died. I never told her all I wanted to say. And then Aleks—
I could have protected him, but I didn't. I let him get killed, too.

"My mother, my father and I, we learned not to take any more chances.
We didn't go to Canada to start new lives. We only went to escape the old
ones. We turned out to be very much alike, my father and I.

"But then the dreams started coming back. I saw the stone again. I saw the
twisting limbs, the grasping hands. I saw the stupid eyes and the evil grin. I
saw I had to take one more chance. The beast was still inside me. I had to get
rid of it. This was the only way I could of…what else could I have done?

"But it was all pointless, wasn't it? I failed again."

He frowned into space. He seemed, once again, to have forgotten I was
there. But then his frown cleared and, to my surprise, he laughed.

"No! I didn't fail," he said. "You're wrong. I've finally done something
right. I didn't kill Dimitri, but he should have been locked up years ago. The
man's crazy!

"So, to hell with you, Inspector. I'm glad I came here. I don't give a damn
about the trouble I caused you. You said I was free to go, so let me go!"

I suppressed my amusement as I regarded this man who'd been my
prisoner for so many days. When I first met him I'd wanted to charge him with
the murder he'd said he'd committed. The truth is that I hadn't cared about
the crime; I just wanted to enjoy the satisfaction of sending this westerner to
trial.

But what would be the point? He was no more to blame for the changes in
my society and my life than he was guilty of murder. I was a policeman. I
couldn't charge him for a crime he hadn't committed, no matter what he or
I wanted.

So the only thing to do was to let Finne go. He had to go on with his life
and I had to go on with mine. I escorted him down the corridors to pick up the
few belongings he'd left in his cell. Then I signed the necessary paperwork
and he was given the things we'd confiscated when he'd first been arrested:
his wallet, his watch, his belt.

Then, instead of just sending him on his way as is normally done, I walked
him outside into the wide sunny courtyard, down the grass-lined walkways
under the tall trees to the front turnstile gate.

I wondered what he would do—if he would say goodbye, or even if he'd
shake my hand. He did neither. He just kept walking. He didn't even look
back. He just pushed through the turnstile into freedom.

Then he stood for a moment blinking in the hot, bright sunlight on Petrovka Street. He seemed oblivious of the cars roaring by and of the people jostling past him to get into the police station. He seemed younger than when I'd first seen him, as if his stay with us had given him new life. Perhaps it had.

He looked right and then left and headed south towards the centre of Moscow, towards the Red Square and the Kremlin, where all the tourists go.

I stood inside the gate and watched as Finne disappeared into the crowds.

"So you let that crazy American go," the turnstile guard said. He must have been the very man Finne slapped to get himself into prison. "Couldn't you find anything to charge him with?"

"No," I answered. "It was outside of our jurisdiction."

Acknowledgements

I WOULD LIKE to thank the following people: Major H.V. Jørgensen, Tønnes Wichmann, Bent Kuhn, Sven Munch Holm, Hans Michael Harild, Sven Harild, Gunvor Harild (née Rønnes), Bent Jacobsen, Silke Fricke, Horst and Christine Beuther, Jens Amsgaard, Andrei Ivanichtchev, Elena Kolmakova, Luydmila Barbolina, Valerie Anderson, Breakwater's intrepid editor Melissa Nance and the late Casper Brown and all the staff at the Labradorian, without whose help this book would not have been born or been able to grow to maturity.

I would also like to thank the Newfoundland and Labrador Arts Council whose valuable assistance gave me time to write *Confession in Moscow*.

—MFJ